"Are You Hurt, Thomas?"

"I'm past all doctoring, friend," Thomas gasped. "I durst not draw the bolt." He groaned in sudden, wrenching agony. "Ah, Jane, love. Has it come to this after all?"

"No, no," she whispered passionately. "Carver will save you, Thomas. Only let me reach him."

Thomas looked down upon the face that was so dear to him, saw through the fast-gathering shadows that her eyes were aswim with tears and could not find it in his heart to deny her anything. He nodded. "Help me, friends," he muttered. "Lay my head in her lap."

Jane stroked the lank hair back from a forehead already chill with the cold dew of hurrying death and, leaning over him, cried soundlessly into the shadow-filled depths with all the force of her terrified spirit: *Help us, Michael! Help us! Do not let him die!*

Books by Richard Cowper

Clone
The Road to Corlay

Published by POCKET BOOKS

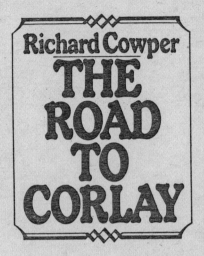

Richard Cowper

THE ROAD TO CORLAY

PUBLISHED BY POCKET BOOKS NEW YORK

POCKET BOOKS, a Simon & Schuster division of
GULF & WESTERN CORPORATION
1230 Avenue of the Americas, New York, N.Y. 10020

ISBN: 0-671-82917-3

First Pocket Books printing September, 1979

10 9 8 7 6 5 4 3 2 1

Trademarks registered in the United States and other countries.

Printed in the U.S.A.

FOR FRANK LEA
best of friends

The Seven Kingdoms
circa A.D. 3000

PART OF 6TH KINGDOM (DYFEDD'S)

SEVERN REACH

■New Bristol

(PART OF 4TH KINGDOM)

BRITTANY

Corlay

MENDIP ISLE

EXMOOR (PART OF 1st KINGDOM)

QUANTOCK ISLE

SOMERSEA

Tellon

Taunton Reach

Chardport

Broadbury

BLACK-DOWN

Sidbury

NORTH DORSET (PART OF 2nd KINGDOM)

FRENCH CHANNEL

7

5

6

4

1

2

3

THE
ROAD
TO
CORLAY

Among the twenty-two books which comprise the Avian Apocrypha, the one which has been called by certain scholars "Old Peter's Tale" and by others "The Book of Gyre," has always occupied a place somewhat apart from the rest.

Recent close textual and stylistic analysis by Professor P. J. Hollins and others would appear to have confirmed the presence of no fewer than three distinct contributing hands, at least two of which have been confidently identified with the anonymous authors of "The Book of Morfedd" and "Orgen's Dream."

In electing to offer to a wider public his new version compiled from the three earliest extant manuscripts I have purposely eschewed the two titles by which the work is generally familiar and have chosen instead that under which the story appears in the "Carlisle m.s." (circa A.D. 3300).

R.J.C.
St. Malcolm's College,
Oxford.
June, 3798.

PIPER AT THE GATES
OF DAWN

Cold curtains of November rain came drifting slowly up the valley like an endless procession of phantom mourners following an invisible hearse. From beneath an overhang of limestone a boy and an old man squatted side by side and gazed disconsolately out across the river to the dripping forest on the far bank. Suddenly a salmon leaped—a flicker of silver in the gloom and a splash like a falling log. The boy's eyes gleamed. "Ah," he breathed. "Did you see him?"

The old man grunted.

"I'm going to try for him, Peter."

The man glanced round out of the tail of his eyes and sniffed skeptically. "What with?"

The boy unfastened the thong of his leather knapsack, delved inside, and pulled out a slender double-barrelled wooden pipe—something between a twin-stemmed whistle and a recorder. He rubbed it briskly on the sleeve of his gray woollen pullover then set the mouthpiece to his lips and blew softly. A note, clear and liquid as a blackbird's, floated out from beneath his fingers. Another followed, and another, and then came a little frisking trill that set the old man's pulse fluttering.

"Who taught you to play like that, lad?"

"Morfedd."

The boy rose to his feet, stepped out into the rain,

and had taken four or five paces down the slope toward the river's edge when the old man called him back. "Here," he said, pulling off his cap and flinging it across. "It'll keep the rain off your neck."

The boy grinned his thanks, dragged the waxed leather scuttle over his untidy mop of black curls, and skipped down to where a flat rock jutted out into the stream. There he squatted, as close as he could get to the hurrying tawny water, and once more put the pipe to his lips.

Squinting through the veiling rain, the old man became uncomfortably aware of a chill area around the back of his neck where his cap had been and he hunched down deeper into the collar of his sheepskin coat. Like wisps of gossamer, odd disconnected threads of music came floating up to him from the rain-pocked waters below and, as he half-listened, there suddenly flickered unbidden across his mind's eye a lightning-sharp vision of a large and succulent dragonfly. So vivid was the image that for a confusing second he was convinced the insect was hovering a mere handspan before his nose. Next instant there was an excited shouting from below, a flurry of splashing and he saw the boy staggering among the rain-wet boulders at the water's edge with a huge silver fish struggling in his arms.

With an alacrity which wholly belied his years the old man scrambled down the bank just in time to prevent the boy from measuring his own length in a pool. He grabbed at the gulping salmon, thrust his thumbs firmly into its gills and contrived to bang its head against a rock. "Blast me, boy!" he cried. "I never saw such luck in all my days! Blast me if I did!"

The boy laughed delightedly. "He's *big,* isn't he? Did you see him jump? Right up at me! *Swoosh!*"

The old man lifted the shuddering fish and contrived to hold it out at arm's length. "I'll swear he's nigh on ten kils," he panted. "A regular whale! What are we going to do with him?"

"Why, eat him, of course."

"Ah, some for sure, lad. The rest we'd best try to smoke. But we've got to get ourselves across the stream first. With all this rain, by nightfall she'll be up to twice your own height, and it's ten lom or more round by Kirkby bridge. Nip you up aloft and fetch the packs. We'll try for a crossing up around the bend."

The boy clambered back up to the overhang and ducked out of sight. The old man selected a stout stick from among a tangle of driftwood, took a clasp knife from his pocket and, having sharpened one end of the stick to a point, spiked it through the salmon's gills and hefted the fish up on to his back.

Twenty minutes later the two of them were over the river and picking their way along the deer track that followed the far bank. By then the rain had eased off to a steady, depressing drizzle. Though it was barely two hours gone noon, the low clouds and the brooding forest dimmed the light almost to curfew gloom. Conversation between the two travellers was restricted to grunts of warning and acknowledgment as the old man negotiated rocks and exposed tree roots which had been made even more treacherous by the rain.

They had covered some two kilometers in this fashion when the track broadened out perceptibly into a discernible path. The boy at once seized the opportunity to move up to the old man's side. "Will we reach Sedbergh before nightfall, Peter?"

"Not without breaking our necks, we won't. But I recall a 'stead hereabouts might lodge us for the night. I've been trying to bring the man's given name to mind, but it's twenty year or more since I last trod this track."

"A farmer, is he?"

"Bit of everything as I recall it. Like most of 'em round here. Newton? Norton? *Norris! That's* the name! Norris Cooperson! Yes, yes, now it comes back. Old Sam Cooperson was a color-sergeant in Northumberland's dragoons. Won his freedom in the Battle of Rotherham in '950. That takes us back a bit, doesn't it? Old Sam leased a stretch of the Lord's grazing down the river a way. Did well enough for his boy to buy the freehold. I seem to recall that young Norris wed a lass from Aysgarth. And didn't her people have property round York? Or was it Scarborough? Funny how his name slipped me. Norris. Norris Cooperson. Aye, that's him."

"Where does he live, Peter?"

"On a bit yet. I seem to mind a beck skipping down from the fells. Old Sam built his 'stead facing south-west, backing right up into the hills. 'Guarding his rear' he called it." The old man chuckled. "Sergeant Cooperson had had a Jock spear up his arse in his time, so he knew what he was talking about."

They came to a waist-high wall of rough stone which had recently been repaired, clambered over it, and headed off on a diagonal course away from the river. After they had gone about five hundred paces the old man paused, lifted his head, and snuffed the air like a dog. The boy watched him closely. "Smoke?" he asked.

"Horses," said the old man. "Smoke too. It can't be far now."

The ground rose slightly and the forest trees began to thin out almost as if they were withdrawing fastidiously from a contact which was distasteful to them. The two wayfarers trudged up to the crest of the rise and saw below them a long bowshot off to their left, the low outline of a substantial stone stable, a bracken-thatched barn, a farm house and a scattering of timber outbuildings. A herd of long-horned, hump-backed cattle was grazing in the meadow which sloped gently down from the homestead to the distant river.

The old man shifted the salmon from one shoulder to the other and nodded with satisfaction. "I wasn't wrong, was I, Tom? But it's grown a fair bit since I last set eye on it. Reckon you'd best get yourself a stick while you can. They're bound to have a dog or two."

The boy shook his head. "They won't bother me."

"It's not *you* I'm feared for, lad. It's our supper here."

The boy unfastened his knapsack and again took out his pipe. "Dogs are the easiest of all," he said scornfully. "They'll believe *anything.*"

The old man studied him thoughtfully, sucked a tooth, seemed on the point of saying something and then, apparently, changed his mind. Side by side they plodded off down the hill toward the farm.

The shaggy cattle raised their heads at their approach, regarded them with mild, munching curiosity and then nodded back to their grazing. They had passed almost through the herd before the farm dogs got wind of them. They came hurtling out from behind the stables, three lean, vicious-looking fell hounds, snarling and yelping in their eagerness to savage the intruders.

The boy stood his ground; calmly waited till the leader was but a short stone's throw distant; then set the pipe to his lips and blew a series of darting notes of so high a pitch that the old man's ears barely caught them. But the dogs did. They stopped almost dead in their tracks, for all the world as if they had run full tilt into a solid wall of glass. Next moment the three of them were lying stretched out full length on the wet grass, whining, with their muzzles clasped in their forepaws and their eyes closed.

The boy played a few more notes then walked forward and prodded the largest of the curs with his toe. The animal rolled over on to its back and offered its unguarded throat to him in a drooling ecstasy of abject submission. "You see," said the boy disdainfully. "They're such ninnies they'll even believe they're puppies."

The barking had brought a woman to the door of the farm house and now she called out to the dogs. Slowly, dazedly, they rose to their feet, shook themselves and loped off toward her, pausing every so often to glance back and whimper perplexedly.

"And who might you be, strangers?"

With his spare hand the old man doffed his cap, allowing the damp breeze to flutter his white hair. "Old Peter the Tale-Spinner of Hereford, ma'am. Legging for York City. This here's young Tom, my niece's lad. We missed our way short-cutting it through Haw Gill. We'd be glad to pay silver for a night's dry lodging."

"My goodman's out timbering," responded the woman doubtfully. "I dursent say you yea or nay without he's back."

"That would be goodman Norris, I daresay, ma'am?"

"Aye," she said, screwing up her eyes to see him better. "Aye, it would."

"Then you must be Mistress Cooperson."

"Aye," she admitted. "What of it?"

"Tell me, Mistress, does Old Sam's halberd still hang bright over the chimney-breast?"

The woman raised her right hand in a strange, hesitant little half-gesture of uncertainty. "You'll have been here afore then, old man?"

"Aye, ma'am. Close on twenty year since. Just agin you and young Norris wed, that would a' been." He cocked an eye up at the sagging, dripping clouds. "If me 'n the lad could maybe step inside your barn yonder, we'd hold it more than kind. This wet strikes a deathly chill into old bones."

The woman flushed. "No, no," she said, backing over the threshold. "Come you in here and dry yourselves by the fire. It's just me and the young lass alone, you see." Then, by way of explanation, she added: "We heard tell there was an Irish raider into Morecambe Bay afore Holymass."

"That's real kind in you, ma'am." The old man beamed, swinging the salmon down off his back and holding it out toward her. "We even thought to bring some supper with us, you see."

"Oh, there's a wild beauty!" she exclaimed. "How came you by him?"

"Singing for our supper, you might say," said the old

man winking at the boy. "I've been thinking we could maybe split master silversides longwise and perhaps smoke one half of him in your chimney overnight. That way you'll have a fine supper and we'll have ourselves fare for our morrow's footing."

"Yes, yes," she said. "There's oak afire this minute. Do you bring him through here into the scullery." She called round over her shoulder: "Katie, lass! Come and liven up that fire right sharp!"

A blue-eyed girl of about twelve, with hair so palely blonde it was almost white, emerged from the shadows, took a long hard stare at the visitors and then vanished. The old man wiped the mud from his boots on the bundle of dried bracken piled for the purpose just inside the doorway, then carted the salmon through into the scullery and flopped it out on the slab of dark green slate which the woman indicated. She reached down a knife and a steel from a shelf and honed a rapid edge. Then with the skill of long practice she slit the fish down the belly and began scooping its insides into a wooden bucket.

The boy meanwhile had wandered through into the long stone-flagged kitchen and now stood silently watching the girl arranging dry oak billets against the smoldering back-log in the huge fireplace. She glanced at him over her shoulder. "You can blow, can't you, boy?"

He nodded, moved across and knelt beside her as she crushed dry bracken up into a ball and thrust it into the space behind the propped logs. "Well, go on then," she commanded. "Show me."

Obediently the boy leant forward and puffed till the white ashes leapt aside and exposed the glowing embers beneath. He reached out, pressed the bracken down and blew again. The kindling began to smoke. Next moment a tiny snakestongue of flame had flickered up. He blew more gently, fanning the flame till the whole ball was well ablaze and then he sat back on his heels and brushed the powder of ash from his cheeks and eyebrows.

The girl laid a few sticks across the flames and turned to him again. "What're you going to York for?"

"To Chapter School."

"What's that?"

"My cousin's spoken me a place in the Minster choir. He's Clerk to the Chapter."

"What'll you do?"

"Learn to read and write. Sing in the choir. Maybe play too."

"Play what? Your pipe?"

He nodded.

She studied him long and hard by the light of the spurtling flames. "I saw what you did to the dogs," she said thoughtfully.

He smiled. "Oh, that was easy. The fish was much harder."

"You did that to the fish too? What you did to the dogs?"

"Sort of," he said.

"How do you do it?"

His smile broadened but he said nothing.

"Can I see your pipe?"

"All right." He got up, walked over to the doorway where he had left his pack, took out the pipe and brought it back to her. She held it in both hands and examined it by the firelight. Deep inside one of the tubes some crystalline facet caught the flames and twinkled like a diamond. She raised the mouthpiece to her lips and was just about to blow when he snatched the instrument from her. "No," he said. "No, you mustn't. It's tuned to me, you see."

"That's daft," she said, her cheeks flushing scarlet. "How could I hurt the silly thing?"

"I'm sorry, Katie. I can't explain it to you." He stroked his fingers in a slow caress all down the length of the pipe and then looked up at her. "You see, Morfedd made it for *me*."

"Morfedd? The Wizard of Bowness?"

"Yes."

"You *knew* him?"

The boy nodded. "Morfedd's in here," he said, lifting the pipe. "And in me."

"Who says so?"

"It's true, Katie. He chose me on my third birthnight—ten summers ago. He twinned my tongue for me. Look." His lips parted and the tip of a pink tongue slipped out between the white, even teeth. As Katie watched, fascinated, the boy's tongue-tip divided and the two halves flickered separately up and down before flicking back into his mouth. "Believe me now?" he asked and grinned at her.

The girl's blue eyes were very wide indeed. "Did it hurt?" she whispered.

"No, not much. He did it bit by bit." The boy held up the pipe and pointed to the twin air ducts. "You see he wanted me to be able to tongue them both separately," he said. "Listen."

He set the pipe to his lips and blew gently down it. Then, without moving his fingers, he sounded two gentle trills, one slow, one faster; yet both somehow intertwined and as sweetly melodious as two birds warbling in unison in a green glade of the deep forest.

Katie was utterly enraptured. She had quite forgiven him his ill-mannered snatching of the pipe. "Play me a tune, Tom," she begged. "Go on. Do. Please."

"All right," he agreed. "What would you like?"

"I don't know. Make one up. Just for me. Could you?"

Tom rubbed his nose with the back of his hand then he turned slowly to face her and gazed deep into her eyes. As he did so he seemed to go very, very still, almost as if he were listening to some sound which only he could hear. For perhaps a minute he sat thus, then he nodded once, set the pipes to his lips and began to play.

Norris and his two grown-up sons returned from the forest at dusk. Well before the others heard them Tom's sharp ears had picked up the distant jingle of traces and the squeal of wooden axles. A moment later the dogs gave tongue to a raucous chorus of welcome. Katie and her mother hustled round making the final preparations for supper while Tom and old Peter sat one on either side of the fire, steaming faintly in the drowsy warmth.

Norris was the first to enter. A thick-set, heavily bearded man, with graying hair and eyes the color of an April sky. He dragged off his hooded leather tippet and slung it up on to an iron hook. Almost at once it began to drip quietly on to the flagstones beneath. "Halloa, there!" he cried. "What's this then? Company?"

Old Peter and Tom had risen at his entry and now the old man called out: "You'll remember me, I think, Norris? Peter the Tale-Spinner. Son of Blind Hereford."

"Sweet God in Heaven!" exclaimed Norris striding to meet him. "Not the Prince of Liars in person? Aye, it's him, right enough! Welcome back, old rogue! I'd given you over for worms' meat years ago!"

They clasped forearms in the pool of yellow lamplight and shook their heads over one another. "And who's the sprig, then?" demanded Norris tipping his chin at Tom. "One of yours?"

"My niece Margot's lad. Tom by given name. Margot wed with a Stavely man. I'm taking the boy to York for her."

"York, eh? And legging it? Ah so, you shall tell us all over supper. Well met, old man. What's ours is yours. And you too, boy. Katie, wench! Is my water hot?"

He strode off toward the scullery, boisterous as the North wind, and soon they heard sounds of noisy blowing and sluicing as he swilled himself down at the stone sink. His wife came into the kitchen and clattered out wooden bowls and mugs down the long table. "He remembered you then?" she said with a smile.

"Aye," said Peter. "I've changed less than he has,

it seems. Not that he hasn't worn well, mind you." He tipped his head to one side. "How comes your lass by that barley mow of hers?"

"Bar me all my folks are fair," she said. "Katie's eyes are her Dad's though. The boys seemed to fall betwixt and between." She stepped up to the fireplace, caught up a corner of her apron and lifted the lid of the iron cauldron which hung from a smoke-blackened chain above the flames. A rich and spicy scent floated over the hearth. She nodded, re-settled the lid and squinted up into the chimney where the other half of the salmon could be dimly seen twisting slowly back and forth in the hot air and the blue-gray woodsmoke. "Let it down again, lad," she said. "We'll souse it just once more."

Tom unhooked an end of the chain and lowered the fish till she was able to reach it. "Hold it still now," she said and picking a brush of twigs out of a pot on the hearth she basted the now golden flesh till it gleamed like dark honey. "Up with it, lad."

The fish vanished once more up the throat of the flue and a few aromatic drops fell down and sizzled among the embers.

As Tom was making the chain fast the door to the yard opened and Norris' two sons came in followed by the three dogs. The men eyed the two strangers curiously and watched without speaking as the dogs bounded up to the hearth and then ranged themselves in a grinning, hopeful semi-circle round the boy who looked down at them and laughed.

Norris appeared at the scullery door toweling his neck and bawled out introductions as though he were calling cattle in from the fells. The young men nodded and flashed their teeth in smiles of welcome. "You must have got a way with dogs, lad," observed one. "That lot don't take kindly to strangers as a rule. They're like as not to have the arse out of your breeks."

Tom eyed the dogs and shook his head. Then Katie came in and summoned them to her. In her hand she held the wooden bucket of fish offal. She opened the yard door, stepped outside, and the dogs tumbled after her, whining eagerly.

Ten minutes later the men and the boy took their places at the long table. Katie's mother ladled out thick broth into wooden bowls and Katie set one before each guest, then one before her father and her brothers and, last of all, one each for her mother and herself. Norris dunked his spoon and sucked up a noisy mouthful. "My women tell me we've got you to thank for this," he said to Peter.

The old man shrugged modestly and winked across at Tom. "You wed a fine cook, Norris," he said. "I've not tasted such a broth since I sampled your mother's."

Norris smiled. "Aye, old Mam taught Annie a thing or two afore she went. How to bear strong men for a start. Now tell us some news, old timer. Is it true there's a new king in Wales?"

"Aye. Dyfydd men call him. They say he's a fierce and cunning fighter."

"That's as may be, but can he keep the peace? Hold off the Paddys? Hey?"

"Maybe. Along the west border there was talk of him laying court to Eileen of Belfast—King Kerrigan's widow. That might do it—if he pulls it off."

"The sooner the better," said Norris, reaching out and tearing a ragged lump from the wheaten loaf before him. "You heard they'd fired Lancaster Castle?"

"There's no truth in that story, Norris. They were held at Morecambe and hanged at Preston."

"Is that a fact?"

"I did a two-day telling in Lancaster myself a month back. On my way up to Kendal. By the time we leg it into York I daresay folk will be telling us the Paddys hold everything west of the Pennines."

Norris laughed. "Aye. If cows grew like rumors we'd none of us lack for beef."

Peter smiled and nodded. "Are you still under Northumberland's shield here?"

"For what it's worth. The last border patrol we saw was nigh on a year back, and they were a right bunch of thieves. No, the only time his Lordship wants to know about us is at the Mid-Summer Tax Harvest. Our trouble here is that there aren't enough of us freeholders to make up more than a token force. And we're spread too thin. The Paddys could pick us off one by one if they'd a mind to, and none of us would be a wit the wiser till it was too late. It's our luck there's not much up here they're likely to fancy."

"You've not been troubled then?"

"Nothing to speak of."

The younger son glanced round at his brother and murmured something too low for Peter to catch.

"Poachers?" Peter asked.

"We had a spot of bother a year or two back. That's all settled now. Let's have some more beer here, Katie, lass!"

The girl brought a huge stone jug and refilled her father's mug. "Dad *killed* one of them," she said to Peter. "With his axe. You did, didn't you, Dad?"

"It was them or us," said Norris. "Don't think I'm proud of it."

"Well, *I* am," said Katie stoutly.

Norris laughed and gave her a cheerful wallop on the behind. "Well, it seems to have taught them a lesson," he said. "We've not been troubled since. Now tell us how the world's been treating you, Tale-Spinner."

"Never better than this," said Peter taking a long pull at his beer. "I crossed the narrow seas; lived a while in France and Italy. Joined up with a Greek juggler and voyaged with him to the Americas. Made some money and lost it. Came home to die two years ago. That's about it, Norris. Nothing you've any call to envy me for."

"You've never felt you wanted to settle then?"

"It's not so much a question of *wanting,* Norris; more a question of *royals.* Some can save money; some can't. Mind you, I'll not say I haven't had my chances. I was three whole years in one town in Italy. Still got connections there in a manner of speaking. But I'll not be putting to sea again. These bones will lie in the Fifth Kingdom. All I'm waiting for now is to see the millennium out."

Katie's mother spooned out steaming portions of rosy fish on to the wooden platters, piled potatoes and onions around them and passed them down the table. Norris stretched out and helped himself liberally to salt. "And just what's so special about the year 3000?" he demanded. "A year's a year and that's all there is to it. Numbers aren't worth a pig's turd."

"Ah, now, if you'll pardon me for saying so, Norris, there you're mistaken. The fact is the world's grown to expect something remarkable of A.D. 3000. And if enough people get to expecting something, then like enough it'll come to pass."

"Peace and Brotherhood, you mean? The White Bird of Kinship and all that froth? I just wish someone would have a go at telling it to the Paddys and the Jocks."

"Ah, but they believe in it too, Norris."

"Oh, they do, do they?" Norris snorted. "It's the first I've heard of it. If you ask me the only time the Jocks and the Paddys are likely to fall on anyone's neck is when they've got a broadsword to hand."

"There'll be a sign," said Peter. "That's how it'll be."

"A sign, eh? What sort of sign?"

"Some speak of a comet or a silver sky ship like they had in the Old Times. In Italy there was talk of a new star so bright you'll be able to see it in the day sky."

"And what do you think?"

"Well, they could be right, Norris. Stranger things have happened."

"No doubt. And telling people about them has kept your old belly nicely lined, eh?"

"Someone has to do it."

"Oh, I'm not belittling you, old timer. In truth I sometimes think we need more like you. Faith, it's a poor look out for folks if they can see no more to life than scratching for food and working up their appetite for it by killing their fellow men." He waved his knife at Tom. "What do you say, boy?"

Tom swallowed his mouthful and nodded his head. "Yes, sir," he said. "There *is* more than that."

"Bravely said, lad! Well, go on, tell us about it."

"Peter's right, sir. About the White Bird, I mean. It *is* coming."

"Oh, yes?" said Norris, winking at Peter. "What'll it be like, son?"

"I mean for some of us it's here *already*, sir," said Tom. "We can hear it *now*. It's in everything—all about us—everywhere. That's what I thought you meant, sir."

Norris blinked at him and rolled his tongue pensively around his teeth. Then he nodded his head slowly. "Well now, maybe I did at that," he said. "Not that I'd have thought to put it just so myself."

"Tom's a piper, Dad," said Katie. "He plays better than anyone I've ever heard."

"Is that a fact?" said Norris. "Then after supper we'll have to see if we can't persuade him to give us a tune. How about it, lad?"

"Gladly, sir."

"Good," said Norris stabbing a fork into his food and turning back to Peter. "You use him in your tellings, do you?"

"Not so far," said the old man. "But the thought crossed my mind just this afternoon. There's no denying he's got a real gift for the pipes. What do you say, Tom, lad? Fancy coming into partnership?"

"I thought you were supposed to be taking him to

the Chapter School at York," said Katie's mother with an edge to her voice that was not lost on Peter.

"Why, to be sure I am, ma'am," he said. "We're legging by way of Sedbergh and Aysgarth. Aiming to strike York for Christmas. That's so, isn't it, Tom?"

The boy nodded.

"I was hoping to make a start two weeks ago but I got an invitation to a telling in Carlisle which held me back." The old man cocked a ragged eyebrow toward Katie's mother. "I seem to recall you to be a native of Aysgarth, ma'am."

"You've got a fine memory, Tale-Spinner."

"I was thinking that maybe you would like us to carry some message to your folks for you?"

"You'd have to leg a deal further than Aysgarth to do it, old man," she said and smiled wanly. "They're dead and gone long since."

"Is that so? Well, indeed I'm truly sorry to hear it."

"It happens," she said.

Supper over, Norris tapped a small cask of strong ale, drew it off into a substantial earthenware jug, added sliced apple and a fragrant lump of crushed honeycomb, then stood the mixture down on the hearth to mull. By the time Tom had finished helping Katie and her mother to clear the table and wash the dishes, the warm ale was giving off a drowsy scent which set an idle mind wandering dreamily down the long-forgotten hedgerows of distant summers.

They settled themselves in a semi-circle round the hearth; the lamp was trimmed and turned low, and old Peter set about earning his night's lodging. Having fortified himself with a draft of ale, he launched himself into a saga set in the days before the Drowning when the broad skies were a universal highway and, by means of strange skills, long since forgotten, men and women could sit snug and cozy by their own firesides and see in their magic mirrors things which were happening at that very instant on the other side of the world.

Like all good stories there was some love in it and much adventure; hardship, breath-taking coincidence and bloody slaughter; and finally, of course, a happy ending. It's hero, the young Prince Amulet, having discovered that his noble father the King of Denmark has been murdered by a wicked brother who has usurped the throne, sets out to avenge the crime. Peter's description of the epic duel fought out between uncle and nephew with swords whose blades were beams of lethal light, held Norris and his family open-mouthed and utterly spellbound. Not for nothing was the son of Blind Hereford known throughout the Seven Kingdoms as "the Golden-Tongued."

When the victorious Prince and his faithful Princess had finally been escorted to their nuptial chamber through a fanfare of silver trumpets the enchanted listeners broke into spontaneous applause and begged Peter for another. But the Tale-Spinner was too old and wise a bird to be caught so easily. Pleading that his throat was bone dry he reminded them that young Tom had agreed to favor them with a tune or two.

"Aye, come along, lad," said Norris. "Let's have a taste of that whistle of yours."

While Tom was fetching his instrument from his pack, Katie made a round of the circle and replenished the mugs. Then she settled herself at her father's knee. The boy sat down cross-legged on the fire-warmed flagstones and waited till everyone was still.

He had played scarcely a dozen notes when there was a sound of frantic scratching at the yard door and a chorus of heart-rending whimpers. Tom broke off and grinned up at Norris. "Shall I let them in?"

"I will," said Katie and was up and away before Norris had a chance to say either yes or no.

The dogs bounded into the kitchen, tails waving ecstatically, and headed straight for the boy. He blew three swift, lark-high notes, pointed to the hearth before him and meek as mice they stretched themselves out at his feet. He laughed, leant forward and tapped

each animal on its nose with his pipe. "Now you be-
have yourselves, dogs," he said, "or I'll scare your
tails off."

Katie regained her place and he began to play once
more. He had chosen a set of familiar country dances
and, within seconds, he had feet tapping and hands
clapping all around the circle. It was almost as if
the listeners were unable to prevent their muscles from
responding to the imperious summons of his jigs and
reels. Even Old Peter found his toes twitching and his
fingers drumming out the rhythms on the wooden arm
of the ingle-nook settle.

With the flamelight flickering elvishly in his gray-
green eyes Tom swung them from tune to tune with
an effortless dexterity that would surely have been the
envy of any professional four times his age, and
when he ended with a sustained trill which would not
have shamed a courting blackbird his audience show-
ered praise upon him.

"Blest if ever I heard better piping!" cried Norris.
"Who taught you such skills, lad?"

"Morfedd the Wizard did," said Katie. "That's right,
isn't it, Tom?"

Tom nodded, staring ahead of him into the flames.

"Morfedd of Bowness, eh?' said Norris. "Me, I
never met him. But I recall how in Kendal the folk
used to whisper that he'd stored up a treasurehouse of
wisdom from the Old Times and Lord knows what
else beside. How came he to teach you piping, lad?"

"He came for me on my third birthnight," said Tom.
"He'd heard me playing a whistle up on the fells and
he bespoke my Mum and Dad for me." He raised his
head and looked round at Norris. "After Morfedd
died," he said, "I composed a lament for him. Would
you like to hear it?"

"Aye, lad. That we would. Whenever you're ready."

Then Tom did a strange thing. He gripped the pipe
in both hands, one at either end, and held it out at
arm's length in front of him. Then, very slowly, he

brought it back toward his chest, bent his head over it and seemed to be murmuring something to it. It was a strangely private little ritual of dedication that made all those who saw it wonder just what kind of a child this was. Next moment he had set the pipe to his lips, closed his eyes and turned his soul adrift.

To their dying day none of those present ever forgot the next ten minutes and yet no two of them ever recalled it alike. But all were agreed on one thing. The boy had somehow contrived to take each of them, as it were, by the hand and lead them back to some private moment of great sadness in their own lives, so that they felt again, deep in their own hearts, all the anguish of an intense but long-forgotten grief. For most the memory was of the death of someone dearly loved, but for young Katie it was different and was somehow linked with some exquisite quality she sensed within the boy himself—something which carried with it an almost unbearable sense of terrible loss. Slowly it grew within her, swelling and swelling till in the end, unable to contain it any longer she burst into wild sobs and buried her face in her father's lap.

Tom's fingers faltered on the stops and those listening who were still capable of doing so, noticed that his own cheeks were wet with tears. He drew in a great, slow, shuddering breath, then, without saying a word, got up and walked away into the shadows by the door. One by one the dogs rose to their feet and padded after him. Having restored his pipe to its place within his pack he opened the door and stepped outside into the night.

It was a long time before anyone spoke and, when they did, what was said was oddly inconsequential: Norris repeating dully, "Well, I dunno, I dunno, I dunno," and Old Peter muttering what sounded like a snatch from one of his own stories—"And the angel of Grief moved invisible among them and their tears fell like summer rain." Only Katie's mother was moved to remark: "He'll not carry such a burden for long, I think," though, had anyone thought to ask her, she would have been hard put to explain what she meant, or even why she had said it.

During the night the wind shifted into a new quarter. It came whistling down, keen and chill from the Northern Cheviots, until the dawn sky, purged at last of cloud, soared ice-blue and fathomless above the forest and the fells.

A bare half hour after sun-up Old Peter and Tom had said their farewells and were on their way. Katie accompanied them to the top of the valley to set them on their path. She pointed to a white rock on the crest of a distant hill and told them that from there they would be able to sight Sedbergh spire. The old man thanked her and said he'd be sure to call and see her again when he was next in the district.

"You may be," she said, "but he won't. I know," and turning to Tom she took from the pocket of her cloak a small, flat, green pebble, washed smooth by the river. A hole had been drilled in the center and through it a leather lace was threaded. "That's for my song," she said. "Keep it. It may bring you luck."

Tom nodded, slid the thong over his head and slipped the talisman down inside his jerkin where it lay cool as a water drop against his chest. "Goodbye, Katie," he said.

He did not look back until they were well down the track and then he saw her still standing there on the hilltop with the wind streaming out her long hair into a misty golden halo. He raised his arm in salute. She waved back, briefly, and the next moment she had turned and vanished in the direction of the hidden farm.

They stopped to eat shortly before noon, choosing the shelter of an outcrop of rock close to where a spring bubbled. The sun struck warm on to their backs even though, but a few paces from where they sat, the wind still hissed drearily through the dry bracken bones. Old Peter broke in two the flat scone

which Katie's mother had given them and then divided one of the halves into quarters. He sliced off two
substantial lumps of the smoked salmon and handed
bread and meat to the boy.

For a few minutes they both chewed away in silence then Peter said: "I'd been thinking of trying our
luck at Sedbergh Manor, but maybe we'd do better
at the inn. There's a chance we'll strike up acquaintance with a carrier and get ourselves a lift to Aysgarth. Better ride than leg, eh?"

"Whatever you say," agreed Tom.

The old man nodded sagely. "If luck's with us
there's no reason we shouldn't pick up a royal or two
into the bargain. Between the two of us, I mean.
Reckon we could milk it out of them, eh?"

Tom glanced across at him but said nothing.

"You've never thought of roading for a living then,
lad?"

"No."

"Ah, it's the only life if you've got the talent for it.
Blast, but we two'd make a splendid team! Think of
legging the high road through the Seven Kingdoms!
York, Derby, Norwich, London. New towns, new
faces! Why, we could even duck it across the French
seas an' we'd a mind to! Taste the salt spray on our
lips and see the silver sails swell like a sweetheart's
bosom! How's that strike you as fare for a spring
morning, lad?"

Tom smiled. "But I thought you said you weren't
going to go to sea again."

"Ah, well, that was just a *façon de parler* as they
say across the water. But with you along it would be
different. We could work up a proper act, see? You'd
feel your way into the mood of each tale and then,
with that pipe of yours, you'd come drifting in along
o' the words like a feather on the tide. Between the
two of us we'd reach right down through their ears
and tickle their pockets. Blast it, Tom lad, I tell you
you've got a touch of magic in those finger-ends of
yours—a gift like nobody's business! You don't want

to chuck all that away while you choke yourself to death on Minster dust! A dower like yours cries out to be shared! You owe it to the Giver of Gifts! Out there on the wide high road you'll be as free as the wind and the birds of the air! Up and off! Over the hills and far away!"

Tom laughed. "But I *am* free. Morfedd taught me that. He unlocked something inside me and let it fly out. Besides, I want to learn how to read and write."

"Pooh, there's nothing to letters, Tom. I'll teach you myself. And more besides! There's only one school for the likes of us, lad. The great high road. Once you've begun to turn the pages of that book you'll never want another."

"And Mum? What would she think? After she's taken all that trouble to bespeak Cousin Seymour for me?"

"Ah, your heart does you credit, lad. Real credit. But I know my Mistress Margot. Been dreaming up plans for you, hasn't she? How maybe you'll catch the Bishop's eye and gain a preference and so on and so forth? Isn't that it? Ah, that's just a mother's daydreams, Tom. Believe you me, lad, the only way to preference in York Chapter for a boy like you is up the back stairs and on to the choirmaster's pallet. Faith, I tried to tell her so, but she wouldn't listen. Said your Cousin Seymour would shield you from anything of that sort. But I know the ways of the world and—"

"People become what you think them, Peter."

"Eh? How's that?"

"Morfedd said so. He said our thoughts are unseen hands shaping the people we meet. Whatever we truly think them to be, that's what they'll become for us."

The old man stared at him, wondering if the Kendal gossips had spoken true and the boy really *was* touched. "Oh, he did, did he?" he said at last. "And what else did he say?"

"Morfedd? Oh, lots of things."

"Well, go on, lad. Let's hear one."

Tom rubbed his nose with the back of his hand and stared out across the hillside. "He used to say that seeing things as they *really* are is the most difficult seeing of all. He said people only see what they want to see. And then they believe the truth is what they *think* they see, not what really is."

"Aye, well, I'm not saying he doesn't have a point here. But I'll warrant he didn't think to tell you how to recognize this truth when you do see it."

"You don't *see* it exactly. You *feel* it."

"And just how's that supposed to help someone like me who lives by his lying? Didn't you know they call me 'Prince of Liars'?"

Tom grinned. "Oh, that's different," he said. "Your stories are like my music. They tell a different kind of truth. People hear it in their hearts."

"Blast it, boy, you have an answer pat for everything! Look here, I'll tell you what. From now till Christmastide we'll work the road 'twixt here and York—Leyburn, Masham, Ripon and Boroughbridge —finishing up at 'The Duke's Arms' in Selby Street. That way you'll get a fair taste of the life I'm offering. Then if you're still set on the Chapter School, why that's all there is to it. Till then you'll have a third-part share in all we take. That strike you as fair?"

"All right," said Tom. "But you must tell me what you want me to do."

"Done!" cried Peter. "We'll set it up while we're legging down to Sedbergh. Have you done with eating? Right then, partner, let's be on our way."

It soon emerged that the book of the open road which Peter had recommended to Tom with such enthusiasm contained at least one chapter which he himself had never read. By the third week of December when they reached Boroughbridge the old man found that rumor, racing ahead like a fell fire, had brought scores of curious people riding into town from as far afield as Harrogate and Easingwold. And the rumors were extraordinary. Even Peter, whose life's philosophy was based on seizing fortune by the fore-lock and never looking a gift horse in the mouth, was genuinely bewildered by them. They seemed to bear no relation whatsoever to the facts which were, as he saw them, that a pair of troupers were working the road down to York for the Christmastide fair. What in the name of the Giver of Gifts could that have to do with any White Bird of Kinship? Yet there was no escaping the fact that it was this which was bringing these credulous country folk flocking in.

Nor was that all. Getting a quarter out of a fell farmer was usually about as easy as pulling his teeth with your bare hands, yet here they were showering their silver into his hat as though it was chaff, and none of them thinking to dip a hand in after it either. Over a hundred royal they'd taken in three weeks, not to mention the new suit apiece that dimwitted tailor in Leyburn had insisted on making for them, refusing even a penny piece for his labor. Why, at this rate, in six months he'd have enough put by for that little pub in Kendal he'd always hankered after. Six months? A bare *three* at the pace things were going! Sure Tom couldn't grudge him that. Meanwhile here was the landlord of "The Bull" fingering his greasy cow-lick and trusting they would favor him with their esteemed custom. No question of *paying!* It would be his privilege. And the inn yard with its gallery would surely be ideal for their performance. It could accommodate three hundred with ease—three fifty at a pinch. The venerable Tale-Spinner had only to give word and the news would be all round the town before the church clock had struck the hour.

"All right, landlord," said Peter magnanimously. "But it'll cost you two royal."

The landlord blenched, made a rapid mental calculation, and agreed.

"Two a *night*," said Peter imperturbably. "For the two nights."

A slightly longer pause followed by a nod of grudging acquiescence.

"And I'll have half in advance."

"There's my hand on it," said the landlord, and suited the action to the word.

A wall-eyed serving wench showed them up to their room which overlooked the inn yard. "There's a spread of clean linen," she informed them shyly, "and coals to the fire. Would you like that I fetch you a bite to eat?"

"Aye, lass. A meat pasty. And a jug of hot punch to help it down."

She bobbed a half-curtsey and ducked out. Tom, who had wandered over to the window, observed that it looked as if it was going to snow.

"More than like," said Old Peter, rubbing his hands briskly and stretching them out to the flames. "Aren't we due a few feathers from the White Bird?" He snorted tolerantly. "Can you make head or tail of it?"

Tom breathed on to the glass before him and drew a "3" on its side. "I think it's like you said to Norris. People *want* to believe it. They're tired of feeling afraid."

"But what's that got to do with *us*, lad?"

"I don't know."

"Oh, I'll not deny you play a very pretty pipe and I tell a stirring enough tale, but what kind of sparks are they to set this sort of kindling ablaze? I tell you true, Tom, if it wasn't that we're coining money hand over fist I'd be sorely tempted to turn around and head right back to Kendal. I don't like the smell of it one bit."

Tom moved away from the window and wandered back to the fire. "There's nothing to be afraid of," he said. "I think we should go along with it."

"Go along with what?"

"Well, tell them the story of the White Bird. You could, couldn't you?"

"And have the crows about my neck? You must be out of your mind."

"But Morfedd said—"

" 'Morfedd said!' That joker said a deal too much for your good, if you ask me! The sooner you start putting him behind you, the better for both of us. Oh, I don't mean to belittle him, lad, but we aren't in the back of beyond now, you know. Down here they're a sight more touchy about such things than they are along the Borders. And as for York . . ."

Tom regarded the old man pensively. "I've been making up a tune to go with the White Bird," he said. "It's not finished yet. Would you like to hear it?"

"I suppose there's no harm. So long as it's without words. But what put that idea into your head?"

"I'm not really sure. The first bit came to me just after we left Katie. When I looked back and saw her standing there on top of the hill. Since then I've been joining things on to it. I've been using some of them for *Amulet*. That scene where the Prince meets his father's ghost is one. And there's another bit later on when he believes Princess Lorelia has been drowned. The last bit I made up at Ripon when you were telling *The Three Brothers*. Don't you remember?"

"To be honest, lad, I can't say as I do. The fact is, when I'm stuck into a tale I don't hear much above the sound of my own words. I'm hearing it and telling it at the same time. Seeing it too. In a bit of a dream I suppose you might say. Maybe that's why my tellings never come out word for word the same. Not even *Amulet*. And, blast me, if I had a silver quarter for every time I've spun *that* yarn there wouldn't be a richer man in Boroughbridge!"

Tom laughed. "And has it always had a happy ending?"

"*Amulet?* Aye. The way I tell it. My old Dad would have the Prince dying at the end. But that cuts too close to life for my taste."

"The White Bird dies too, doesn't it?"

"Look, do me a favor, will you, lad? Just forget about that Holy Chicken. Leastways till we're shot of York. Down south in Norwich we'll like enough get away with it, tho' even there it could still be a bit risky."

Tom who had taken up his pipe now lowered it to his lap. "But we're not going to Norwich," he said. "Just to York. That's what we agreed, wasn't it?"

"Aye, so it was," said Peter easily. "The fact is, Tom, I've grown so used to having you along I can't think of it being any other way. Tell me straight now, hasn't this past month been a fair old frolic? Remember that flame-headed wench at Masham, eh? Blast me but she was properly taken with you! And yon whistle wasn't the only pipe she was pining for neither! I tell you that between us we've got it made, lad! Stick with me and I swear that six months from now you'll be taking such a bag of royals home to your mam as'll topple her on the floor in a fit! You *can't* just let it drop now!"

Tom raised his pipe and slowly lowered his head above it as Peter had seen him do once before in the farmhouse kitchen. For a full minute he said nothing at all, then: "I must go to York, Peter. I must."

"Well, and so you shall. Show me him as says otherwise. We struck hands on it, remember? 'Sides I had word only this morning from Jack Rayner at 'The Duke's Arms' that he's looking to us for Friday. The way I've planned it we'll just work out the Christmas fair and then you'll trot round and pay your respects to your Cousin Seymour at the Chapter House. You can't say fairer than that, can you?"

Tom nodded. "I'm sorry," he said. "I really am, Peter. I think you're the finest story-teller that ever was. Listening to you is like sharing in a golden dream. But you see I promised Morfedd I'd go to York, and I can't break my promise."

"*Morfedd?* What's he got to do with it? I thought this was all Mistress Margot's idea."

"She thinks so," said Tom. "But really it was Morfedd. He planned it years ago. Long before he chose me. Before I was even *born*. It was a secret between us."

"I'm not with you, lad. Planned *what*? That you should get yourself schooled in York Chapter? Is that supposed to make sense?"

"Oh, that's nothing to do with it. I just have to be in York at Christmas. For the forthcoming."

"Blast it, boy, why must you speak in riddles? What 'forthcoming'?"

Tom lifted his head and gazed into the flickering coals. Then in a gentle sing-song he recited: " *'The first coming was the man; the second was fire to burn him; the third was water to drown the fire, and the fourth is the Bird of Dawning.'* " So saying he took up his pipe and began to play very softly.

It seemed to the old man that the tune came drifting to him from somewhere far away like the voice of a young girl he had once heard singing on the far side of a twilit lake high up in the Appenines, strange and sweetly clear and so magical that he had scarcely dared to breathe lest he should miss a note of it. He closed his eyes, surrendering himself wholly to the enchantment.

At once there began to drift across his inward eye a series of glittering pictures that were not quite real and yet were more than mere daydreams, memories almost, of not quite forgotten moments woven into the long tapestry of years that had gone to make up his life; instants when, wholly in spite of himself, he had seemed about to reach out towards something that was at once so simple and yet so profound that he just could not bring himself to accept it. And yet it *could* be grasped because it was not outside him but within him; a vision of what might be, as when he, and he alone, by stretching out an arm in thought could wrest the deadly weapon from the Uncle's hand and grant Prince Amulet life. The power was his—was *anyone's* —was . . .

The thread of the melody snapped. Peter's eyes blinked open and the room seemed to rock into stillness around him. He felt his cloudy identity distill itself like mist on a windowpane and trickle downwards in slow, sad drops. There was a *tap-tap* at the door and, to Tom's summons, in came the serving girl bearing a tray on which was a jug and two earthenware cups and the steaming pasty which Peter had ordered. She set it down on a stool before the fire, then turned to where the boy was sitting on the edge of the bed. "It's true what they're saying," she whispered. "I stood outside the door and listened. I was feared to come in while you was a-playin'."

Tom grinned at her. "What *are* they saying?" he asked.

"That the White Bird's a-coming. It is, isn't it?"

"Do *you* think so?"

"Aye, young master," she said. "I do *now*."

The night before they were due to leave for York there was a heavy frost. The landlord of "The Bull" lit some charcoal braziers in the yard and Peter and Tom gave their final performance at Boroughbridge under a sky in which the stars seemed to quiver like dewdrops in an April cobweb. Peter was perched up on a rough dais made of planks and barrels and Tom sat cross-legged at his feet. As the recital was drawing to its close the old man caught sight of a figure slipping away from the outer fringe of the crowd. Lamplight gleamed briefly on polished metal and, a minute later, Peter's alerted ears caught the brisk and receding clatter of iron-shod hooves on cobblestones.

Later, while settling accounts with the landlord, he inquired casually whether any "crows" had been pecking around.

The landlord glanced quickly about him, saw that they were unobserved and murmured: "Aye, there was one."

"Happen you know what he was seeking?"

"Not I," said the landlord. "He asked nowt of me."

Peter took a bright gold half-royal out of his purse and laid it on the table between them. With his extended fingertip he nudged it delicately an inch or two toward his host. "Flown in from York, I daresay?"

The man's eyes swivelled away from the coin and then back to it again as though tethered by an invisible thread. "Aye, most like," he said.

"And home to roost by starlight," mused Peter, coaxing the coin back toward himself again. "I wonder what sort of song he'll be croaking in the Minster?"

The landlord leant across the table and beckoned Peter closer by a tiny jerk of the head. "Know you aught of the White Bird of Kinship, old Tale-Spinner?" he whispered.

Peter clucked his tongue, chiding ironically. "Did you think to speak heresy with me, landlord?"

" 'Twas you that asked, and that's the carrion the crows are pecking for. They've smelt it blowing down strong from the hills these twelve months past. Don't tell me you've not heard the talk."

"Aye, some to be sure. Along the Borders."

The landlord shook his head. "No longer. It's in the open now. Seems even the field mice have got bold all of a sudden. Me I keep my thoughts to myself."

"So you'll live to raise wise grandsons like yourself," said Peter, nodding approval. He tapped the coin with his fingernail. "Was that one I saw asking after us?"

"Aye, he was. Where you hailed from. Whither bound."

"And you told him, of course."

"Not I. But anyone with ears in Boroughbridge could have done so. You've not kept it any close secret."

"That's true. Well, I'm obliged to you, landlord. The boy and I have a mind to ride horseback the rest of our way. Can you manage us two hacks to 'The Duke's Arms' in Selby Street?"

"I can that, and gladly," said the landlord, quite at

his ease once more. "A quarter apiece they'll cost you."

Peter nodded, opened his purse once more, joined a second half-royal to the first and pushed them across the table top. "You'll not be out of pocket by our stay, I think."

The landlord shrugged and pocketed the coins. "They weren't an over-thirsty lot, but there were plenty of them."

That night the old tale-spinner's dreams were troubled by shapes of vague ill-boding, but the shadows they cast soon lifted next morning as he urged his hired horse at a trot out of Boroughbridge along the ancient road to York. Frosty icing glittered as the early sunlight splintered off diamond sparks from the hedgerow twigs; frozen puddles crackled briskly beneath the clopping hooves; and breath of horse and rider snorted up in misty plumes along the eager nipping air.

"Hey, Tom, lad!" Peter called back over his shoulder. "How's it feel to be entering York in style? This is the life, eh? Beats legging any day!"

Tom shook his own nag into an arthritic canter and eventually lumbered up alongside. "No one can hear us out here, can they, Peter?"

"What about it?"

"There's something I've been wanting to ask you."

"Well, go ahead, lad. Ask away."

"It's about the White Bird."

A light seemed to go out in Peter's eye. He sighed. "Well, go on, if you must," he said. "Get it off your chest."

"Just before he died Morfedd told me that the Bird *will* come down and drive the fear out of men's hearts. But he didn't say *how*. Do you know, Peter?"

"I thought I'd made it pretty clear what I think, Tom. Why don't you just let it alone, lad?"

"But you know the story, Peter."

"I know how it *ends*," said the old man grimly.

"The other bird, you mean?"

"Aye, lad. The Black Bird. Me, I prefer my stories to have happy endings."

Tom rode for a while in silence considering this. "Maybe it *was* a happy ending," he said at last.

"Not the way I heard it, it wasn't."

"Then maybe we should all hear it different," said Tom. "Perhaps that's what Morfedd meant. He said true happiness was simply not being afraid of anyone at all. He called it the last secret."

"Did he, indeed? Well, let me tell you I'm a great respecter of Lord Fear. That's how I've lived so long. If you want to do the same you'd better start by speeding all thoughts of the White Bird clear out of your mind—or into your pipe if you must. I've more than a suspicion we'll find plenty of ears in York ready pricked for heresy, and plenty of tongues ready to run tattle with it. It's a dangerous time to be dreaming of the White Bird of Kinship, Tom. Have I made myself plain enough?"

"Aye, that you have," said Tom and laughed cheerfully.

As they clattered over Hammerton Bridge a solitary horseman dressed in doublet and breeches of black leather, wearing a studded steel casque helmet, and with a lethal-looking metal cross-bow slung across his shoulder, emerged from behind a clump of trees and came cantering after them. "Good morrow, strangers," he hailed them civilly. "You ride to York?"

"Aye, sir," said Peter. "To York it is."

"For the Fairing, no doubt."

Peter nodded.

"You buy or sell?"

The old man doffed his cap. "A little of both, sir. Old Peter of Hereford, Tale-Spinner. At your service."

"Well met indeed, then!" cried the bowman. "How better to pass an hour than by sampling your goods, Old Peter. And the lad? Does he sing, or what?"

"He pipes a burden to my tales, sir."

"A piper too, eh! Truly fortune beams upon me." The stranger drew back his lips in a smile but his eyes remained as cold and still as slate pebbles on a river bed. "So, what have we on offer?"

Peter rubbed his chin and chuckled. "On such a morning as this what could suit better than a frisky love story?"

"Nay, nay, old man! I fear you might set me on so hard my saddle would come sore. I'll have none of your rutty nonsense. In truth my tastes are of a different order. Inclined more toward the fable you might say." The smile was gone as though wiped from his face with a cloth. "I'll have The White Bird of Kinship, Tale-Spinner, and none other."

Peter frowned. "Faith, sir, I'm famed to know a tale for every week I've lived, but that's a new one on me. No doubt I have it by some other name. That happens sometimes. If you could, perhaps, prompt me. . . ."

"We'll let the lad do that for us, old rogue. Come, sprat! Put your master on the right road!"

Tom smelt old Peter's fear, rank as stale sweat, and felt a quick stab of pity for the old man. He looked across at the bowman and smiled and shook his head. "I do have an old hill tune of that calling, sir. But it has no words to it that I know. If you wish I can finger it for you." And without waiting for a reply he looped his reins over his pommel, dipped into his knapsack and took out his pipe.

The bowman watched, sardonic and unblinking, as the boy first set the mouthpiece to his lips then turned his head so that he was facing the newcomer directly across the forequarters of Peter's horse. Their glances met, locked, and, at the very instant of eye-contact, the boy began to play.

Whiteness exploded in the man's mind. For an appalling instant he felt the very fabric of the world rending apart. Before his eyes the sun was spinning like a crazy golden top; glittering shafts of light leapt up like sparkling spears from hedge-row and hill-top; and all about his head the air was suddenly awash with the slow, majestic beating of huge, invisible wings. He felt an almost inexpressible urge to send a wild hosanna of joy fountaining upwards in welcome while, at the same time, his heart was melting within him. He had become a tiny infant rocked in a warm cradle of wonder and borne aloft by those vast unseen pinions, up and up to join the blossoming radiance of the sun. And then, as suddenly as it had come, it was over; he was back within himself again, conscious only of a sense of desperate loss—of an enormous insatiable yearning.

The bowman sat astride his horse like one half-stunned, the reins drooping from his nerveless fingers, while the old man turned to the boy and whispered: "What in the name of mercy have you done to him? He looks like a sleep-walker."

Tom ran his strange forked tongue across his upper lip. "I thought of him like I think of the dogs," he murmured, "not as a man at all. Perhaps he *wanted* to believe me. Do you know who he is?"

"Aye. He's a Falcon. Each Minster has a brood of them. They have a swift and deadly swoop. I glimpsed one of them at the telling last night." He turned back with a broad guileless smile to the bowman. "Well, sir," he cried cheerfully, "now you've sampled the lad's skill, how about a taste of mine? Myself I'm in the mood for a good spicy wenching tale, if you're agreeable?"

The man nodded abstractedly and the old storyteller launched himself without further ado into a tale of lechery whose bones had been creaking long before Rome was young and yet which, for all its antiquity, lacked neither spirit nor flavor.

By the time the last score had been settled, the last knot tied, the three riders were within a strong bowshot of the city walls. Peter reined up his horse and doffed his hat with a fine flourish. "Your servant, sir," he said. "And may your nights be as lively as my tale."

The man reached absently toward the purse that hung at his belt but the old man stopped him with a lordly gesture. "Your personal recommendation is all we crave, sir," he said. "We come to work the Fair."

"So you shall have it," said the bowman. "I give you the word of Gyre." He stood up in his stirrups and looked back along the road they had ridden as though he were searching for something he could no longer see. Finally he shook his head, turned back, and glancing at Tom, said: "I am sorry I didn't get to hear your piping, lad. Some other time, eh?"

Tom nodded and smiled and patted the neck of his horse.

In brief salute the bowman touched his left shoulder with his clenched right fist. "Well met, then," he said. He shook his reins, kicked his heels into his horse's flanks and cantered off toward the west gate of the city.

As they watched him go, Peter muttered uneasily: "Was that his idea of a joke, d'you think?"

"No," said Tom. "He meant it."

"But he can't have *forgotten*."

"I think he has," said Tom. "He remembers *something,* but he's not sure whether we had anything to do with it. Didn't you see him looking back along the road? Perhaps he thinks I offered to play for him and he refused."

"And he *won't* remember?"

"I don't think so. Not unless I want him to."

"I once knew a man in Italy who could entrance people," said Peter. "But he did it with words."

Tom nodded. "Morfedd could do that too."

"He did it to you, did he?"

"Often."

"And how do *you* do it?"

"I tell them too—only without words."

"Tell them what?"

Tom looked into the old man's eyes and smiled faintly. "I told *him* about the White Bird," he said. "He wanted to believe me, so it was easy."

Peter stared at him. "Do you *know* how you do it?"

"I know when someone wants me to."

"But *how,* lad? What is it you *do?*"

Tom sighed faintly. "I join myself to them. I build a bridge and walk to them over it. I take their thoughts and give them back my own." He glanced at Peter and then away again. "One day I'll do it for everyone, not just one or two."

"And Morfedd taught you that, did he?"

"He taught me how to find the right keys. A different one for each person. But I believe there's a master-key, Peter. One to unlock the whole world. I call that key the White Bird."

Peter shook his head slowly. "Well, I'm scarcely wiser than I was before, but I'm mighty glad you did it. I had an ill vision of the two of us lying spitted at the roadside like a couple of sparrows. That little toy he carries at his back can put a bolt clean through an oak door at thirty paces."

Tom laughed. "I liked the story anyway."

The old man treated him to an enormous wink. "Come on, lad!" he cried. "We're still alive so let's make the most of it! My throats as dry as a brick oven." Slapping his horse's haunch with the reins he led the way into the city.

York was the first city that Tom had ever laid eyes on. As soon as he had recovered from his initial astonishment he found it put him irresistibly in mind of an ancient oak that grew on a hillside near his home in Bowness. Known locally as "the Wizard's Oak" this once lordly tree had been completely shattered by lightning and given up for dead. Then, a year later, it had begun to generate a few leafy shoots and, within ten years, had become a respectable living tree again. Now as he wandered about the bustling streets and squares and nosed into the dark alleys, Tom's sharp eyes picked out the dead skeleton branches of ancient York still standing amidst the new, and he found himself wondering about the race of men, long since dead and forgotten, who had erected these incredible buildings. He even conceived the odd notion that the builders must themselves have been shaped differently from ordinary men and women, not rounded but squared off and pared to sharp edges, as if their gods had first drawn them out on a plan with rule and line and then poured them into molds, row upon row, all alike like bricks in a brick works.

Yet even underneath those stark bones he perceived faint traces of a structure yet more ancient still: great blocks of gray granite cemented into the foundations of the city's walls and, here and there, twisting flights of stone steps worn thin as wafers by the feet of generations all hurrying on to death long long ago. Once, wandering near the Minster he had seemed to sense their hungry ghosts clustering all about him, imploring him with their shadowy charnel mouths and their sightless eyes to tell them that they had not lived in vain. He had fled up on to the city walls and, gazing out across the Sea of Goole, had tried to imagine what it must have been like to live in the days before the Drowning. He strove to visualize the skies above the city filled with Morfedd's "metal birds" and the great sea road to Doncaster thronged with glittering carts drawn by invisible horses. But in truth it was like believing that the world travelled round the sun—something you accepted because you were told it was so—and a good deal less real than many of Old Peter's tales. Even the importunate ghosts of the dead were more alive in his imagination as they came flocking grayly in upon him, unaccountable as the waves on the distant winter sea.

Staring into the setting sun, lost in time, he heard, deep within himself, yet another fragment of the melody he was always listening for. At once the smothering weight lifted from his heart. He turned, and skipping lightly down the steps, headed back to the inn.

Late on Christmas Eve a message was brought up to Clerk Seymour at the Chapter House that a man was below asking to speak with him on a matter of urgency.

The Clerk, a gray, cobwebby man with a deeply lined face and bad teeth, frowned tetchily. "At this hour?" he protested. "What does he want?"

"He didn't say, except that it was for your own ear."

"Oh, very well. Send him up."

A minute later there were steps on the wooden stairs, a deferential knock at the door and Old Peter appeared on the threshold with his hat in his hand. "Clerk Seymour?"

"Aye, sir. And who are you?"

Old Peter closed the door carefully behind him and came forward with hand outstretched. "Old Peter of Hereford," he said. "Tale-Spinner by calling. You and I are related by wedlock through my niece Margot."

"Ah, yes. To be sure. You are bringing her boy to me. Well met, cousin." They shook hands formally and the Clerk gestured the old man to a seat. "I have heard many speak highly of your skill, Tale-Spinner," he said. "But am I not right in thinking you are over a week in York already?"

The old man made a self-deprecating gesture. "Truly I would have called sooner," he said, "but I guessed these weeks would be a busy time for all at the Chapter. Is it not so?"

The Clerk smiled faintly. "Aye, well, we are none of us idle at the Mass. That goes for you too, I daresay. You will take a cup of wine with me?"

"That I will and gladly, cousin."

The Clerk fetched cups and a stone bottle from a

cupboard. "And how goes the Fairing for you?" he inquired amiably.

"Faith I've never known one like it," said Peter. "I vow I could fill Cross Square four times over and I had the voice to carry. They flock in like starlings."

The Clerk poured out the wine carefully, re-corked the bottle, handed a cup to Peter and lifted his own in silent toast. Having taken a sip he resumed his chair. "You are not working alone, I gather."

"Ah, the lad you mean?" Peter nodded indulgently. "Well, he pleaded with me to let him take a part and I hadn't the heart to deny him. He has a mighty engaging way with him has Tom. But of course you'll know that."

"Not I," said the Clerk. "I've never set eyes on the boy. In truth, until Margot's letter I'd thought he was another girl. What is it he does with you?"

Peter licked a trace of wine from his lips. "I let him pipe a burden to my tales. A snatch or two here and there. It helps things along and it keeps him happy."

"He does it well?"

"I've had to coach him, of course. But he learns quickly. He has a good ear for a tune."

"Then it's clear that I must make time to come and hear you." The Clerk took another sip at his wine. "You see the Fairing out?"

"Aye. I had thought to leg to Doncaster for the New Year but while things go so well . . ."

Clerk Seymour nodded, wondering when the old man was going to get round to saying whatever it was that he had come to say. Surely it was not just to pass the time of day? "To Doncaster," he murmured. "Aye, well . . ."

Old Peter set down his cup and plucked his lower lip thoughtfully. "Tell me, cousin Seymour," he said casually. "The Chapter School. Am I right in thinking they take lads of all ages?"

"Well, within reason, yes, that is so."

"Fourteen years would not be thought too old?"

"By no means. But surely I understood Margot to say . . ."

"Yes, yes," said Peter quickly. "Young Tom won't span fourteen for a five-month yet. What I am anxious to know, cousin, is whether his place could be held open for him till then?"

"I'm not sure that I . . ."

"This would be in the nature of a personal favor to me, you understand, and naturally I should be prepared to recompense the Chapter for any inconvenience it might cause." The old man hesitated a mere half second, glanced sharply sideways and added, "Fifty royal?"

The Clerk did his best to conceal his astonishment and did not succeed. After all, the sum mentioned was as much as he earned in a six-month! He stared at Peter. "Forgive me, Tale-Spinner," he said. "But do I understand you right? You wish to postpone the boy's entry till he reaches his fourteenth year?"

Peter nodded.

The Clerk waved a hand. "Why this, I'm sure, could easily be arranged. But *why?*"

Old Peter sank back in his chair and let out his breath in a long sigh. "Cousin Seymour," he said, "you see before you an old man, friendless, alone in the world, with the final curtain about to come down upon his last act. For this month past I have found in Tom's constant companionship a source of solace and comfort I had not dreamed could be mine. My sole wish is to make one last farewell tour through the Seven Kingdoms and then back home to Cumberland and the long rest. Without Tom I could not face it. With him along it will be my crowning triumph. There now, *that* is the answer to your question."

The Clerk nodded, pursing his lips pensively. "And the boy? Presumably he is agreeable?"

"Oh, he loves the life! Fresh faces; fresh places. Why this last six weeks a whole new window has opened in Tom's world!"

"Then there would seem to be no problem."

"On the face of it, you are right, cousin. But the truth of the matter is it's not quite so simple. For one thing there's still the lad's mother."

"You mean you haven't discussed it with her?"

"Well, until the lad expressed his desire to join up with me, the question didn't arise. Since then we've got along like a house a-fire. But it's only natural he should feel a good son's duty to abide by his mother's wish."

A gleam of belated understanding kindled in the Clerk's eye. "Ah, I *see*," he murmured. "So it would suit you if we could make this delay 'official'?"

Peter slipped his hand beneath his cloak, fumbled for a moment, then drew out a soft leather bag which clinked faintly as he laid it on the table. "What harm could there be in gratifying an old man's whim, cousin? I will cherish that boy as if he were my own son. I'll even undertake to school him in his letters. And I shall return him here to you, safe and sound, before the Midsummer High Mass. All I'm asking of you is that you write a letter to Margot explaining that the place you had bespoken for the lad will not be open to him till the summer; and that when I bring Tom along here you say the same to him. That done we can all go our ways contented."

The Clerk reached out, uncorked the wine bottle and poured out a second careful measure into the two cups. "There is but one thing troubles me," he said. "I have only your word for it that the boy is happy with you. I would have to speak to him alone before I could agree."

"You would not tell him that I have spoken with you, Cousin Seymour?"

"Naturally not," said the Clerk, lifting his cup and touching it against Peter's. "That is clearly understood. Nevertheless, for his mother's sake, I feel bound to insist upon it as a condition of our confidential 'arrangement'."

"Agreed then," said Peter, and with his free hand

he gathered up the bag of coins and shook it gently. "The moment you have satisfied yourself that matters are as I say, these will be yours to distribute as you think fit. To your health, cousin."

At the very moment when the Clerk to the Chapter was chatting so amiably to the old tale-spinner, a very different sort of discussion was taking place in a tall gray tower block at the far end of the Minster Close. This building, which was known locally as "The Falconry," was the headquarters of the whole Secular Arm of the Church Militant throughout the Seven Kingdoms. Its reputation was just as bleak as its appearance. Cold, functional, efficient; the only sign of decoration on the walls of The Falconry was an inscription in burnished steel characters riveted fast to the stonework above the main door: *Hic et Ubique.* This, when translated from its archaic tongue, read simply: "Here and Everywhere." Nothing further was needed.

The man responsible for overseeing all the multifarious activities of the Secular Arm had the official title of "Chief Falconer" though he was more generally spoken of as "the Black Bishop." Born in 2951, the illegitimate son of a Cornish tax-collector, he had been brought up by the Black Fathers and had risen to his high eminence by dint of great intellectual ability, an outstanding capacity for organization, and an appetite for sheer hard work which had already become something of a legend before he had reached the age of twenty-five. In the seven years since he had been appointed to his present office he had completely re-vitalized the moribund structure he had inherited and rumor had it that his heart was set on doing the same throughout the whole of Europe. Others maintained, *sotto voce,* that here rumor lied, since it was a proven fact that the Black Bishop had no heart at all.

What he did have was a fanatical sense of dedication and a will that brooked no obstacle. It was not ambition in the commonly accepted sense of that word, rather a kind of steely conviction that he and he alone was privy to the Truth. Long ago he had been vouchsafed a vision that would have struck a responsive chord in the imagination of many a nineteenth-century engineer, for he had dreamed of the Church Militant as a vast and complex machine in which every moving part functioned to perfection, and all to the greater glory of God. In such a machine, with fallible men as its components, fear was the essential lubricant, and none knew better than the Black Bishop when and where to apply the oil can. Yet he derived no particular pleasure from watching men tremble—indeed it was debatable whether he derived particular pleasure from anything—but if he deemed it necessary he did it, and he deemed it necessary quite often.

Besides the Bishop there were four other men present in the Council Chamber high up on the fifth floor of The Falconry. They were seated two to each side of a long table. The Bishop himself sat at the head. For the past half an hour he had listened in silence while his four District Marshals gave him their verbal reports and now, with the last one concluded, he simply sat there, his left elbow resting on the arm of his chair, his chin resting on the knuckles of his left hand, and slowly looked at each of them in turn. And one by one they quailed before his eyes, their own glances seeking the shelter of the table top or the candlelit corners of the room.

"So," he said quietly, "I ask for facts and you bring me rumors: I ask for the firebrand and all you can offer me is a cloud of smoke. Meanwhile every road into York is choked with credulous fools hurrying in to witness the miraculous advent of . . . of *what*? A goose? A swan? A seagull? What *is* it they're expecting? Surely one of you has discovered!"

The four officers continued to stare down at the table top. Not one of them cared to risk opening his mouth.

The Bishop thrust back his chair, stood up and

walked over to the wall where a map of The Seven Kingdoms was hanging. He stood for a moment, with his hands clasped behind his back, contemplating it in silence. Finally he said: "And why here? Why York? Why not Carlisle? Edinboro? Newcastle? Belfast, even? There must *be* a reason."

One of the Marshals, Barran by name, observed tentatively: "In the legend, my Lord, the White Bird—"

"Yes, yes, I know all that, Barran. Lions and unicorns. Fairytale nonsense. But I sense a guiding hand behind it. I feel it here, in my bones." He turned away from the map and moved back restlessly toward his chair. "Why do men and women *need* miracles?" he asked. "Can any of you tell me that?"

They shook their heads.

"It is really very simple. If the life they know already is all there is for them to believe in, then most of them would be better off dead."

The marshals' eyes widened as each one wondered whether the perilous boundary which demarcated heresy from orthodoxy was about to be re-drawn.

"It has always been so," continued the Bishop somberly. "And what happens ultimately is that they are driven to create their own. Miracles born out of sheer necessity—out of spiritual starvation! Our danger is that unless we are very careful they may do it here. The time is full ripe and there are sufficient gathered for the purpose."

"We could disperse them, my Lord."

"You think so, Thomas? That would be a miracle indeed! By tomorrow night, at the rate things are going, they will out-number us by hundreds to our one."

"So many, my Lord?"

"I have it on the Mayor's authority. And there's another thing. So far there's been no whisper of civil trouble in the city. They're meek as sheep, all of them. Most have even brought in their own provisions for the week. All they do is wander up and down gawping at the Minster. Quiet as mice. Waiting. Just waiting. *But for what?"*

The Marshal called Barran cleared his throat and murmured: "I have heard it referred to as 'the forthcoming,' my Lord."

"Go on."

"It is said that at the start of each millennium mankind is given another chance. They would have it that the Drowning in 2000 wiped the slate clean so that a new message could be written on it in the year 3000." He tailed off apologetically and turned his hands palm upwards on the table as if to disclaim any responsibility for what he had said.

The Bishop snorted. "The Drowning was the direct result of humanity's corporate failure to see beyond the end of its own nose. By 1985 it was already quite obvious that the global climate had been modified to the point where the polar ice caps were affected. Besides, the process itself lasted until well into the 21st Century. Such dates are purely arbitrary."

"But, my Lord," Barran protested, "the teachings of Jos—"

"Yes, yes," cut in the Bishop irritably, "because it suited the Church's purpose to denounce it as a Divine Judgement upon the Materialists—which of course it was. But that does not mean that the Church was not fully aware of the *physical* causes which underlay it. At the end of the 20th Century disaster could have struck in any one of a dozen different ways. By allowing us just time enough in which to adjust to it, the Drowning proved to be the most fortunate thing that could have happened. So five billions perished. When you consider the alternatives you can only allow that God was exceedingly merciful."

The Marshals, back once more on firm ground, nodded in agreement.

"So," said the Bishop, "let us discard speculation and concentrate upon the practical aspects of our present situation. The one thing to be avoided at all costs is any sort of direct confrontation. The symbolic features of this ridiculous legend must on no account be permitted to gain a hold over their imaginations. Five days from now, *Deo volente,* they will all have dispersed to their homes, hopefully a good deal wiser than when they left them. In the meantime I wish our men to be seen, but nothing more. They must keep themselves in the background. Let them lend their assistance to the Civil Watch. But tell them to keep their eyes and ears open. At the first sign of anything out of the ordinary—anything which might conceivably be exaggerated into some spurious 'miracle'—get word back to me *at once,* and leave it to me to decide what action should be taken. Is that understood?"

The Marshals nodded, relieved that it had been no worse.

"Have you any further questions, gentlemen?"

There were none.

Two days after Christmas Clerk Seymour sent a message to "The Duke's Arms" that he wished to speak with Tom. Old Peter accompanied the boy to the Chapter House. Of the two visitors there was no question who was the more nervous. Hardly had the introductions been made than Peter, pleading the afflictions of advanced age, scuttled off to relieve his bladder. It took him rather longer than might have been expected. When he reappeared it was to learn, to his well-simulated dismay, that Tom would not be joining the Chapter School until the summer.

He clucked his tongue and shook his head dolefully, then brightened up. "No matter, lad!" he cried. "It's not the end of the world, is it? And the days twixt now and then will pass in an eyeblink, eh, Cousin Seymour?"

The Clerk nodded. "I have been suggesting to Thomas that he might do a great deal worse than to keep you company on your spring travels, Tale-

Spinner. Would such an arrangement be acceptable to you?"

"Nothing could please me better!" exclaimed the old man. "Why, Tom, we'll make that round tour of the Seven Kingdoms I spoke of. That'll give you something to brag about to your school-fellows, eh? What do you say, lad?"

Tom smiled. "It's very kind of you, Peter."

"Pooh! Stuff!" cried the old man, clapping an arm round the boy's shoulders and hugging him tight. "We're a team, you and I. We stand together against the world, Tom. Artists both, eh? A few days more in York then off down the high road to Doncaster. We'll follow the coast as far south as Nottingham, then, if the wind's fair, take ship to Norwich. How does that like you?"

"It likes me very well," said Tom.

"I shall be writing to your mother, Thomas," said the Clerk, "to let her know that you are in good hands. As soon as you have decided what your plans are, Tale-Spinner, I will be happy to include the information in my letter. We have a Church messenger leaving for Carlisle next Wednesday. I will see that he delivers it into her own hand."

"That's most civil of you, Cousin Seymour. Most civil."

"Myself I depart for Malton directly," continued the Clerk, "but I shall be back on the eve of the New Year. Perhaps you would drop in on me then?"

"Indeed I shall. In the meantime I'll have roughed out some details of our trip."

The Clerk accompanied them to the door of the Chapter House where they shook hands before making their way through the crowds which thronged the Minster Close. As they were passing The Falconry a man emerged from beneath the overshadowing porch and caught sight of them. He paused a moment, watching them through narrowed eyes, then ran lightly down the steps and plucked the old man by his sleeve. "Greetings, old Tale-Spinner," he murmured. "Dost remember me?"

Peter turned. "Aye, sir," he said. "Even without the casque. How goes it with you, Falcon Gyre?"

The man glanced back over his shoulder. "I was at the telling last night," he said.

"I am indeed honored," returned Peter, with the merest hint of irony in his voice. "Didst prefer it to the other?"

"I would talk with you, old man. But not here."

Peter flicked a quick glance at Tom who appeared supremely unconcerned. "Aye, well," he muttered uneasily. " 'Tis not the best of times, friend Gyre. We have a telling billed within the hour. Would not tomorrow be—"

"Tomorrow would be too late," said Gyre. "I know of a place hard by." As he spoke he tightened his grip perceptibly on the old man's arm and steered him, gently but firmly, toward a narrow alley.

By a series of twists and turns they were conducted into a courtyard which fronted on to a backstreet market. There in a dingy shop which was part ale house, part general store, Gyre ordered up three mugs of spiced wine, guided the old man and the boy into a corner settle and said: "You must quit York tonight."

For some seconds Peter was too taken aback to say anything at all, then he managed to stutter: "By whose authority comes this? We break no law."

Gyre shook his head. "I, Gyre, tell you this, old man. For three nights past I have had the same dream. I wish no harm to befall you. Stay not in York." He spoke in little impetuous rushes, like one who has run hard and snatches for his breath.

Old Peter gazed at him, noted the unnatural brightness of eyes which he had first seen cold as the pennies on a dead man's sockets, and he remembered the way this licensed bird of prey had stood up in his stirrups and stared back along the sunlit road to Hammerton Bridge. "A dream, eh, friend?" he murmured mildly. "And three nights running. Is that all you can tell us?"

Gyre looked from the old man to the boy and back again. "I noose my own neck by speaking of it with you," he said. "Will you not be warned?"

"Aye, man, we are truly grateful. Think not otherwise. But this dream of yours. Could it not have some other reading?"

"Perhaps," said Gyre, and all the urgency had suddenly drained from his voice. He sounded almost indifferent.

"You cannot tell us?"

"It comes and goes again," said Gyre and frowned. "I know when it has been, but I know nothing of its nature."

"And yet you sought us out to warn us?"

"Aye, well." Gyre shrugged. "Something came over me." He got up and, without another word to them, walked out of the shop and disappeared, leaving his drink untasted on the table.

Old Peter stared after him, kneading his chin with his thumb knuckle. "What make you of that?" he asked.

"He meant it," said Tom.

"Yes. But meant *what,* lad? Did you see his eyes?" Tom sipped his drink and said nothing.

"I'll warrant he'd been chewing 'drasil root."

"But we could go, couldn't we, Peter? We don't have to stay now, do we?"

"Ah, you're forgetting your Cousin Seymour. He won't be back from Malton till Monday. Besides, lad, this place is a regular gold mine for us. Close on twenty royal a day we're taking. A *day!* And I can recall plenty of times when I've not taken one in a week!"

"All right," said Tom. "So we'll stay."

"Me I'm not superstitious," said Peter. "I can't afford to be. Still I wouldn't like you to feel that I . . ."

Tom laughed. "And abandon a gold mine? Never!"

"Ah, I thought you'd see it my way," said Peter complacently, and catching up Gyre's abandoned mug he swigged it off in a single draught.

At the tenth hour of the New Year's Eve, Old Peter shrugged on his heavy cloak and set out to keep his appointment at the Chapter House. That afternoon he had totted up the sum of their takings over the past fortnight and found it came to the staggering total of one hundred and seventy eight royal. Even allowing for the fifty he had pledged to the Clerk this was still a golden harvest the like of which he had never known. It had driven him, for the first time in his life, to seek the services of the bankers. Now, folded flat and stowed away in a concealed pocket within the lining of his doublet, he carried a letter of credit which would see them both round the Seven Kingdoms and back again to York even if they never took another quarter. Truly, as far as Peter was concerned, the advent of the millennium had already proved wholly miraculous.

As he approached the Chapter House he was astonished to find the Minster Close almost deserted. On this night of all nights he had expected to see the crowds milling in readiness to celebrate the midnight chimes. Then he recalled how an Order had been promulgated from The Falconry that very morning banning all such gatherings within the city walls on account of a case of plague which had been discovered. He looked about him. Over the roofs to the south he saw the low clouds already tinted a coppery red from the flames of invisible bonfires that had presumably been kindled on the open ground beyond the southern gate. He decided that as soon as his business with the Clerk was concluded he would take a stroll along the walls to watch the sport.

He was kept waiting for a cold half hour at the Chapter House before Clerk Seymour could receive him and by the time all the details of the transaction had been settled, the cash handed over and a pledge drunk in wine, the last half-hour chime before midnight was sounding from the Minster. Peter stepped back out into the night to find that the air had become alive with snowflakes, large and soft as swansdown.

There was no wind at all, and where the two wall torches flamed beside the entrance to The Falconry the currents of rising air were setting the drifting flakes into a swirling dance like twin clouds of golden moths.

As the old man hefted up the hood of his cloak and re-tied the leather laces at his chin a solitary horseman came spurring into the Close. He reined up outside The Falconry, flung himself from the saddle and, without even bothering to tether his mount, raced up the steps and into the building. Reflecting that no news travels faster than bad news, Peter made haste to quit the scene. He was hurrying toward the southern gate when a troop of five Falcons, helmeted and with their bows at their backs, galloped past him down the main street, the steel-shod hooves of their horses striking showers of sparks from the snow-slippery cobblestones. So uncannily silent was the town that Peter could hear their clattering racket long after they had passed out of his sight.

The last quarter-chime had just died on the air as he set foot on one of the ancient stairways that led up to the top of the city wall. Pausing to gather breath for the climb, the old man suddenly remembered Tom. The thought came to him in the form of a brilliantly clear mental image of the boy's face as he had once seen it lit up by the flamelight from Norris' hearth. As if a hand had been thrust violently into his back, the old man began scrambling up the stairs two at a time. Heart pounding, lungs wheezing like a blacksmith's bellows, he staggered up on to the battlements and peered dizzily over. The sight that met his eyes all but brought his heart to a full stop. By the light of a dozen bonfires an enormous crowd was assembled, a silent sea of blank white faces gazing upwards toward the city wall. The only sound to be heard was the crackle of flames as a log broke in two and a fountain of sparks swept up to meet the ceaseless downward sift of the snowflakes. The *only* sound? "Dear God," groaned the old man in what was part prayer, part incantation, "Dear God, no."

He set off in a shambling, broken-winded run along the battlements, pausing every now and again to peer downwards. He came upon other silent watchers, first in ones and twos, then clustered ever more closely together, leaning over the parapet, rapt and still. He elbowed his way between two of them and saw that a little way below and some thirty paces to his right, a rough wooden scaffold had been erected by masons working to repair an inward-curving section of the wall. A ladder led down from the parapet to a boarded platform, and there, seated so casually that one leg hung dangling over the airy gulf below, was Tom. His back resting against a rough pine joist, the snow already beginning to settle unheeded upon his bent head, he was playing his lament for The White Bird of Kinship; playing it really for nobody but himself, unless perhaps it was for the spirit of a man he had once loved who had dreamed an impossible dream of human kinship long ago among the hills and valleys of Bowness.

As Peter stared downwards it seemed to him that the whole scene was becoming oddly insubstantial: the pale upturned faces of the silent crowd beginning to swirl and mingle with the drift and swirl of the pale flakes; the stones along the parapet touched with the rosy firelight until they appeared to glow with the warm inward glow of molten glass. All about him he seemed to sense a world becoming subtly transformed into something wholly new and strange, yet a part of him still realized that this transformation must lie within his own perception, within himself.

—*I believe there's a master-key, Peter. One to unlock the whole world. I call that key The White Bird.*

As the boy's words came whispering back into his memory an extraordinary excitement gripped the old man. Fear slipped from him like a dusty cloak. He began to hear each separate note of the pipe as clearly as if Tom were sitting playing at his side and he knew that every listener in that vast concourse was hearing the same. So it was that, despite himself, no longer caring, Peter found his head had tilted backwards until the feathery snowflakes came drifting down upon his own upturned face. And gradually, as he surrendered himself to the song, he too began to hear what Gyre had once heard—the great surging downrush of huge wings whose enormous beat was the very pulse of his own heart, the pulse of life itself. He felt himself being lifted up to meet them as if he were being rushed onwards faster and faster along some immense and airy avenue of cool white light. Of their own accord his arms rose, reached out in supplication, pleading silently— *Take me with you . . . take me . . . take me . . .* But, ah, how faint they were becoming, how faint and far away. Ghostly wingbeats sighing fainter and ever fainter, washed backwards by an ebbing sky-tide, drifting beyond his reach far out over the distant southern sea. Away. Gone away. Gone.

The old tale-spinner opened his eyes without realizing that he had ever closed them. What had happened? There was a mysterious sighing in the air, an exhalation, as if the held breath of the whole world had been released. *Gone away. Gone. Our bird. Our own White Bird. Why hast thou forsaken us?* He shook his head like a wet dog and blinked round at the vacant, dream-drugged faces beside him. And it was then that he realized the music had stopped. A sound most like an animal's inarticulate bewildered growl broke from his throat. He lunged forward, thrust himself half over the parapet and squinted down through the lazily drifting petals of the indifferent snow.

The boy was lying, head slumped, limbs twisted askew on the wooden platform. Through the left side of his chest a single crossbow bolt fledged with ravens' feathers was skewering him to the pine joist behind him. One hand was still clutched around the projecting shaft of the bolt as if to pull it free. On the snowy boards blood was already spreading outwards in a slow, dim puddle.

Forcing his way through the press of stunned spec-

tators the old man gained the ladder by which Tom
must have descended and, heedless of his own safety,
clambered down to the platform. As he set foot on it
the Minster bells suddenly unleashed their first great
clamorous peal, flighting out the Old Year and wel-
coming in the New.

Accompanied by Marshal Barran the Chief Falconer strode furiously along the top of the city wall.
In the distance he could make out a little huddled
knot of on-lookers, lit by flickering torch light, gathered around the top of the scaffolding. Down in the
meadows below, the mounted troopers were already
dispersing the crowd. For the third time he asked the
same question: "And you are absolutely *certain* this
was the same boy?"

"There could not be two such, my Lord. He fits the
Boroughbridge report perfectly."

"Insane," muttered the Bishop. "Absolutely insane.
Whose troop is the madman in?"

"Dalkeith's, my Lord."

"And why *that* way when he could have slit the
pup's throat in a back alley and no one a wit the
wiser? Now we've got ourselves five thousand eyewit-
nesses to a needless martyrdom. And on this one
night of all nights!"

"Aye, my Lord. They're already murmuring about
Black Bird."

"And for how long do you suppose it will stay a
murmur? In a month they'll be shouting it from the
rooftops. What they'll be saying by this time next year
is anybody's guess."

Already the snow was falling more heavily and a
breeze had sprung up, blowing in from the sea, bringing the smoke from the dying bonfires billowing up
along the battlements. Two members of the Civil
Watch had found a plank, had laid the boy's body
upon it. Having covered it with a piece of sacking,
they were now arguing about how best to get it down

the narrow steps. The Chief Falconer strode into the center of the group. "Back!" he commanded.

As they shuffled to obey he stooped over the make-shift bier, twitched aside the sacking and stared down at the pale calm face of the dead boy. He caught sight of a leather lace about the throat and, thinking it might be a crucifix, jerked it clear. All he found was a bloody fragment of a shattered green pebble. "The bolt," he said. "Where is the bolt?"

"I have it safe," said a voice from the shadows.

The Bishop raised his cowled head and peered into the shadows. "Who are you?"

"Peter of Hereford. Tale-Spinner. He was my lad."

Marshal Barran leant across and whispered something into the Bishop's ear. The Chief Falconer frowned. "What know you of this sad accident, Peter?"

The old man stepped forward into the pool of quivering torchlight. From beneath his cloak he produced the black-fledged bolt, its crumpled feathers already stiff with congealed blood. "This was an accident, sire?" he said. "Your birds flew here this night to shed innocent blood."

"Have a care for your tongue, old man."

"Fear you the truth, my Lord Bishop? Know then there should by rights have been two of us down there. I to tell the tale and he to breathe the breath of life into it. Ask any man or woman who heard Tom play whether or not the White Bird of Kinship hovered here tonight."

The Bishop glanced swiftly round at the circle of impassive faces and felt suddenly as if the sea wind was blowing right through his bones. Why was this old scoundrel not afraid to speak these heresies to his face? Men had been racked to death for less. Something was stirring here that even he might well be powerless to quell. There was a rank smell of false faith in the air. Well at least there would be no more public martyrdoms this night. He touched the bier with his foot. "Get this down to the gate-house. As for you, Tale-Spinner, present yourself at the Falconry by the tenth hour of forenoon. Meanwhile you would be well advised to place a closer guard over that precious tongue of yours."

The snow stopped shortly after dawn. When Peter made his way to The Falconry next morning it was through streets muffled as if on purpose to honor the dead. Everywhere along his route people, recognizing him, came up and touched hands and went away. Few said more than: "I was there," but their eyes were eloquent.

The ghost of an old fear brushed against him as he mounted the snowy steps to The Falconry but it no longer had the same power to freeze him from the inside out. He strode into the building, stamped the ice from his boots and told the doorkeeper who he was. The man directed him down an echoing passage into a room where a log fire was burning. Crouched on a stool beside the fire was Falcon Gyre.

Peter gazed at the bowman in surprise then walked across and placed a hand on his shoulder. "Well met, friend," he murmured. "Would that we had heeded those dreams of yours."

Gyre looked up but there was no hint of recognition in his eyes. They seemed to look right through the old man to something far beyond that only he could see. Peter remembered how he had stared back along the sunlit road across the moors to Hammerton and wondered what thoughts were going through his mind. "You did your best, friend," he said. "No one could have done more."

As though by a superhuman effort Gyre brought his eyes to focus on the face above him. His lips trembled loosely and, suddenly, with a shock of real pity, Peter saw the man was weeping silently, the tears runneling down his unshaven cheeks and dripping unheeded from his chin. At that moment the door opened and the Chief Falconer walked in. He stood for a moment gazing with obvious distaste at the blubbering Gyre, then he turned to Peter and said: "What do you wish done with him?"

Peter glanced round, half convinced that the Bishop was addressing someone else in the room whom he had not yet seen. "I?" he protested. "Why should I . . . ?"

"He has not told you?"

"He has not spoken a word. I thought perhaps he was . . ."

"He is in a state of profound shock," said the Bishop. "He remembers nothing. Nevertheless he was responsible for the accidental death of the boy."

"*Gyre!* Never!"

"So you know his name?"

"Aye. We rode into York together. My Lord, I assure you there has been some mistake. This cannot be the man."

"There has been no mistake," said the Bishop testily. "Gyre loosed the bolt by accident. Think you we would have *ordered* him to do it? Surely even you must have the wit to realize that it was the last thing on earth we could have wished."

Peter stared down at the silently weeping man and then back to the Bishop. "No man could have fired that shot by accident," he said slowly. "It would have been difficult even for a skilled marksman. Upwards—against the falling snow—with only the fire-light to aim by? That was no accident. But whoever did it it was not Gyre."

The Bishop drew his lips back against his teeth with a faint sucking sound. "And just what makes you so certain?" he asked curiously.

Peter shrugged. What had either of them to lose by it now? "Because Gyre tried to warn us to leave the city three days ago."

"*Warn you?* How?"

"He told us to quit York. He said he had had a dream."

The Bishop gazed at the old man, seeing the ripples of superstition multiplying, crowding thick upon each other, ringing outwards wider and wider with every minute that passed. "A dream," he said flatly. "What dream?"

"He would not tell us. But he said he had the same dream three nights running. He just warned us to leave. Would to God we'd listened to him. But I had arrangements still to make with the Chapter Clerk for the lad's schooling."

"Schooling?" echoed the Bishop. "Are you telling me the boy was to enter the Chapter School?"

"Aye, my Lord. That's why I brought him here to York."

"But in that case he was certainly destined for the Ministry."

"I know naught of that, my Lord."

The Bishop punched one hand into the other. "Oh, he was, he was," he said. "There can be no question of it. Besides, the Clerk will certainly confirm it. You must realize that this puts a very different complexion on the matter."

"How so, my Lord?"

"Why naturally he must be interred in the Minster crypt with all due honor as befits a true son of the Church. How like you that, old man? Better than a public grave in the wall ditch, wouldn't you say?"

Peter looked hard at him. "I daresay Tom will not be minding much either way," he said. "But make it a grave in the open Close if you must. Those Minster stones would lie too heavy on his heart."

"So be it," said the Bishop. "Leave it to us, old man. I promise you he shall lack for nothing."

"Except a little breath, my Lord."

Frost laid an icy finger on the Bishop's smile. "Have a care," he murmured, "or that golden tongue of yours may buy you a grave of your own."

And so it came to pass that on the third of the New Year the Minster bells rang out once more. The pine coffin, decked with blood-berried holly, was borne from the gatehouse through the twisting streets to the doors of the Minster and vanished inside. By the time it re-emerged the crowd of mourners in the Close had swollen beyond computation, lapping out even to engulf the steps of the Falconry itself.

Gazing down somberly from his fifth floor eyrie the Chief Falconer was moved to question his own wisdom in acceeding to the old man's wish that the body be buried outside the Minster. Where had they all appeared from, these massed ranks of silent watchers? What marvelous sign were the fools hoping for? He watched with growing impatience as the bearers made their slow way through the crowd toward the heap of upturned earth beside the newly dug grave. As they laid the coffin across the leather straps, the first feathery flake of new snowfall came drifting downwards outside the window. Another followed and another, and then the Bishop saw faces here and there in the throng lift and gaze upwards. In less than a minute only the officiating clergy appeared concerned in the burial, the rest were reaching upwards, hands outstretched in supplication toward this miraculous manna softly falling feathers of the immortal White Bird of Kinship whose song once heard would never be forgotten.

The Bishop turned to Marshal Barran with a mirthless smile. "I suppose you realize that it is more than likely we are witnessing a future miracle."

Barran nodded. "You did well, my Lord, to claim him for the Church. Think what this might have become had it taken place below the city walls."

"I hope you're right," said the Chief Falconer. "Myself I'm not so sure. What if this fledgling we've taken into our nest should prove to be a cuckoo?"

Barran returned his attention to the scene below just in time to see the coffin disappear jerkily out of sight. The priest scattered a handful of soil into the grave and stepped back. As he did so those nearest to the graveside shuffled forward and each appeared to drop something white on to the lid of the hidden coffin. Soon a long procession had formed. As it wound slowly past the heap of raw earth each man, woman and child stretched out an arm and dropped a single white feather into the open grave.

Barran debated whether to draw the Bishop's attention to this new development and decided against it. Instead, he remarked: "Do you recall, my Lord, how the fable ends?"

"With the death of the bird, of course."

"Oh, no, my Lord. They would have it that when the blood of the dying white bird splashes the breast of the black, then the black bird becomes white itself and the cycle is repeated."

The Bishop swung round on his Marshal, his eyes seeming to smolder like dark red coals. "In God's name, Barran, don't you see what you're saying? Why didn't you tell me this before?"

"My Lord," stammered the Marshal, "indeed I would have done so, but you assured me you were familiar with the legend. As I recall it you—"

"Aye, man, I remember. Lions and unicorns I called it. Stupid fairy tale nonsense. Well, so it is. So are they all. Credulous idiots. Children. Fools." He sighed. "Ah, well, it's done now—for better or worse. I only wish I could believe it was for the better."

Standing beside the grave, with the snow falling all about him, a lone piper had begun to play a hauntingly familiar lament.

"Amen to that, my Lord." murmured the Marshal.

Three days after the funeral two men rode out of the city by the south gate and took the shore road for Doncaster. One rider was Old Peter of Hereford; the other an ex-Falcon by the name of Gyre. Around Gyre's neck was fastened a thick hinged band of studded brass clamped at the throat by a steel padlock. The key to this lock was in Old Peter's purse. The Collar of Servitude was the punishment which, as near kin, he had elected at the behest of the Secular Court; the rejected alternative would have been ritual blinding with a white-hot iron.

When they were fifteen kilometers clear of the city, Old Peter signaled Gyre to dismount then climbed down off his own horse. He beckoned the Falcon to him, unlocked the brass collar and flung it far out into the Sea of Goole. The key followed it. "That's the way Tom would have wanted it," said the old man, panting from his exertions. "You're free, Gyre."

Gyre, who had spoken no intelligible word to anyone since loosing the fatal bolt, produced a sort of bubbling gurgle from deep inside his throat. Then he turned away, went back to his horse and unfastened one of the leather saddlebags. From inside it he took out something wrapped in a piece of blue cloth which he brought to Peter.

"What's this?" said the old man. "An exchange, eh?" He unwrapped the cloth and then drew in his breath in a painful hiss. "Man, how came you by this?"

Gyre looked down at the pipe which the Wizard of Bowness had fashioned for Tom and then he laid his clasped hands against his chest and crouched down in the damp sand at the water's edge and whimpered like a dog.

"Why did you do it, Gyre?" muttered the old man. "What made you, man?"

Gyre raised his head, unclasped his hands, and with his right forefinger gently touched the barrel of the pipe. As he did so the sun thrust aside the clouds and shone down upon him. An expression of childlike wonder softened his ravaged face. His fingers closed round the pipe, eased it from the old man's grasp, and then set it to his own lips. Closing his eyes he blew gently down it and then began to move his fingers falteringly over the stops.

To his dumb amazement the old man heard the unmistakable air of one of the themes which Tom had first devised for *Amulet* and then incorporated into his Lament for the White Bird. Gyre played it all through once, and then again, gaining assurance as he proceeded. As Peter listened in a sort of trance, understanding broke over him in a foaming wave of revelation. It was as though the music had brought him the answer to his own question. And it lay back there behind him on a road fifteen kilometers to the northward where the boy had once said to him in that quiet, supremely confident way of his—"I told *him* about the White Bird. He wanted to believe me, so it was easy." But what was it you had wanted to believe, Gyre? That the Bird was a living reality which would indeed come winging out of the winter sky? If you believed that, then you would have to believe all the rest too. Which meant believing that the Bird *must* die in order to live again!

Like bright bubbles rising to the swirling surface, memories began to cluster together in the old man's mind: remembered things that Tom had said: "They are such ninnies they'll believe anything"—"I thought of him like I think of the dogs, not as a man at all"—"I take their thoughts and give them back my own." And others too: "Our thoughts are unseen hands shaping the people we meet"—"Morfedd planned it all years ago. Long before he chose me. Before I was even born." The old man began to shiver right deep down in the very marrow of his bones. What manner of being had this boy been? What latent power in him had Morfedd recognized and nurtured? Was it possible Tom could have *known* what he was about—or even *half* known—enough to stamp a picture of his own destiny on Gyre's too willing mind? *Could he have chosen his own death?* Every instinctive fiber in Peter's being rejected the notion. And yet . . . and yet . . . the pattern would not go away. One by one the nails thudded into the coffin and among the hands wielding the hammers one was his own. "I thought you'd see it my way." *Thud!* "A few more days in York then off down the high road to Doncaster." *Thud!* "You're forgetting your Cousin Seymour. He won't be back from Malton till Monday." *Thud!* "What harm could there be in gratifying an old man's whim, cousin?" *Thud!* Nailed down by the strength of an old man's weakness. That collar should have been round his own neck not Gyre's. With everything to lose, poor crazed Gyre had at least seen the boy as an end in himself. "I, Gyre, tell you this. I know when it has been but I know nothing of its nature." Why was it that men could never value things truly till they were gone?

Far out to sea a ship with silver-white sails was dipping and plunging in and out of the slanting shafts of sunlight. Eagerly the blue-gray waves hurried in, stumbled, and creamed up the gently shelving beach as they had done for a thousand years. The old tale-spinner looked down at the man still crouched at his feet. A huge calmness descended upon him. He stretched out his arm and gripped Gyre gently by the shoulder. Then he walked down to the water's edge and dipped both his hands into the sea. Returning he tilted back Gyre's head and with a wet finger drew across his forehead the sign that Tom had once drawn on a misty window of an inn—a child's representation of a flying bird. "Come friend," he said. "You and I together have a tale to tell. Let us be on our way."

THE
ROAD
TO
CORLAY

Chapter One

IT WAS JONSEY who saw him first, "One-Eye" Jonsey whose single eye, so they said, could see more and see further than many another coaster's two good ones. Three hours out of New Bristol on the long tack into Taunton Reach a snowflake-swirl of sea birds caught and held the attention of that one bright eye as Jonsey squatted up in the bows of the "Kingdom Come" bending floats of tarred cork on to the seine net. Over the slide and dip of the April sea, where the laggard ebb met the rip off Blackdown Head and the bewildered waters jumbled all ways at once, a dot of darkness was hoisted momentarily on the shoulder of a wave for just long enough to bring Jonsey to his feet with a shout to his brother Napper at the helm.

Young Napper masked his eyes against the shimmering sea-glare and, obedient to Jonsey's directions, leant his weight against the stout oak tiller bringing the boat's head butting hard round into the eye of the east wind. "What is it?" he yelled.

Jonsey had clambered up on to the gunwale and wrapped his right arm round a stay. The patched brown mainsail clattered at his back and the shadows of the wheeling gulls flickered to and fro across the rocking deck. His single gray-green eye raked the water's face. Suddenly he flung out his left arm toward the distant coast of North Dorset. "There!"

Napper eased off the helm, the mainsail tautened

again and the boat crabbed slowly off in the direction
of Jonsey's pointing arm. Within minutes they had
drifted close enough for Napper to make out the
shape of a man's head as it lolled above the wooden
spar to which the upper arms had been lashed. He
maneuvered the boat round and then let it drift back
before the breeze until the spar's end rapped against
the lee boards and Jonsey was able to get a line
around the man's waist. While Jonsey heaved, Napper
abandoned the helm, leaned out over the side and
sawed through the hemp lashings with a gutting knife.
Then, together, they dragged the water-logged body
aboard.

They rolled it over so that it was lying face downwards across a pile of nets, then Napper went back
to the helm and brought the "Kingdom Come" back
on course. Jonsey resumed his work on the floats but
every now and again he glanced over his shoulder at
the sodden corpse wondering whose it was and how it
came to be drifting so far out in the Somersea and
why the gulls had left the eyes alone.

Beneath the body's open mouth draining water
formed into a swelling puddle. As the boat heeled the
puddle broke free and trickled off toward the scup-
pers. Idly Jonsey watched it wriggle its way past the
hand of the sprawled left arm and, as it did so, he saw
one of the dead man's fingers slowly crook itself. The
movement was so slight—scarcely a nail's breadth—
that for a moment Jonsey doubted the evidence of his
one good eye. Then it moved again. Starting to his
feet with an oath the coaster flung himself astride the
back of the "corpse" and began pumping its arms
backwards and forwards while at the same time he
contrived to rock the body from side to side on its rib
cage.

From his station at the helm Napper observed his
brother's actions with amazement. "You're crazy!" he
cried. "Why he's so soused he didn't even bleed where
I snicked him!"

"Could be a spark still," Jonsey panted. He stopped

pumping, tilted the body on its side and ripped open the lacing of the sodden leather jerkin. Then he pressed his ear to the cold chest, listened, shook his head, thumbed up an eyelid to expose an eyeball seemingly as blind as a peeled egg and finally resumed his pumping.

Ten minutes later Napper heard a crow of triumph. "He's alive, boy! Leastways his heart's beating."

Jonsey straightened up, palmed the sweat from his forehead and scrambled down into the hold to emerge a moment later clutching the spare foresail. He made his way back to where the unconscious body lay and contrived to bundle it up in the canvas. Satisfied that he had done all he could he made his way back to his brother's side.

Napper brought the "Kingdom Come" round so that she was running free down the middle of the channel toward the tiny harbor of Tallon, the last outpost on the Isle of Quantock. Twenty-five fathoms below her keel the long-drowned borough of Taunton slumbered beneath its thousand year old quilting of red silt. The sky above Exmoor was speedwell blue and the breeze out of Salisbury sharp with the promise of spring on the 12th day of April in the year A.D. 3018.

Jonsey took the mainsheet from his brother's hand and shook out more canvas. "What do you make of it?" he asked indicating the shrouded figure with a jerk of his head. "He didn't tie those ropes himself, did he?"

Napper nodded. "You reckon he's off a wreck?"

"I dunno," said Jonsey. "There's marks of the lash on his ribs. From not so long since I'd say."

"Flogged and drowned too!" Napper grinned. "Maybe the poor bugger won't thank us for saving him from the crabs. Who d'you think he is?"

Jonsey cleared his throat and spat a gob of phlegm at an escorting gull. He wiped his lips with the back of his hand. "I dunno who he is," he said. "But *what* he is, now that's another matter."

"Go on," said Napper curiously.

"I'd lay you ten to one he's a Kinsman."

Napper's head jerked round. "You're joking."

"Not I, boy."

"But how can you tell?"

For answer Jonsey opened his mouth, stuck out his tongue and flicked his thumb down its underside.

"Are you *sure?*"

"See for yourself. He won't stop you."

Napper relinquished the tiller, picked his way forward and peered down at the unconscious figure. He saw a tiny pulse in the man's neck flutter faintly and noted where a scrap of feathery red seaweed had entangled itself in the short dark beard. Stooping, the boy placed his thumb on the man's chin and eased the jaw downwards. Cold blue lips and white teeth parted to expose the pink tongue. Very gently the young coaster inserted the tip of his index finger behind the lower teeth, slid it under the man's tongue, and lifted. Sliced neatly in two right down the middle to its root the tongue fell apart like a snake's and, as the finger was withdrawn, closed up again. Napper gave a sudden, violent shiver, straightened up and returned to the helm. "Oh, Christ, Jonsey," he said. "What are we going to do?"

"Get him ashore, boy. What else?"

"At Tallon?"

"Aye. It's as good as anywhere else. Maybe better."

Napper stared back along the deck to where the man lay in his sun-warmed canvas shroud, unmoving but indubitably alive. A faintly speculative expression tightened the sunburnt skin around the boy's eyes. As if to himself he murmured: "I did hear as how they're offering five royal a live head in New Exeter."

"Tempted are you?" enquired Jonsey.

"No more than most. Still, it's a lot of money."

"Blood money only buys ill luck."

"So they say," agreed Napper. "But I reckon there'll be a few in Tallon as would gladly take the risk for half of what they're offering."

"You're wrong there," said Jonsey. "The combers are a close lot but they're no carrion crows. But we'd best get him down below out of sight all the same. I'll have a word with Pots Thomson when we get in. He's Kin and if I read it right he'll take him off our hands. 'Sides, we've no call to know *what* he is, have we?"

Shortly after noon the "Kingdom Come" nudged up alongside the deserted quay at Tallon. Jonsey scrambled ashore, made the boat fast, and then set off up the steep, cobbled street of the village. Some twenty minutes later Napper saw him returning. He was accompanied by a brown-bearded, barrel-chested man who pushed a long fish-barrow loaded with two wooden crates. With them was a young woman who carried a covered basket.

The little caravan halted beside the moored boat. "Well met, Napper," called the bearded potter. "We've got two cases of fired glazings here. They're for Sam Moxon at Chardport. Jonsey tells me you've got those powders I ordered."

"Aye," said Napper. "They're ready for you, Pots. 'Lo, Jane. Coming aboard?"

The young woman gave the coaster a brief, abstracted smile, handed him her basket and then jumped down on to the deck. Napper indicated the companionway with a jerk of his head. She took the basket from him and vanished down the steps leaving the men to deal with the two crates.

The second crate was no sooner aboard than the young woman reappeared. She drew a deep breath and shook her head sending her short, dark hair tumbling around her pale face. Pots joined her on the deck. "Well, lass," he murmured. "Is it him?"

"I don't know, Dad," she said. "I can't reach him. We'll have to get him home."

The men exchanged glances and Pots said: "What do you mean you can't reach him?"

She shrugged and pushed her hair back off her face. "I just can't, that's all. He's closed off and"—she hesitated, frowning—"I don't know. There's something not right about him—muddled—foggy sort of—it's just a jumble. Maybe when he comes round . . ."

Pots scratched the back of his neck and glanced round at the blank windows of the waterside houses. It was the dead hour of the day but, even so, he knew that curious eyes were sure to be watching him. "That stuff you've got for me, Jonsey," he said thoughtfully. "Is it in sacks, or what?"

"Four small bags and a box," said the coaster.

"So if we trussed him up all shipshape there's a chance we could pass him off along with it. You boys would give us a hand to the top, wouldn't you?"

The two brothers looked at one another, hesitated, and then nodded.

Pots noted the momentary pause and grinned. "I'll see to it you're not short of a royal for all your trouble, lads. And you'll take a bite with us. More I can't do."

The "Kingdom Come" sailed from Tallon on the four o'clock tide, its crew the richer by a gold piece and a comfortable conscience. As they set course for the port of Chard some forty kilometers to the south-east, neither Jonsey nor Napper were a wit the wiser as to how the man had come to be drifting in the Somersea for he was still unconscious when they took their leave of the potter. Nor were they unduly troubled by curiosity. There were a lot of things which it was safer not to know in A.D. 3018.

The drowned man lay naked beneath gray woolen blankets in the back parlor of Kiln Cottage, cold as a fish despite the three oven-warmed bricks which the potter's wife had wrapped in scraps of flannel and placed, one at his feet, and one at either side of his chest. Only the faint misting of a close-held glass betrayed that he breathed at all.

The girl came into the room, drew up a stool, sat down and stared at the mask-like face. Then she leant forward so that her lips were no more than an inch from his ear and whispered urgently: "Kinsman? Kinsman, can you hear me?"

There was no response at all. She sat back, laced her fingers together and bowed her head over them for a long minute. Then she sighed deeply, leant forward once again, laid her right hand, palm flat, across the cold forehead and closed her eyes.

Stillness descended upon the room like twilight as she sank slowly into the darkness within him like a carp sinking down into a deep pool. With the spread fingers of her mind she winnowed through the cloaking mists until at last wisps of his memories began to flicker dimly at the fringes of her awareness—tiered boxes with luminous windows, each holding a wriggling worm of light; a man's anxious face looming close; a square white building glimpsed from high above as though by a bird; a girl with red hair, bare breasted, laughing down at him; and an endless, swirling tunnel of shifting shadow out of which drifted the frail echo of a whisper: *"Carver."* But it was all so faint, guttering like a candleflame in a draft, and she was about to withdraw, exhausted and despondent, when suddenly a whole cascade of strong, brilliant images came pouring into her consciousness; the sickle moon racing through a tattered cloud wrack; sea birds wheeling and crying all about her; a group of men, women and children with laughing faces running forward to embrace her; and an old man with white, wind-blown hair lifting a hand that glittered wet in the sunshine as it sketched upon her up-turned forehead the Sign of the Bird. So intense was the radiance of this final vision that she cried out aloud and opened her eyes. As she did so she felt the man stir beneath her hand. She saw his eyelids flutter uncertainly, then his eyes were staring up blankly into hers.

The door opened and the potter came in. He took in the scene at a glance. "Well done, lass," he murmured. "I was beginning to think he was lost to us." He leant over his daughter's shoulder and grinned down cheerfully at the man. "Welcome back to the land of the living, friend. Dos't know where'st been?"

The man's lips parted slightly and then closed again.

The potter called out: "Susan! Bring us in a drop of that warmed spirit and a bowl of milk." He patted the girl on the arm. "You look ready for a sup yourself, Jane, love. Hard work, was it?"

She nodded wanly, got up from her stool and kneeling down beside the hearth laid two fresh logs upon the sulky fire. She felt utterly drained and exhausted as though some vital part of her were still far away, wandering lost in the dark and lonely catacombs with the wraith called "Carver." She felt too tired even to weep.

The potter's wife came in carrying a bowl and spoon in one hand and a stone bottle in the other. She handed the bottle to her husband who poured a generous measure of French spirit into the warm milk then bent over the man on the bed and lifted him up into a half-sitting position. His wife sat down on the stool Jane had vacated, dipped the spoon, touched it against the rim of the bowl and then lifted it to the man's lips. "Sup, friend, sup," urged the potter. "'Tis better than salt water."

The spoon slowly emptied, some running down the man's beard but most ending up inside him. Susan gave him another, nodding and smiling encouragement as she saw his throat working laboriously. "Ah, poor drowned wight," she crooned. "Drink up. Drink up."

The man contrived to swallow four or five spoonfuls and then sank back exhausted against the potter's arm and closed his eyes again. "Set the bowl down against the hearth to hold warm," murmured the potter. "Happen he'll take some more by and by. Jane, love, ye'd best have a drop yourself."

He eased the man down on to the bed and gathered the blankets up under his chin. Then he went out into the kitchen with Susan, fetched a cup, poured a measure of spirit into it, and handed it to his daughter. "Sup it up," he commanded.

Jane took the cup from his hands, raised it to her lips, sipped, and promptly choked.

Pots laughed and patted her on the back. "It's come a long way, lass," he said. "It's a pity to waste it."

She took another sip and then handed the cup to him. "You finish it," she said. "It makes my eyes water."

The potter tilted his head and drank off the brandy at a gulp. "You've done a good day's work, Jane."

"Where was it they found him, Dad?"

"Out in the Reach somewhere. Off Blackdown Head I think Jonsey said. Why?"

"I don't know. I just wondered."

"But you got through to him, didn't you?"

She nodded.

"Well?"

"I don't think it *is* Gyre," she said. "He's not old enough, is he? But I'm sure I saw Old Peter baptize him, and I felt the Boy there too. But there's something else. Something I can't understand at all."

"Go on."

"But it doesn't make sense." She looked up at him shaking her head. "You see, before I reached him there was another man—someone else. I just don't understand it."

"Someone else?"

She nodded. "He was terribly deep down—faint and far away. But he *was* there, Dad. I'm sure of it."

"Could have been early memories, couldn't it?"

"That's what I thought at first. But now I'm sure it wasn't. It was someone from the Old Days before the Drowning." She sat back on her heels and said with a sudden conviction: "Yes! *That's* what I was getting on the boat! I couldn't understand it at all. But it *was* the same man! And his name's 'Carver,' Dad."

"Carver, eh? I don't know of any Kinsman called Carver."

"No, no," she insisted. "Carver's the *other* one. The one I got to first. I saw this place, Dad—a sort of long white house—and a whole room full of those magic

mirrors like in the stories—and a girl with red
hair . . ." Suddenly, for no reason at all, she was
weeping bitterly, the tears runneling down her cheeks
as she wailed: "Oh, he's lost, Dad. He's lost. He's lost!"

Pots, totally bewildered, took her into his arms and
comforted her as he had not done since she was a
small child mumbling to him through tear-swollen lips
that the other kids were calling her *huesh*. "There,
there, lovey," he soothed. "Don't you take on so.
There's no call for tears. You've brought him back to
us, haven't you? Without you he'd be lost and gone for
sure."

He held her head to his shoulder, murmuring to her,
and patting her with his broad and gentle hand, until
the flood tide of her misery slowly ebbed away.

One of the two logs which Jane had thrown on the
fire smoldered through, broke, and rolled sideways on
the stone hearth. A tongue of flame licked along the
scorched bark which began to spit and crackle. The
man lying on the bed opened his eyes and blinked
up at the dancing shadows of the ceiling rafters. Almost at once he became aware of a dull ache in the
muscles of his shoulders and upper arms, and crossing
his hands over his chest he began abstractedly to mas-
sage the bruised flesh. It was then he discovered that
a dressing had been bound round his left arm just
above the elbow. He explored its surface with the
finger-tips of his right hand and so came upon the
tender area of the gash made by Napper's knife.

Like a baby investigating an unfamiliar building
block he picked up the idea "wound", turned it over
curiously in his mind for a while and then laid it
aside. He rolled his head over slowly, heard the faint
rustle of dry straw from the mattress and saw the
flame tongues wavering in the hearth. These too he
contemplated dully for a while, then let his gaze drift
round to the window. Each separate perception he
weighed and examined before passing on to the next,

seeking for some link which would connect the present to the past and finding none.

When Jane looked into the room some twenty minutes later she found the man crouching beside the hearth with the blankets wrapped round him. "Why didn't you call out?" she said. "Have you been awake long?"

The man raised his head. "To whom should I have called?" he inquired mildly. His voice was low and husky; his question oddly direct, devoid of all subterfuge; and in the flamelight his dark eyes seemed to flicker as if with a gentle and secret amusement.

"I'm Potter Thomson's daughter and Jane is my given name," she said, coming into the room and closing the door behind her. "What's yours, Kinsman?"

"Thomas of Norwich, Jane."

"Oh, then you're not Gyre?" Her question was faintly tinged with disappointment.

"No," he said. "Why? Did you expect me to be?"

"Yes," she said simply. She took a candlestick from the windowsill, moved across to the fire and touched the wick to the flames. When it was alight she carried it back to the window, drew the curtains across, and set the candlestick down before it.

The man watched her gravely. Finally he said: "Gyre is lying ill on Black Isle in the Western Borders."

Jane frowned, shook her head slowly, then came and knelt down beside him. "Tell me, Kinsman Thomas," she said. "How come you were found drifting along in the Somersea?"

"Found by you?"

"No," she said. "By Jonsey and Napper. They're coasters. They brought you ashore at noon in the 'Kingdom Come'."

Thomas pondered for a long moment and then said: "Where am I, Jane?"

"Why, at Tallon," she replied.

"Tallon?" he repeated. "And where is that?"

"Well, on Quantock Isle, of course."

He stared at her without speaking for fully half a minute and then he nodded. "And what day is this, Jane?"

"The twelfth day of April."

"Are you *sure* of that?"

"Why, yes," she said. "The moon was at first quarter yesterday."

"And the storm? When was the storm?"

"The big blow was three days ago. Why do you ask?"

Thomas shivered violently and Jane cried: "Lord! What am I about? I'll fetch you some clothes of Dad's. He told me I was to call him as soon as you came awake." She scrambled to her feet and scuttled out of the room leaving the candle flame flapping like a banner behind her.

She was back within minutes with a bundle of clothes in her arms. "Your own aren't dry yet," she informed him, "but these will serve to keep you warm. Shall I help you?"

"Thank you," he said. "I seem to have lost the knack of standing. No doubt it will come back to me by and by."

She shook out a thick woolen jersey from the bundle and pushed it down over his head. Then she unwrapped the blankets and winced as she caught sight of the scars on his back. "Ah, cruel!" she exclaimed. "Who did that to you?"

Thomas contrived to insert his arms into the sleeves of the jumper and between them they got it on to him. He twisted his hair and beard free. "You read the script of the Gray Falcons," he said. "They write with sharp pens."

Jane fetched the stool from beside the bed, helped him on to it, and then guided his bare feet into the legs of her father's trousers. "Hold on to my shoulders, Thomas," she commanded. "Now. Up!"

He rose shakily to his feet and stood, rocking unsteadily, while the blankets slid to the floor. Jane ducked down, pulled the trousers up over his naked-

ness and made the buckle fast at his waist. "There,"
she said. "Isn't that better?"

"Much better," he agreed with a wan smile and sub-
sided on to the stool, drawing in a deep breath of
relief.

Woolen socks and leather slippers followed and
finally a potter's smock of blue sailcloth. Jane surveyed the finished effect with satisfaction. "We'll have
some supper now directly," she said, "and then you
shall tell us all." She gathered up the blankets, shook
them, folded them deftly, and laid them on the bed.
When she had finished she turned to him and said:
"Will you tell me one thing first, Thomas? Just one."

"Of course," he replied. "If I can."

She took a pace toward him and clasped her hands
together so tightly that her knuckles gleamed white
in the candlelight. "It's Carver," she whispered. "Who
is he, Kinsman Thomas? Who's Carver?"

The man called Thomas stared back at her blankly
and yet she sensed that he was not really looking at
her at all but at someone or somewhere far, far beyond her. "Carver," he murmured. "Yes . . ."

She waited, hardly breathing, watching his face as
a cat watches a bird, seeing the shadows of doubt and
incomprehension dusking across it like the shadows
of clouds on the Somersea. At last he shook his head.
"I'm sorry, Jane," he said. "I do not know the answer
to your question. What made you ask?"

"It doesn't matter," she said. "We'll talk of it some
other time. I'll go and tell them you're ready now."

Chapter Two

ACROSS THE SODDEN pastures of Sedgemoor the rain came rolling in from the Bristol Channel in a seemingly endless series of slow, gray waves. Though it was only two o'clock in the afternoon the cars on the M5 motorway drove with dipped headlights dragging clouds of spray behind them like trailers of smoke. One of the vehicles on the southbound carriageway— a dark blue Volkswagen—turned off at the junction before Taunton, crossed over the motorway, drove through the village of North Petherton and then turned west, climbing slightly as it headed toward the Quantock Hills. A mile and a half beyond the village it slowed and swung left through a wide stone-pillared gateway beside which stood a white signboard bearing the legend "LIVERMORE FOUNDATION. HOLMWOOD HOUSE. POST-GRADUATE RESEARCH CENTER."

The blue car drove on down the wide graveled driveway, between huge, dripping beech trees, negotiated the roundabout in front of the Georgian mansion, and followed a macadamed road which led round to what had once been the stable block of the Marquis of Ridgeway's ancestral home. There in the stable courtyard the Volkswagen came to a halt among a score of assorted vehicles on the parking grid. The engine was switched off, followed by the lights and the windscreen wipers; the driver's door opened and a young woman climbed out.

She reached over into the back seat and dragged

out a bright yellow waterproof plastic jacket which she draped over her shoulders. This was followed by a shiny black plastic sou'wester hat which she jammed down over her chestnut curls. Then she slammed the door to and set off at a trot across the deserted courtyard, passed under another arch and headed through the teeming rain toward a long, white building which stood some three hundred yards from the main complex. She pushed through the swing doors, dragged off her coat and hat and shook them over the mat. A uniformed porter seated behind a desk at the foot of the stairs looked up and grinned at her "Afternoon, miss. Fine weather for ducks."

"Hello, Harry," she responded. "Is Doctor Richards in number 5?"

The porter glanced down at his console and nodded. "That's right, miss. Do you want me to give him a buzz?"

"Don't bother. He's expecting me."

She walked past him down a long corridor and turned into the cloakroom where she hung up her jacket and hat and ran a comb through her hair. Then she pushed her way out, walked another twenty paces down the passage and knocked on the door numbered "5." She could hear voices from inside but no one appeared to have heard her, so she pressed down the lever handle and walked in.

At the far end of the room three men—two of them wearing white lab coats—were standing beside a wheeled trolley on which a fourth figure was lying. The three looked round as the door opened and the one who was without an overall called out: "Ah, there you are, Rachel. Come on in."

The girl closed the door behind her and walked forward past the benches banked high with cathode ray encephalographs, sine wave frequency generators and oscilloscopes, and festooned with heavy-duty electric cable. She nodded to the two white-coated technicians and peered down apprehensively at the still figure on the trolley whose head was largely concealed beneath a molded plexiglass helmet from which a multitude of colored wires depended like the locks of a psychedelic medusa. "Good God!" she exclaimed. "That's not Mike, is it?"

Doctor Richards nodded.

"Is he asleep?"

"Yes, I suppose you could say he was asleep."

"You don't sound too sure."

"I'm *not* very sure," he admitted.

"But he *is* all right, George?"

Doctor Richards gestured to where a fluorescent screen was registering a slow and regular pulse of electronic blips. "His heart-beat's as steady as a rock," he said. "Nothing to worry about there."

"Then why did you phone me?"

Doctor Richards looked down pensively at the figure on the trolley, then he pushed back the cuff of his jacket and consulted his wristwatch. "Mike should have come round just after twelve o'clock. Now it's coming up to half-past two. He's been out for just over three and a quarter hours."

"Well, why don't you *bring* him round? Give him a shot of something? You can, can't you?"

He shook his head. "We've tried. Twice in fact. I daren't risk a third yet."

"Why didn't it work?"

"I don't know," he confessed. "I simply don't understand it. It was just a routine scanning trip. Mike and I have done it a hundred times. Ian and Ken have both done it."

One of the technicians said: "That's right, miss. It's just a bloody bus ride for us."

Rachel unzipped her shoulder bag and took out a packet of cigarettes and a lighter. She lit a cigarette, inhaled, and then blew the smoke up into the air above her head. "When you say 'routine trip,' what am I supposed to understand?"

"How much has Mike told you about the present program?" countered Doctor Richards.

"Not much. I know you're trying to find some new

way of displaying neural impulses. I think I got the general drift."

George Richards nodded. "We've been following up a line suggested to me by a chap called Klorner. I met him at Stanford last year. Apparently he'd been researching in the same field down at Hampton way back in the '60's. According to him they'd had some pretty startling results, though he didn't specify exactly—"

"Hey up!" called one of the technicians. "There's something coming through on Number 4 again."

Doctor Richards swung round and bent over the still figure on the trolley. "No sign of R.E.M., Ian."

"There's a strong trace showing on Number 7," said the other technician.

"That's P/E and P/G. Four times in the last hour," said Doctor Richards.

Rachel looked from one to the other and intercepted the excited glances they were exchanging. "What's going on?" she demanded. "Is he coming round?"

The three men were gazing as if spell-bound at a single cathode-ray tube which was pulsing out faint circles of bluish light like phantom smoke rings. "Well, I'm buggered," murmured Ian. "Does that signify what I think it does?"

The other two shook their heads leaving Rachel to ask: "Well, go on, Ian. What *does* it signify?"

"Some sort of contact—we think," said Ian.

"What sort of contact?"

"Ah, there you have me," he said. "Maybe Doctor Carver will be able to tell us when he comes round."

"I still don't understand," she persisted. "What sort of 'contact'?"

Doctor Richards turned to her. "Let's go and get ourselves a cup of coffee, Rachel, and I'll try to explain. Ian can give us a buzz in the canteen if anything develops. O.K., Ian?"

The technician nodded and Rachel allowed George

Richards to take her by the arm and guide her out of the laboratory.

The canteen was all but deserted, lunch having finished over an hour earlier, but George was able to obtain two cups of coffee and a packet of cheese and crackers. He carried them across to the window table where Rachel was sitting gazing morosely out at the rain-drenched park. "At least it's hot and wet," he said. "But that's about all you can say for it." He pulled out a chair and sat down opposite her.

Rachel nodded. She picked up her cup, raised it to her lips and then set it down again untasted. "Mike *is* going to be all right, isn't he, George?"

"Well, of course he is." George stripped the cellophane wrapping off his packet of biscuits, rolled it briskly into a ball and dropped it into the ashtray. "His autonomic system's functioning perfectly. Heart going like a metronome. Well, you saw it."

"Then why doesn't he come round?"

"Oh, he will, Rachel. It isn't as if he'd been concussed or anything. He's just taking his time about it, that's all."

"But it hasn't happened before, has it?"

"Not to this extent, I grant you. But these compound neurodrugs we're using are tricky things at the best of times. Any slight variation in the body chemistry is liable to affect them. I suppose you and Mike didn't by any chance have a row this morning?"

"No," she said. "Why?"

"It was just a thought. A thundering old bust-up can upset the chemical balance for hours afterwards." He poised a lump of cheese on a cracker, pushed it into his mouth and crunched it noisily.

Rachel raised her cup again and sipped at her coffee. "What *did* Ian mean by 'contact'?"

"Ah," said George. "That was really rather naughty of him. I mean it's just pure speculation. Nothing more."

"Go on."

George crooked his little finger, inserted it in his

mouth and dislodged a lump of half-masticated cracker from his upper gum. "Well," he said, "when Mike and I started mapping out the cortical hemisphere we divided it up into separate zones. Those proximate to the pineal gland we labelled 'P'. P/E and P/G are two encephalic contact points which we've been concentrating on for the past couple of weeks."

"But that wasn't what Ian meant by 'contact', was it?"

"No," admitted George with a grin. "He meant something much more spooky."

"*Spooky?*"

George nodded. "Has Mike ever talked to you about O.O.B.E's?"

Rachel shook her head.

"It stands for 'Out of the Body Experience.' They have quite a respectable ancestry if you're prepared to accept purely subjective evidence."

"And what are they?"

"It's not easy to say, exactly. But, briefly, when the body's placed in a state of artificial sensory deprivation it's apparently sometimes capable of perceiving things through some unspecified medium other than its own physical senses. The phenomenon has been known to operate over quite extraordinary distances."

"Telepathy, you mean?"

"That's not a word we like very much. It's too hazy: too emotional."

"All right, but I still don't see what any of this has to do with Mike."

"You may well be right at that," said George, spooning sugar into his coffee. "But you wanted to know what Ian was talking about and that's it, more or less. We're pretty sure those impulses on the 'P' points signified that Mike was in some sort of O.O.B. contact."

Rachel stared at him. "But Mike isn't *in* a state of sensory deprivation. Don't you have to be floated in a tank and be blindfolded and God knows what else for that?"

"Not any more you don't. Y-dopa does it just as effectively."

"And what is hell's name is 'Y-dopa'?"

"Dihydroxyphenyalamine and a synthesized extract originally derived from a South American plant called the Yucca."

"Christ Almighty! And that's what Mike's had?"

"It's what we've all had, Rachel."

"You're crazy," she said flatly. "You really are *crazy*, George."

"Far from it," he protested. "We're just operating along the frontier, that's all. There may even be a Nobel in it somewhere. I'm quite serious, Rachel. I think we're on the verge of uncovering facts about the human psyche which will totally revolutionize our conception of what we are."

Rachel shook her head slowly. "Well, bully for you, George," she said. "And if it makes you feel any better I'm revolutionizing my own conception of you, right now."

Doctor Richards grinned indulgently and was about to frame a retort when the telephone rang. He thrust back his chair, skipped across to the domed booth and lifted the receiver. "Extension two five. Richards here. I'm listening, Ian . . . Yes . . . Are you *sure?* . . . O.K. I'll be right down."

"What's happened, George?"

"Mike's pulse has just dropped to below thirty. Come on."

Ian met them at the door of the laboratory. "I don't know what the hell's going on, Doc. There's nothing except auto. registering anywhere apart from P/E and P/G." He glanced quickly across at Rachel and then murmured: "Should I phone for an ambulance?"

"Hang on a minute," said George.

He hurried down to the trolley, lifted the unconscious man's wrist and felt for his pulse. The others watched him intently. After thirty seconds he let go and stood staring down at his colleague, shaking his head. "It just doesn't make sense," he muttered. "His heart-beat's still as strong as a horse; his breathing's regular; yet somehow or other he's just letting go—gradually drifting off."

" 'Drifting off'?" Rachel's voice trembled.

"Into a deep physical coma by the looks of it."

"For God's sake, George! What are you going to *do* about it? *Let* him?"

"I'm afraid we'll have to get him into hospital, Rachel. There's nothing else for it. But look at that!" He pointed toward the screen labelled "7" which was still pulsing out its ghostly circles of pale blue light. "If that isn't evidence of intense mental activity, what is? All right, Ian, get hold of Harry and tell him to send out an S.O.S. buzz to the hospital."

As Ian hurried out of the lab, Doctor Richards walked over to the control panel and made a slight adjustment to a calibrated dial. The light in number 7 screen intensified perceptibly. "Incredible," he murmured. "What time did the first trace show up, Ken?"

"Just after 12," said the second technician. He consulted a notepad. "12.02 I've got down: duration 32 seconds. Second trace 12.48: duration 3 minutes 7 seconds. Third at—"

"That's O.K.," said Doctor Richards. "We've got them all on tape?"

"Sure."

"We'll use it as the enceph. base for the new converter. We may learn something that way." He turned back to where Rachel was standing forlornly beside the trolley. "What can I say, Rachel? I can't tell you how sorry I am that it's happened to Mike. It could just as easily have been any one of us lying there."

She raised her head, gave him a long, level look, and then she nodded. "Yes, I know," she said. "I realize it's not your fault. But, oh God, George, I only wish it wasn't him."

Chapter Three

THOMAS OF NORWICH, holding on to Jane's arm for support, walked slowly through into the kitchen of the cottage. Pots was sluicing his face over the stone sink and Susan was standing beside the glowing range stirring something in a steaming iron saucepan. The Kinsman stood still for a moment savoring the scene—the spread table, the soft cone of yellow light falling from the chain hung lamp, the rose pink fire flush on Susan's downcast face, the cat dozing beside the fender, the waterdrops flickering in a golden shower from the potter's busy hands—and lifted it entire into the jumbled storehouse of his memory.

Pots swung round, groping for a towel, and caught sight of them. "Welcome, Kinsman Thomas," he called. "I see the clothes fit."

"Most well, potter. I have much to thank you for."

Pots buried his face in the towel and scrubbed energetically to hide his embarrassment. "What's ours is yours, so long as we live. You know that."

"So long as we live," murmured Thomas. "Aye."

"Now sit you down, Kinsman," said Susan. "This will be ready directly. Jane, love, run and fetch in some fresh ale."

Jane guided Thomas into a seat and went out. As the passage door closed behind her, Thomas said: "Jane tells me that today is the 12th of April."

"Aye, 'tis so," acknowledged Pots, flinging the towel over a hook. "Though you'd not guess it from the trees. There's scarce a bud to be seen breaking yet. And we had snow lying on Lydeard Hill till the third week in March." He picked up a wooden comb from

98

the windowsill and raked it through his hair and beard. " 'Tis the same elsewhere, I don't doubt."

Thomas frowned down at the table. "And the storm . . ." he began, and then left his sentence hanging broken in mid-air.

"Aye," said Pots, eyeing him curiously. "What of it?"

"It blew for two days and two nights?"

"No less, surely," said Pots. "Hard as iron straight out of the west. If Jane hadn't warned me I'd like as not have ruined a whole firing."

"Warned you?"

"She's *huesh,* Thomas. Did you not guess?"

"I do not know the word."

"Jane has the gift, Kinsman," put in Susan. " 'Twas for that we were expecting you."

"Expecting me?" repeated Thomas emptily.

Pots laughed. "Aye, friend, but you were late arriving. We had you coming ashore two days ago. And not by boat either. You were to be washed up in the Jaws on the day the storm blew itself out."

"Gyre," murmured Thomas. "She told me she had expected me to be Gyre. I did not know what she meant."

"She wasn't sure," said Pots pulling out a chair and seating himself opposite Thomas. "It's like that sometimes. The lass and I near froze our fingers off hunting for you down in the sea-wrack. She would have it that you must be there somewhere. And since she'd *hueshed* the storm it seemed like enough she was right about you too. Well, in a way she was, eh? Except in the small matter of your being drowned."

"You wrong her," said Thomas slowly. "She did see right, Potter." He lifted his right hand and pressed his fingertips against the flesh of his cheeks like a blind man exploring the face of a stranger. "I tell you this body you see before you has been drowned."

"Ah, well," said Pots uneasily. "You were indeed fortunate, Kinsman. No mistake about that."

"Four days, Potter? Three nights and four days?

You ask me to believe that a body can stay alive floating for four days in the April Somersea?"

"A miracle," said Pots cheerily. "For here you are as large as life and hungry with it. So where's the lass got to with that ale? *Jane!*"

Even as he shouted her name they heard the passage door open and a moment later Jane came in carrying a stone flagon in a wicker basket. "The lantern blew out," she panted, setting the flagon down at her father's side and turning to help her mother who was ladling broth into bowls. She lifted a filled bowl, carried it carefully over to the table and set it before Thomas.

When everyone was seated Pots called upon the Kinsman for a blessing.

"I have more need of that than any one of you," murmured Thomas. "Good people, may your peace soothe my troubled soul. Let the blood of the Boy ransom us: let the Bird of Dawning hover over us: grant us the Bliss of Kinship for Eternity." He raised his right hand and sketched the Sign over them.

Everyone intoned "amen" and Pots unstoppered the flagon, poured foaming ale into a mug and pushed it down the table to his guest. "Eat and drink, Kinsman Thomas, there must be a howling wolf inside that soused belly of yours. Our Kinsman tells me he was in the water for all of four days, Jane. What make you of that?"

"Then it *was* the storm," said Jane, glancing sideways at Thomas over her lifted spoon. "I knew it. Will you tell us what happened?"

"Oh, let him sup awhile, girl," said Susan. "He'll tell us all when he's ready."

"I will tell you what I can," said Thomas. "But first you must tell me of *huesh*. Where does the word come from?"

"That's one thing I *do* know," said Pots. "I had it all from an old cobweb of a clerk in the library at New Exeter. Seemingly it's a wild Cornish word which comes from way back when the fisher folk used to station a man at the top of the cliffs to watch for the pilchard shoals. They called him the *huer*. Over the years the word came to mean someone who could see what was hidden from others. *Huesh* grew out of it. Or at least that was *his* story." He dunked a lump of bread in his broth and sucked it down with noisy relish. "Round here every one takes it for granted," he said. "But I could never do that. Maybe because I'm not native to these parts. I held out against it for years, didn't I, wife? As I saw it the thing went against all reason. But in the end I had to give in. It got so I was tying myself in knots to keep myself from seeing what was right there under my very nose. Now I reason that if the Giver of Gifts has chosen so to dower our Jane, who am I to refuse it?"

Susan got up from her place, fetched the saucepan from the stove and ladled out more broth into the men's bowls.

Thomas said: "And what made you change your mind?"

"That's quite a story," said Pots. "It happened five years back when Jane was just coming into womanhood. We were visited for the Tax Culling of '14. A whole bunch of them arrived on horseback. There was a Census Clerk, a Tax Assessor, one of the Black Friars, half a dozen birds of prey, and the Collector himself—a great, fat, greasy fellow with a laugh like a cracked trumpet who carried the Earl Robert's seal.

"We'd had word by sea that they were on the way so we were able to put on a very convincing show of pitiful poverty. But that didn't stop us getting the Friar billeted on us for the night. At the time I thought it was just our bad luck but I found out soon enough that he'd got me singled out for a local informer on account of my quarterly trips to New Exeter and me being able to read and write. He was well primed too was Brother Benjamin. Knew all about a charge of sedition that had been laid against me in Banbury way back in '92 and he made it as plain as a poke in the eye they'd rake it all up again if I didn't co-operate. It was a nasty moment I can tell you.

"He was a real bad-un that Friar. As soon as Jane came into the room he was gobbling her up with his eyes in a way that made my skin creep. I knew he was just itching to get his hands on her. But she wouldn't look at him. Just wouldn't. Not *at* him, that is. At his shoes, or his beads, or his hands, but not into his face. And this really got him on the raw. In the end he laid hold of her by the arms and *ordered* her to do it—charged her in God's name—while Susan and I just stood there and looked on, and I wondered if I could get away with strangling a Holy Friar with my bare hands and stuffing his poxy corpse into the firing kiln.

"Well, she did. Looked at him, I mean. As though he was some sort of nastiness crawled out from under a stone. She must have stared at him for a full half-minute before he let go of her arms and fell to crossing himself and muttering a lot of Roman gibberish as though he'd just discovered he'd got the plague. Jane ran out into the yard and, after a bit, I went out to see what had become of her. I found her curled up in a corner of the pottery shivering like a mackerel. I asked her what ailed her—tho' in truth I knew well enough what it was. Then she told me she'd 'seen' Brother Benjamin lying stark naked in a ditch with his throat cut.

"Now if you give or take a murderous detail or two, that was more or less the picture I'd been toying with on my own account, so I didn't make as much of it at the time as I might have done otherwise. I just did what I could to cheer her up and told her he'd be gone by the morning and that she wasn't to worry because we'd see no harm came to her.

"And that's about all there is to it, except that the whole thieving bunch of them was ambushed in Crowcombe forest at noon the very next day by a gang of Welsh raiders. Every man jack was stripped to his skin and sent into the next world with a brand new mouth half way down his throat. We got the news two days later. From that day to this I've always given the lass the benefit of the doubt. And believe me, Kinsman, she's come far since then."

Throughout this recital Jane had sat mute. Now she rose quietly to her feet and began helping her mother to collect up the bowls. She took care to avoid Thomas's eye.

"Tell me, Jane," he said. "Why would you not look at the Friar?"

"He had the power," she said simply. "And I was frightened."

"But how did you know he had?"

"You know very well how," she replied with a faint smile. "So why do you ask?"

"Perhaps because I need to hear it from your own lips."

She paused, her face suddenly rapt and intent. "I saw the dark flame around him and within him," she whispered. "And he knew that I saw it."

Thomas leant back in his chair and stared at her, thinking: "Yes, Jane, you are right. Who could know better than I that dark flame and the fear that it feeds upon?" His eyes dwelt on her pensively, noting the square, firm chin; the wide, generous mouth; the broad forehead beneath its boyish helmet of dark hair; and, gradually, he became convinced that he was poised upon the threshold of a stupendous revelation. Bathed by the golden lamplight the very features of her face seemed to shift and glow as if they were being illuminated from some mysterious inward source. Brighter and brighter they shone while all around her the room slipped away into the darkness until it appeared no more substantial than a dim curtain of shadow against which her face, hovering in mysterious isolation, grew ever more dazzling and, at the same time, curiously, supremely innocent. He felt the world lurch and rock all about him; he heard a voice intoning the burden of the Testament: "Lo! He shall return and all things old shall be made new" and he knew beyond all possibility of denial that he was gazing upon the face of the Boy.

But even as he struggled to encompass his exploding vision a black wave rose up out of the past, hung brooding over him, menacing and huge, and though he cried out to stay it, the light and the room and the divine face all were swept away to be lost among the inrushing welter of the darkness.

The Kinsman's swoon lasted for barely a minute. He came to with a ringing in his ears and opened his eyes to find that he was lying on the kitchen floor and that Susan and Jane were bending over him. "Forgive me," he muttered. "These sudden storms have afflicted me from childhood."

They helped him back into his chair and Pots said with a nervous laugh: "Faith, you had me worried sure. I thought maybe it was the ale had taken you. You not having eaten for so long, I mean."

"Maybe a little of that too," said Thomas with a pale smile.

"We have baked mackerel to hand," said Susan. "Will that be to your liking?"

"Indeed it will," said Thomas, "though 'tis not long since I was thinking the fishes were like to be feasting upon me."

"Ah, you don't want to dwell on that, I'm sure," said Pots.

"But I do," said Thomas, "for I think that Jane may well be the one to throw some light into my dark corners. Even, perhaps, to telling me why the Bird brought me to her door, eh, Jane?"

If Jane heard his question she gave no sign.

"Did you not ask how I came to be floating out in the Somersea?" he pursued.

"You do not have to tell us," she said. "I should not have asked."

"You have a right to know," said Thomas. "So I trade my story for yours. Is that a bargain?"

"But I have no story to trade," she protested.

"I think you have," he said, "even though you may not know it yet. Besides, have you forgotten what it was you asked me?"

She glanced at him across the table, seemed on the point of denying it, and then shook her head as if to say: "What could you tell me that I don't already know?"

For a while they ate in silence then Thomas pushed his empty plate to one side, swallowed a mouthful of ale and said: "I took ship at Port Maenclochog in the south of Dyffydd's Kingdom. It was not the boat I would have chosen if I'd had a choice but by then they were right on my heels. They had picked up my tracks in Monmouth and were hoping I would lead them to Gyre. I decided to put my trust in Dyffydd's shield. Besides, there was nothing better once the Edict of Proscription had sealed off the land route to the north. Did you know they've put a price in gold on our heads in five of the Seven Kingdoms?"

"Aye," said Pots. "Five royal they've billed in New Exeter."

"That's Simon of Leicester's doing. Constant has entrusted him with the task of implementing the Edict. Having met the man I can well believe he relishes his new duties. The Falcons who trailed me across the Welsh mountains were members of a troop calling themselves the Gray Brotherhood. They have secular license to range the Kingdoms and owe allegiance only to Lord Simon. The days when each brood was firmly tethered to its own roost are over and done with."

"But you still managed to give them the slip."

"Only just. The brig sailed on Monday's midnight tide with a cargo of wool and Welsh hides, bound for the Isles of Brittany. By noon on the Tuesday the wind had swung round to the southwest and by the time the coast of Cornwall was in sight it was clear we were heading into trouble. The mate and the crew were all for making a run into New Barnstaple but the Captain had once lost a vessel in those waters and elected to ride it out in the Channel. They hove to, made all fast, set a storm rig and threw out a drag anchor.

"For a time all seemed well, but as the wind blew harder the boat began to roll like a barrel and then some of the cargo started to shift in the hold. Two of the sailors went below to try and secure it and one of them got his leg crushed against a stanchion. It was then that they began muttering about having a Jonah aboard.

"The Captain was the only man who knew what I was and he spoke up for me. He was not Kin, just an ordinary, decent human being, and I daresay that if the wind had dropped a bit they'd soon have forgotten all about me. But, alas, it blew harder. By midnight you could hardly hear yourself speak for the screaming of the rigging and the roaring of the black waters. The Captain came into the cabin and told me the anchor cable had parted. "Pray for us, Kinsman," he said, "and for yourself too, for I cannot stay them now."

"They took me and lashed my arms to a spar and cast me overboard. I saw the light of the ship's lantern glimmer through the darkness once, then once again, and then it vanished. Later the clouds thinned and I saw the new moon swimming among them like a silver fish. Later still the sun rose and I saw the coast of Exmoor.

"All that day I drifted with nothing for company but the gulls, though once in the distance I glimpsed a barque with white sails. Then, gradually, I began to slip away from myself, traveling back to the scenes of my childhood. Out and back again, out and back. And sometimes when I returned I found it was night, and sometimes it was day, and sometimes it was betwixt and between. And that was the second day.

"By the third day I suppose my body was already drifting in the Somersea. I hovered over it with the circling gulls, grieving for it as it nodded there open-mouthed, awash upon its spar, and nuzzled up against it with the gray seals. The bond which tethered my soul was thinner than a lace and yet still it would not break. And so passed the third day.

"By the fourth day that lace had shrunk to a thread of gossamer. I floated in a world of rose-red mists where there was neither pain nor heat nor cold, and yet I knew that I was not alone. It was as though I was lying awake in the night and listening to someone breathing quietly in the darkness beside me. It lasted for only a moment but somehow I knew that because it *had* been there, the thread which had all but parted the link between myself and that poor sodden thing on the spar, was being restored for a little while longer."

He lifted his hand and stroked his beard and then said abruptly: "And that ends my story. The rest you know better than I know it myself."

Pots blinked across at him then got up from his place, carried the flagon round the table and replenished the Kinsman's tankard. "You spoke more truly than I gave you credit for, friend, when you told me you had been drowned. Faith, I know not what to make of it. Jonsey said you were less than a heart-beat away from death when he dragged you aboard."

Thomas nodded. "Less than a heart-beat," he murmured. "Aye, potter, he spoke true. But the question which troubles me so deeply is, Whose was the heart?"

Chapter Four

THE EDICT OF Proscription outlawing the Kinsmen had been promulgated at the express command of Archbishop Constant, supreme head of The Church Militant throughout the Seven Kingdoms. For the first fifteen years following the martyrdom of the Boy Thomas at York in the year A.D. 3000 the doctrine of Kinship, though never officially recognized, had been permitted to flourish under the tacit aegis of the True Faith. By boldly claiming Thomas for the Church the Black Bishop (as Constant was then known) had sought to neutralize the power of the resurgent myth of the Forthcoming, and the advent of the White Bird of Kinship. But the spirit of the Boy had refused to be shackled. Blown by the breath of the old Tale Spinner, Peter of Hereford, and the renegade ex-Falcon Gyre, the spark of the Boy's faith had flown out along the highways of the Kingdoms starting hungry fire in the dry kindling of men's hearts.

Before the year 3001 was out pilgrims were beginning to trickle into York, humble folk for the most part, but one or two traveling on horseback. They came to pray at the graveside in the Minster Close and at the station on the city wall where the fatal bolt had been loosed and the Boy had died. Thenceforward, each year, the numbers grew until the trickle had become quite a sizable stream and there was even talk of building an oratory in the cathedral precinct. Then, at midnight on the last day of December 3015, the first miracle was reported. A child who had been blind from birth was standing with her parents below the wall station listening to a Kinsman playing Thomas's "Lament" when she had suddenly cried out that she could see the White Bird hovering in the starlight above the piper's head.

By the next day the whole city was humming with the news. There seemed little doubt that something extraordinary *had* occurred. Certainly the child could see, and everyone who had known her swore that she had been sightless from the day she was born. Nevertheless, the Church in its wisdom hesitated to acknowledge the miracle, choosing instead to send a certain Brother Francis as Advocate Sceptic to ferret out the truth.

To the Archbishop who had selected him personally, Brother Francis seemed an ideal choice. A man whose devotion to his faith bordered at times upon the fanatical, he had lost no time in questioning not only the girl herself but every single member of her family together with all the inhabitants of the little Cotswold village where she lived. In so doing, for the first time in his life, Brother Francis came into close contact with a complete community who had embraced the doctrine of Kinship. Thus it was that during the long watches of the night he found himself wrestling with a faith that

was large enough to contain even his own. Being the
kind of man he was, he rode back to York and delivered his report personally into the hands of the
Archbishop.

Their meeting took place in the Falconry, the grim
tower block of gray stone which housed the headquarters of the whole of the Secular Arm of the Church
Militant throughout the Seven Kingdoms. From a window of the sparsely furnished fifth floor eyrie which
constituted the Archbishop's personal quarters a group
of pilgrims could be seen making their way across the
Minster Close to the Boy's grave. While Constant pe-
rused his report, Brother Francis gazed down upon the
tiny figures now kneeling in prayer beside the plain
slab of sandstone that marked the Boy's tomb and was
moved to wonder at the nature of the power that lay
beneath it.

The Archbishop concluded his reading, tossed the
sheets of parchment on to the table before him and
moved across to the friar's side. "Fifteen years ago,"
he observed somberly, "I stood with Marshal Barran
at this very window and watched them interring the
lad's body. I had my doubts as to the wisdom of what
we were doing even then."

"How so, my Lord?"

"I had not paid sufficient heed to the myth, Francis:
I smelt heresy in the air—smelt it sharp as burnt
feathers—and yet I did not trust my own nose. Now it
is all coming to pass as Barran said it would."

"The Brotherhood of Mankind is no heresy, my
Lord."

"You think not, Francis?" The question was so gently voiced that anyone who knew the Archbishop less
well than the friar might well have taken it for a mere
conversational formality.

"My Lord, the *corpus juris canonici* . . ."

"Go on, Francis. Go on."

The friar turned and stared into his master's face.
"The Kinsmen preach only love for their fellows, my
Lord, and the doctrine of the Kingdom of the Holy
Spirit which lies within our grasp. Their White Bird is

no more than a fanciful symbol of their . . ." his words
faltered and died upon his lips.

"To you, Francis, I am sure it is," returned the
Archbishop mildly. "But to them? This bird which the
child claims she saw, was *that* a symbol? And the gift
of sight which your report would appear to confirm,
was that also symbolic? I only ask."

"I sincerely believe it to have been a reward for the
maid's pure faith, my Lord."

"But her faith in *what*, Francis? That is what troubles me. We can hardly suppose it to be her faith in
the Holy Mystery we serve. Faith in the Boy Thomas,
then? Or is it perhaps faith in something which he has
let loose in the world and which now, like a pernicious
mole burrowing secretly in the darkness of superstition,
threatens the very foundations of our Holy Church!"

"How so, my Lord?"

"By undermining Her supreme spiritual authority,
Francis. Do you really believe that if we decline to accept this 'miracle' it will make the slightest difference
one way or the other? Go out into the City and ask the
shopkeepers for their opinion. Their answer is already
lying in their moneybags. What better evidence of au-
thenticity could they imagine? Give them sufficient
time, Francis, and the Boy and his Bird will have the
very streets of York paved with gold."

"But the miracle, my Lord. What of that?"

"You really believe it *was* a miracle, Francis?"

"I do, my Lord. It fulfils every requirement in the
codex transcendentalis. At no point could I shake her."

Archbishop Constant pursed up his lips, drew a
deep breath and then expelled it in a prolonged sigh.
"A thousand years ago men had such miracles at their
fingertips, Francis, and yet what did it avail them?
They held the whole natural world cupped in the
palms of their hands and all they could contrive to
do with it was to ravish it and then drown it. They
had the knowledge and the skill and yet they lacked
the wisdom which alone can make skill and knowledge meaningful. Indeed some of them appear, in all

sincerity, to have believed that they were responsible
not *to* God but *for* Him! And when at last they awoke
from their hubristic dream and saw what they had
done they wrung their hands and blamed each other.
That any of them were spared is surely the greatest
possible tribute to the infinite mercy of the Almighty."
He glanced back at the table where the report lay and
shook his head. "I have learnt to distrust all miracles,
Francis—even ones as well authenticated as yours.
Especially ones as well authenticated as yours!"

"But surely you cannot deny that they constitute
our only evidence of true *sanctitas,* my Lord? I have
always assumed that it was your awareness of this
that made you insist upon the Boy being interred in
consecrated ground?"

"Oh, I was aware of *something,* all right," said the
Archbishop. "It was in the air all that year and growing stronger month by month as the millennium approached. By Christmastide the rumors were flying
around like feathers and with about as much substance. The 'Forthcoming" the fools called it."

"True, my Lord."

The Archbishop snorted derisively. "And where
does that leave us? A legend: an old rogue of a story-
teller; and a boy who plays the pipes. Smoke, Francis.
Moonshine. Nothing."

"Surely enough, my Lord, in all conscience, if God
chooses them."

"The rebuke is justified," said the Archbishop with
a thin smile. "But the Church has no need of Birds
of Kinship. The truth enshrined in Holy Writ must
suffice us."

The Friar nodded. "Then you have made up your
mind, my Lord?"

"You have done it for me, Francis. Far better than
I could. You have shown me the error of my ways."

"My Lord?"

"Yes, indeed. Fifteen years ago I overlooked a
small but highly significant detail of the legend. It was
Barran who first drew my attention to it. He told me

how in the very moment of its death, the blood of the White Bird splashed the breast of the Black Bird which had destroyed it, and from that moment the Black Bird became white itself and the whole cycle was repeated. Like that other fabled *rara avis,* the Phoenix, its death contained the seed of its own rebirth. Had I realized the implications even a bare twenty-four hours earlier than I did, that grave you now see below you would be an unmarked hole in the wall ditch and this whole farrago would have been forgotten. Well, perhaps it is too late to undo the damage, but what option have I but to try? I am debating whether to prepare an Edict of Proscription branding Kinship as heretical and having it promulgated throughout the Kingdoms. As for your report, Francis, that will go to join a hundred others—each in its own way not one scruple less convincing than your own—in the Secular Archives." He eyed the friar. "You are disappointed?"

"I live only to serve, my Lord."

"Yes, of course you do. So do we all. Well, now I have another commission for you. I think it may be that we shall have to discredit the Boy, Thomas. To do this it will be necessary to discover all we can about him. So this is your next task, Francis. Find out where he was born, his parentage, upbringing and so forth. All I know for certain is that he hailed from Cumberland. There is an old clerk in the Chapter House, Seymour by name, who knows something about him. Start there. I can spare you for two months. That should prove ample for our purposes. After all, as I recall it, the whelp had seen scarce thirteen summers when he died."

Confidential. Into the hand of Archbishop Constant at York. Under Seal.

The Priory of St. Margaret, Kentmere.
Quadragesima Sunday. February 3018.

"My Lord,

"I write to you in all humility and great haste concerning the mission with which you entrusted me. I have been diligent in your service having questioned many people who knew the Boy, Thomas. All here speak of him as 'Tom' and, for convenience, that is the form I propose to adopt.

"He was born on Midsummer's Eve 2986, the first born son and fourth child to Margot and Andrew Gill, a wheelwright of Stavely in Cumberland. Baptized on the 5th Sunday after Trinity, given names Thomas Andrew. His mother continued to suckle him until he was past his second year—a common practice in these parts. He appears to have been of a notably independent disposition even in infancy—'a mind of his own,' 'knew what he didn't want,' were two phrases commonly applied to him by his sisters. As soon as he had learned to walk he was wont to wander off into the woods and fells and was lost more than once. His father chastized him but to little avail.

"On his second birthday his father made him a present of a wooden whistle which the boy had soon taught himself to play with remarkable skill, learning to copy the calls of birds so well that he was said to be able to charm down the birds from the trees. His musical talent brought him to the notice of one Morfedd of Bowness (2910–2296), known as 'the Wizard of Bowness,' who approached Andrew and Margot Gill and 'bespoke' the boy on his third birth-night (2989), offering in exchange the sum of thirty gold pieces and promising that he would gift the mother with a second son within a twelve month should she and her husband accede to his wish.

"The size of the sum offered and Morfedd's reputation were such that they could have had little option but to agree. The bargain was accordingly sealed and Tom went to live with the wizard on the Isle of Cartmel. Ten months later (April 2990) Margot was indeed brought to bed of a second son, Stephen, who now lives and plies his father's trade in Stavely.

"With regard to the man Morfedd I have found it well nigh impossible to disentangle fact from fantasy. He is, of course, credited with all the conventional powers of the sorcerer but, unless hearsay lies most grievously, he appears to have employed them with singular discretion, seemingly content to rely upon his formidable reputation to achieve his ends. However, when Irish raiders threatened to lay waste the coastal town of Windermere in 2840 the townsfolk approached Morfedd and begged him to protect them. This he is said to have done by 'devising magic thunderbolts of such force that two of the raiders' ships were sunk without trace and the rest fled.' To the best of my belief that was the only occasion when he was directly responsible for the taking of human life. Nowhere have I encountered anyone who is prepared to speak against him, though whether this is due to fear or reverence is hard to say. The terms most often applied to him are 'good' and 'wise,' and though he has now been dead for nearly twenty years the ineradicable impression he has left upon people's minds is of a remarkable sage, benign and wholly fearless who revered life in all its forms.

"Tom spent seven years in Morfedd's tutelage, returning home every third month to pass seven nights with his family. His sisters report him as having been well cared for and remarkably happy if somewhat reluctant to tell them how he passed his days—'it was like a lock had been placed on his tongue.' But occasionally he let slip some remark which made them wonder whether he was not fey, as when he told his sister Angela that he was learning how to talk 'plant talk.' Challenged to prove it he took her out into the kitchen garden, sat down cross-legged amid the young cabbages and 'fell into a kind of a dream, sitting so still that the butterflies alit upon his head and I was afeared to say owt or e'en to go nigh him.' Shortly after Tom had returned to Cartmel Angela noticed that the plants surrounding the place where he had sat were all growing far bigger and stronger than the others, so that in a month they had attained the size of full-grown plants while the others still stood little more than a span.

"Late in his sixth year (or early in his seventh) his mother observed that the tip of the boy's tongue had been cleft and, taxing him with it, learned that Morfedd was responsible. Tom explained to her that it was being done so that he could play a new kind of pipe which his teacher had devised for him. Strangely enough, his mother does not appear to have been unduly perturbed by this for, as she herself put it to me, 'the good wizard had promised me that no harm should ever befall my Tom at his hands, and I did so trust him to keep his sworn word for I knew full well he loved the lad more than his own life.'

"By the boy's eighth year the initial preparation had been completed and on his birthnight in June, Morfedd himself brought his pupil to Stavely. Tom handed out gifts to all his family—things he had made for them with his own hands over the year. Angela showed me a comb of deer's bone which she treasured. It was indeed a true work of art, most marvelously contrived and painstakingly decorated. After supper, at Morfedd's command, the boy played his pipes to them.

"Everyone who was present that evening recalled the occasion with a vividness which struck me as quite exceptional, and they all used the same word to describe Tom's playing—'magic.' Angela, who seems to cherish the boy's memory more than any of them, described it to me as 'like hearing the whole world cry tears of pure happiness.' When the performance was over Morfedd had placed his hands on the boy's shoulders, gazed at him 'with something akin to wonder' and said: 'So you are ready then, Tom? It is well. Now we can begin.'

"For two years thereafter his family did not once hear Tom play his pipes though they often asked him. He still came to visit them regularly but they found him oddly withdrawn as if he was 'only half there with us, the other half away listening to some tune or other inside his own head.' Angela recalls walking with him high up on the fells above Sleddale and watching an eagle soaring up into the clouds. When it disappeared Tom turned to her and said: 'That's what I'll do one day, Angie. I'm learning how.' And she remembers that: 'I found I half believed him even as I laughed because he said it so ordinary-like.' I asked her whether Tom had ever spoken to her of the White Bird of Kinship. She said that many people had asked her the same question but the truth was that he never had, though of course there had been much talk of it in the district as the century drew near to its close.

"In the autumn of 2996 Morfedd died. He had been ailing for some months previously. Tom returned from Cartmel to Stavely. With him he carried a letter for his parents and a further small sum in gold. Since neither Andrew nor Margot were literate they took the message to their priest, Father Robert, and asked him to read it to them. Anxious to obtain confirmation of Margot's own account of what this letter contained I questioned the priest myself. He is now an old man but his memory is unclouded and he was well able to recall the event having, I suspect, already done so on numerous occasions.

"The message was apparently couched in the form of a rambling, rhyming prophecy, the gist of which appeared to be that the boy, Tom, was the one for whom the world had waited for three thousand years —he who was destined *'to Unlock the Gates of Dawn.'* This particular phrase was repeated more than once—both the priest and the boy's mother were agreed upon it. (His father I was unable to question, Andrew Gill having died four years ago.) Nevertheless, if their recollection is even passably accurate, this document would appear to have been truly prophetic when viewed from the standpoint of what has, to my own knowledge, occurred during the years since it was written. The Boy's own death was clearly prefig-

ured, though I believe it to have been couched in
such a way that the author had intended it should be
interpreted as a profound spiritual triumph. (The par-
allels here are too obvious and too disturbing to re-
quire any further elaboration on my part.) There was
also a gnomic reference to the Boy's 'return'—or at
least so Margot would have it: Father Robert could
not recall it, though he thought there might have been
some suggestion of it contained in an obscure passage
alluding to the coming of the 'Child of the Bride of
Time.' There was a verse describing a Black Bird
whose wings of scarlet flame would set fire to its own
nest and also that reference to the 'Forthcoming'
which now forms a part of the creed of Kinship, viz:

> 'The first coming was the Man;
> The second was Fire to burn Him;
> The third was Water to drown the Fire;
> The fourth is the Bird of Dawning.'

"As you may imagine, my Lord, I was most anxious to peruse this remarkable document for myself,
but Margot had entrusted it into the safe keeping of
her uncle, Old Peter of Hereford the Tale-Spinner,
when he visited Stavely in the winter of 3002. Peter
died at an advanced age somewhere in the far north
of Scotland four years ago and I believe that the document (known as *Morfedd's Testament*) passed into
the hands of Kinsman Gyre—the ex-Falcon who was
responsible for the Boy's death and who had been
the old man's inseparable companion ever since. Rumor has it that Gyre is now proselytising along the
Borders. I will speak more of this later.

"Tom's father was anxious that his son should now
join him at his trade and, though the boy appears to
have accepted this without rancor, at the same time
it seems he secretly prevailed upon his mother to in-
quire of her cousin Seymour, the Clerk to the York
Chapter, whether a place could not be procured for
him in the Chapter School. This she did, in spite of

knowing her husband's wishes, and an arrangement was concluded whereby the Boy was to enter the School at Christmas in the year 2999. I asked Margot how it was that she had persuaded Andrew to agree and she said that it was none of *her* doing—Tom had 'soothed him with his music and talked him round.'

"It is at this point that Old Peter enters the story. Hearing that he was in the neighborhood Margot persuaded him to take the Boy to York, offering to pay him five of Morfedd's gold pieces for his pains. The old man agreed and the two of them set off early in November, traveling by the way of Leyburn, Masham, Ripon and Boroughbridge, and reaching York in the second week of December.

"Already an all but impenetrable wilderness of legend has sprung up along the track they followed. On my way to Stavely I talked with many people who had attended the 'tellings' but it was not until I reached Sedbergh that I met somebody who had actually spoken to the two of them. She sought me out herself, presumably having heard that I was making inquiries in the neighborhood.

"Her name is Katherine Williams, 27 years of age, a woman of remarkable beauty and the daughter of a freeholder, one Norris Cooperson (now deceased), who held title to a lonely fell farm on the upper reaches of the River Lune. She told me how the Boy and the old man had appeared at their homestead one cold, rainy afternoon in November 2999 and had begged a night's lodging. Katherine was a girl of 12 years at the time and the Boy seems to have made an impact upon her youthful mind that can only be described as 'revelationary.' Her words concerning him impressed me so deeply that I inscribed some of them from her own lips, viz: 'It was as though all the promise of life was twinkling inside him like sunshine in a waterdrop . . . So bright and so clear was it that I knew it could not last . . . Even though I live for a thousand years I shall never meet another like him, for he took my heart from me and breathed his music

THE ROAD TO CORLAY   119

into it and gave it back to me . . . Oh you, holy men, how can you ever, *ever* hope to understand? You come sniffing after him, poking and prying, and all the time Tom is everywhere about you, just as he always has been and always will be. He came to show us what we have it in ourselves to be, and you blind priests killed him because you could not see what we saw!'

"It is not easy, my Lord, to convey the impression her artless words made upon me. I felt that I was listening to one who had drunk the spring pure at its bubbling source before the trampling hooves of the cattle had muddied it. And at the same time I was conscious that I was hearing again the voice of young Josephine Wilmot—the child who was given the gift of sight. I have become wholly convinced that there *was* some strange power in the Boy—a unique spiritual quality which the sage Morfedd first recognized and nurtured, and I would be doing less than my bound duty to you and to our Faith, my Lord, if I did not beseech you to reconsider your decision to brand the Kinsmen as heretical and drive them into open conflict with our Holy Mother Church.

"In the weeks which remain of the eight you granted me I propose to travel to the Western Borders where I shall, with God's help, locate the man Gyre and, hopefully, learn from him the contents of that 'Testament' which the Boy's mother entrusted into the care of the old Tale-Spinner. Should I prove successful in this I shall convey its import with all the speed at my command into your Lordship's hands.

> Yr. obt. servt. *in Deo,*
> Fr. Francis.

The interim report from Brother Francis was delivered into the hands of Archbishop Constant at the end of February. He read it through, pondered its contents, then scribbled one cold word of comment in parenthesis below the signature *"(Apostata!)."* A week later he received the *Ceremonarius* confirming his appointment to the Sacred College and summoning him to the Vatican in Turin. His last official act before setting out for Italy was to seal an Edict of Proscription outlawing the sect known as "The Kinsmen" throughout the Seven Kingdoms, and commissioning Bishop Simon of Leicester to ensure that it was prosecuted with all possible despatch.

Chapter Five

"WILL YOU SPEAK to me of *huesh,* Jane?"

It was the evening of the day following the Kinsman's rescue, a miracle of a pink and silver twilight, and he had strolled with the potter's daughter along the track that followed the curve of the hillside above Tallon until they had reached a sheltered viewpoint. The air was motionless, sweet as milk, and from the harborside cottages below them the smoke rose straight upwards in slim, gray rods. Far to the east the Mendip coast lay bathed in the mauve afterglow, and midway out in the Somersea a three masted barque, its white sails drooping like tired petals, floated becalmed above its own reflection. High above it a solitary star twinkled, a silver drop suspended from an invisible thread.

Jane gathered her skirt, sat down upon the close-cropped turf and gazed out to sea. "What is there to speak about?" she said. "Dad told you all there was to tell last night."

"I'm sure there's a great deal more to it than that," said Thomas, "though what he told me was marvelous enough to beggar belief. What did he mean when he said you'd come far since then?"

"You didn't think to ask him?"

"Does it not frighten you a little sometimes?" he mused, sitting down beside her. "Where does it come from, this strange power you have. Have you any control over it?"

"No, it doesn't frighten me," she said. "It's just something I was born with like red hair or cross eyes. Besides, it isn't as if I *made* these things happen. I just see them."

"But *how*, Jane?"

"I don't know *how*," she said. "It's just bright and clear and then it's gone. But I remember it."

"Like a dream?"

"Perhaps. A bit."

Thomas fingered his beard. "Was that how you saw me?"

"Yes." She smiled faintly. "Except that it wasn't you, was it?"

"I don't know," he said. "I think perhaps it should have been me—*would* have been. Only something happened to prevent it. Something I cannot understand." He gestured with his chin over the tranquil waters of the distant Reach. "Out there in the Somersea, Jane. Do you know what I'm talking about?"

High overhead a lone gull winging southwards, swung round to the west with a melancholy cry and caught a last flush of rose upon its breast. Bats emerged from crannies in the cliff and began to swoop and flicker among the thickening shadows. The lop of waves drifted up from the cove below.

"Out there," murmured Jane, "under that water, long ago, there was once a town with men and women in it. Do you believe that, Thomas?"

"Of course. Was it not called Tauntown?"

Jane nodded. "I often think about it—wonder what it was like when the waters came—what happened to them all."

"The Drowning took many years. Some say ten,

some twenty, some fifty. It didn't really happen over-night. That's just a story."

"But *why* did it happen? Do you know, Thomas? Was it really a punishment from God?"

"I believe so," said Thomas. "But maybe it was just a final warning—God's way of saying: 'Turn back, fools. No further. That path will lead you only to destruction.' Joseph of Birmingham says that if it had not been for the Drowning, the Devil would have triumphed and men would have perished utterly with-in a century because they knew only fear and had forgotten how to love."

"And that was why they died?"

"We think so."

Jane frowned. "Then why is it that men are still afraid?"

"Everything new is fearful until it has been faced," he said. "How we can learn to face it is what the Boy taught us. He showed us what we have it in ourselves to be—that the choice is ours alone. But in you, Jane, I sense something scarcely less marvelous in its own way than Tom's dazzling vision of Kinship—some-thing which, like that, is capable of reaching out and shaping anew the human spirit. It burst over me last night like an explosion of pure white light. Since then I have been tormented by the thought that it was you who came to me when I was drifting out there in the Somersea—you who would not let me die."

"And if it was not?"

Thomas turned his head and looked into her face. "Tell me what you know, Jane. For that you *do* know something I will put my life at stake."

Jane drew in a long slow breath. "When you were lying so close to death on Jonsey's boat I tried to reach your innermost soul," she said. "I can do that too, sometimes. It's what Dad was talking about."

He nodded. "And . . . ?"

She raised her hands and lowered her face into them so that when she spoke again her voice was muffled and he had to lean close to catch what she was saying. "I found somebody," she murmured. "Someone within *you*, Thomas. He was clear but so far away. It was like a far-off voice coming across still water in the evening. I think he was from The Old Times before the Drowning. But how could that be?"

"Was this the man you called 'Carver'?"

Jane raised her head and nodded.

"You think he was the one?"

"I don't know," she said. "But he was there, Thomas. I know he was because I found him again just before I reached you properly. Don't you remember?"

"I remember you asking about him. Nothing else . . . at least . . ." He shook his head. "The *name*," he said. "There *is* something about the name 'Carver.' Like a dream I've forgotten. Or perhaps one I do not care to remember."

"He's lost," she said simply. "That's all I know. I think perhaps he tried to save you and then got himself trapped somehow. But how could he be a thousand years old?"

"The spirit is immortal," said Thomas. "It cannot die."

"But his soul pictures are all of the Old Time," objected Jane. "I saw *machines*."

"And is he still there?"

For a moment Jane became very still and watchful. Staring into her face, Thomas thought he saw the pupils of her eyes suddenly dilate until they seemed to swallow up the whole of the gray iris. Next moment she had scrambled to her feet. "Come, Thomas," she cried, "it grows dark. We will surely miss our footing on the path home if we linger here."

"But you *will* tell me, Jane?"

"I think perhaps *he* will be the one to tell *you*," she said. "But I do not know if you will listen."

An hour later, as they were sitting down to supper, they heard a knocking at the back door of the potter's cottage. With his spoon half raised to his lips, Pots frowned, glanced from his wife to his daughter and finally down the table at Thomas.

Jane thrust back her chair and was about to answer the summons when her father said: "I'll go, lass. Likely it's Rett."

He crossed to the dresser, picked up a candle and touched it into flame at the glowing range. The knocking was repeated. Calling out: "Coming! Coming!" the potter stumped out into the passageway and pulled the kitchen door shut behind him.

They heard the click of the distant latch and the mutter of voices. Then a door banged and there was the sound of nailed boots on flagstones. "That's not Rett's step," murmured Jane as the door opened and Pots returned closely followed by a young man who had the beginnings of a beard upon his chin and was clutching a leather cap in both hands.

"Well met, Willy," said Susan. "And what brings you into Tallon at this time of the night?"

" 'Lo, Mrs. Thomson," the boy greeted her. " 'Lo, Jane."

"Willy's just ridden down from Crowcombe," said Pots, blowing out the candle and snuffing the smoldering wick between finger and thumb. "Sit yourself down, lad, and share a bowl with us."

The boy smiled shyly and murmured that he didn't wish to be a trouble to them.

"No trouble at all, lad," said Susan, placing another chair beside Jane's. "There's more than enough and to spare for the five of us." She set a bowl and spoon before him, fetched the saucepan from the range and ladled out thick broth. The pungent steam rose cloudily in the lamplight as Pots resumed his place.

"Dad thought it best to let you know right away, Mr. Thomson," said Willy, picking up his spoon. "He reckons they're sure to be here afore noon tomorrow."

"Who are?" asked Jane.

"Falcons," said Pots. "Seems there's a troop of them been combing the coast along Exmoor and the Brendon hills. They crossed the north channel yesterday. How many was it, Willy?"

"A score all told," said the boy. "One lot headed up toward Bicknoller and the other toward Aisholt. Each one's got a crow along for company."

"What are they looking for?" asked Susan.

Willy put down his spoon and darted a quick, shy glance along the table to where Thomas sat gazing down at his empty bowl abstractedly crumbling a hunk of bread. "I'm not rightly sure, Mrs. Thomson," he said, "but Dad said they'd been asking if any Welsh boats had put in to shelter from the storm."

"And had they?" asked Pots.

"Not that I know of, Mr. Thomson."

"That was all they were asking?"

Willy picked up his spoon again, dipped it, and then shook his head. "They wanted to know if we'd seen any strangers about this last day or two."

Pots stretched out and poured himself a mug of ale. "Strangers?" he repeated. "What sort of strangers, Willy?"

"Kinsmen, Mr. Thomson."

Pots nodded. "It follows," he growled. "As night follows the day, that follows. Those carrion don't give up easily once they've found a scent, eh, Thomas."

Thomas shook his head. "The crows you spoke of, lad," he said. "Did they have gray feathers?"

Willy nodded.

"And was one of them deaf—a short, fat man with a bright red beard?"

"Not deaf," said Willy. "But for the rest, one of them was as you say."

"He hears with his eyes," said Thomas, "and reads men's speech from their lips."

"You know him then?" said Pots.

"Yes, I know him," said Thomas. "We last met in Newbury Falconry. You might say I'm privileged to carry his personal signature upon me. His name is Brother Andrew, and if there is one thing certain in this world it is that he will not make the same mistake twice. He will not let me go alive a second time."

It was Jane who broke the silence this somber observation evoked. "What will you do, Thomas?"

Thomas smiled faintly. "Believe me, Jane, I am giving that very question my most urgent consideration. Certainly it will serve no purpose except theirs to have me found here."

"They won't find you here," she said. "That I do know."

"And what makes you so certain, lass?" asked Pots.

"Because I *hueshed* Thomas with the Magpie this evening. Just before we came back."

"The Magpie? Are you sure?"

"Of course I'm sure. I was going to tell you anyway."

"Where's it to be?"

"I don't know."

Willy spooned in the last of his broth, pushed back his chair and stood up. "Reckon I'd best be on my way, Mr. Thomson," he said. "Dad bound me not to linger."

"You're a good lad, Willy," said Pots. "And we're all beholden to you and your Dad. Tell him that from me. But best tell him no more. You follow?"

The boy nodded, "Good night, Mrs. Thomson. Good night, Jane. And good night to you too, sir. I'm glad to have been of some service."

"Good night, Willy," said Thomas, raising his right hand and sketching the Sign of the Bird over the boy. "Peace go with you."

Pots saw Willy to the door, wished him Godspeed, and then rejoined the others. "If you're to be clear away before morning, friend Thomas," he said, "there's no time to lose. You'll have to be off the Reach by daybreak or some sharp eye's bound to spot you and the hunt will be up on the other side. How come they be so hot on your heels, anyway? Sure they can't still be hoping you'll lead them to Gyre."

Thomas shook his head. "I have two things which

Brother Andrew craves: my own carcass, and something far more precious which was entrusted into my keeping by Gyre himself." He touched the left shoulder of his sea-stained leather jerkin with the fingers of his right hand. "We Kinsmen know it as 'Morfedd's Testament.' Gyre has bound me on oath to deliver it to the Sanctuary at Corlay in Brittany."

Pots' eyebrows rose. "Brittany, eh? Then that trading brig you scuttled aboard in Wales wasn't quite such a blind chance as you made it seem last night?"

"Believe me, potter, she was not the vessel I would have chosen," said Thomas. "But I take your point."

The sickle moon had just crept over the shoulder of the eastward Mendips when three cloaked and hooded figures emerged from the potter's cottage, and after a whispered farewell to Susan made their way silently along the grassy track that followed the contours of the hill above Tallon. A breeze was already stirring among the gorse and the dead bracken fronds and muting the hush of the breaking waves. Jane who was the last in the line edged up close to Thomas and whispered: "This breath will surely carry us across the Reach before cock crow. Truly the Bird favors us." As if to lend substance to her words a hunting barn owl chose that moment to ghost down, huge and silent above their heads, before swooping away over the huddled roofs of the village.

Twenty minutes later Pots produced the lighted lantern he had been carrying concealed beneath his cloak and led the way down the steep zig-zag track into the cove where Jane's boat was beached. He set the light down on the stones and flung off his cloak. "We'd best rig her at the water's edge," he muttered. "Take the other side, Thomas. You bring the lantern, lass."

Her keel bumping and grinding over the damp shingle the little boat was hauled down the beach to where the ebbing waves were breaking in faint lines of starlit foam. Pots swiftly hoisted the yard of the brown lugsail and cleated the haul fast to the mast. The canvas hung dark against the star-pricked sky and trembled like a batswing. Jane slotted the rudder home on its pins and set the oars in the crutches. Pots heaved the boat out until the water was washing about his thighs. "In you get," he said.

The Kinsman scrambled aboard and Jane followed him. Pots moved back toward the stem. "I reckon the tide turn will shove you into Culmstock Cove by daybreak, Janie," he observed. "But if you're finding it doesn't, head straight for Keardley Point. Whichever it is we'll expect you back for supper unless the weather breaks."

Jane put her arm around his neck and kissed him.

Pots turned to Thomas and thrust out a hand. "Well met, Kinsman," he said gruffly. "Let's hope this voyage is luckier than your last, hey? God speed, man, and good fortune, attend you. Here, take this. It may come in useful." He produced a leather purse and thrust it into the Kinsman's hand. " 'Tis not much but it will buy you a meal or two. Perhaps we'll meet again one day—live to laugh about it all, eh? Now, away with you!"

"God's blessing and my thanks, potter. If ever man deserved them, you are he."

"What's ours is yours, Thomas. Grab those oars, man! You're off!" Pots stooped and thrust the little boat bouncing out over the waves, watched it for a minute, then turned and waded back to the shore.

Thomas soon lost sight of the potter in the shadows but he saw the wink of the lantern and guessed that he was still gazing out to sea after them. Then the breeze plumped out the sail and he was able to ship his oars. "You are indeed fortunate to have such a father, Jane," he murmured. "I have never met a kinder man. How came he to Tallon?"

"By boat, Thomas," she said and laughed. "Dad was born in Lutown in the Fourth Kingdom. His dad and his grandad were both potters. He came to Tallon five years before I was born."

"And when was that?"

"My birthdate? The first day of this century. The first *minute,* Dad says. Me I don't remember a thing about it."

"So you drew your first breath just as the Boy was drawing his last."

"Aye, so it seems. Truth to tell I've sometimes wondered if Tom knew much more about his end than I did about my beginning. I mean no sacrilege, Thomas."

The little boat bobbed over the swells buoyant as a duck. Thomas rested his back against the quietly creaking mast and gazed up at the rocking stars. "Would that I had my pipes with me," he murmured, "for my heart is full of music at this moment—the selfsame song that led me into Kinship all those years ago."

"And where are your pipes?"

"Who knows, Jane? Swimming around in the Somersea as like as not. The sailors would have flung them after me for sure. But no matter, I shall fashion another set as soon as maybe. Meanwhile I am free to play them in my own head. Ghost piping is sometimes better than the real thing."

"Have you heard Gyre play?"

"Indeed I have. Many times."

"Is it as wonderful as men say it is?"

"Gyre plays well—sometimes *very* well."

"But . . . ?"

"Ah, you see through me too clearly, Jane. I can hide nothing from you. Once, when I was a year or two younger than you are now. I first heard Old Peter telling the Tale of the Boy, and Gyre played with him. And that *was* wonderful. The White Bird hovered over my head all that soft summer night. I felt I could do anything I set my heart to, and most of all I wanted to stretch that moment out to the end of time —beyond death even—just as the Boy had done. I knew the supreme joy of possessing something that can only exist in the giving. The next day I knelt be-

fore Old Peter and received my baptism at his hands.
For three years I followed them through the length
and breadth of the Seven Kingdoms and then, one
winter's night right up along the northern Borders,
Gyre was taken sick and could not play. Old Peter
asked me to take his place even though there were
two other pipers in our company more experienced
than myself he could well have called upon. I knew
everything by heart and yet that night it was as if I
was hearing it all for the first time. And when Peter
reached the point in the Tale where the Boy plays for
the farmer and his young daughter the pipes seemed
to come to my lips of their own accord and the Boy
played *through me,* was *in me, was me!* Thomas of
Norwich no longer existed—had no being of his own
and wanted none. I knew then that though Gyre lived
for a thousand years he would never play like that."

The boat, now running free, had drawn clear of the
Quantock shore, swooping and sliding over the long,
slow, dark swells in the open Reach. Behind them,
faintly phosphorescent in the pale moonlight, the wake
bubbled and glimmered and was lost.

"When I first saw you," said Jane, "down in the
hold of the 'Kingdom Come' and tried to reach your
soul, I found something which I have never found before in anyone. It was like a strange, bright smoke, and
yet I knew it was something to do with the Boy. That
was when I thought you must be Gyre because
it seemed to me that only someone who had known
the Boy in life could have had that sort of feeling of
him. But now I can see that for you he *does* live, and
he lives *in* you."

"The Boy lives in all of us, Jane. Perhaps in you
even more than in me. We who drink from his cup
know that it is always full to the brim and spilling
over."

"To me those are just pretty preaching words,
Thomas. The Boy can't *really* be in you—not like
Carver is."

"I know nothing of that," said Thomas.

"But Carver *is* there, Thomas. I *know* he is. Doesn't it worry you?"

"It might, if I could really believe such a being exists."

"But it was you who told us that you owed him your life!"

"I owe so many people my life, Jane. You and your father among them."

"You know that's not what I mean. Carver made you go on living when you wanted to die. That's what you said."

"Well, perhaps he did. But I did not ask him to."

Jane shook out a little more sail, then deftly made the rope fast again to its wooden cleat. She turned her head and peered back at the dark hump that was Quantock Isle then forward to the other line of looming darkness that was Blackdown. "We must be about over Taunton now," she said. "When I was little, out in the boat with Dad, I used to make believe I could hear the bells ringing down below."

"And could you?"

"Sometimes. But only in my own head. Day says that any bells down there would have rusted away long since. But I still wonder about it sometimes. About what it must have been like in the Old Times, I mean. Do you believe it's true they flew about the sky in metal birds and had carriages pulled by invisible horses?"

"Yes, Jane. It's all true."

"Then why couldn't they save themselves from the Drowning?"

"But many of them did. If they hadn't you and I wouldn't be here today."

Jane pondered this in silence for a while, then she said: "Do you think it *had* to happen, Thomas?"

"What? Our being here now?"

"Everything. The Drowning: the Seven Kingdoms: the Boy. All of it."

"What do *you* think?"

"That's just it, Thomas. I don't know what to think.

Do the things I *huesh* happen *because* I *huesh* them; or do I *huesh* them because they're going to happen?"

"But am I not your living proof that they don't always come true?"

"That's what I can't understand, Thomas. It's the only time in my life that a *huesh* hasn't happened. Yet I saw you being tumbled there naked in the sea-wreck as clear as I've ever seen anything. I was so sure I'd find you that I even went back twice more on my own to look for you."

"It could still happen."

"Don't *say* that!" she cried with sudden passion. "It's all past and done with now. It has to be."

"I'm very glad to hear it," he replied with a smile. "I have had quite enough of drowning for one lifetime."

"You laugh because you do not believe in *huesh!*" she said.

"Not so," he replied. "I laugh because I am still alive, Jane. And because you are here with me. And because the stars are laughing over my head. And because I am once again on my way to Corlay. When I can no longer laugh I shall know that the time has come for me to die."

"Those are good reasons," she said, "but you still haven't told me if you believe in *huesh*."

"I believe in *you*, Jane. And I know *you* believe in it. Will that not suffice?"

"Yes," she said. "It will suffice."

Chapter Six

THE INTENSIVE CARE Unit was situated in the North Wing of the General Hospital. From its fourth floor windows those patients capable of looking out had a view westward across the Vale of Taunton to the Brendon Hills and northwards to the Quantocks. Few took advantage of it, for in June 1986 the vista which should have lifted the spirits served only to depress them.

Rachel Wyld was no exception. She gazed with blank eyes at the sodden landscape while the raindrops pattered against the windowpane of Ward No. 3 and trickled downwards in slow, interminable tears. On the bed behind her the man she loved lay like a corpse while the saline and glucose drips suspended above him mimicked in slow motion the weeping on the windowpane. Only the monitor screens, flipping out their indifferent impulses, insisted that Michael Carver was still technically alive, three days after being brought in from the Livermore Research Center.

Rachel turned away from the window, walked slowly over to the bedside and stared down at the impassive face. "Where in God's name are you, Mike?" she whispered. For all the response her words evoked she might as well have been addressing an effigy on a tomb. She lowered her head until her lips were just touching his and felt, faint as a moth's wing brushing her cheek, the minute exhalation of his breath. Then, hearing footsteps in the corridor, she straightened up and returned to her station by the window.

The door opened and a staff nurse came in. She flashed Rachel a brisk, antiseptic smile, rustled crisply over to the bed and checked the state of the drips. Then she unhooked a clipboard from the foot of the bed and consulted the monitor dials. "Isn't this just terrible weather we're having?" she observed.

Rachel agreed that it was.

"They say the floods are reaching right up to Nyne-head. You can hardly credit it." The nurse jotted down some figures in a rapid scribble and hung the clipboard back on its hook. "And now I think it's time we did a little tidying up," she remarked. She bent over the bed, produced a battery razor from her pocket and began buzzing it around the unconscious man's cheeks and chin.

Rachel watched her with a sort of horrified fascination. "Is that really necessary?" she asked weakly.

"Dr. Phillips will be on his rounds in five minutes," the nurse informed her. "We wouldn't want our Mr. Carver looking scruffy, would we? There. Isn't that better?"

Rachel found herself in the grip of a mild hysteria. "Christ," she spluttered. "Oh, Christ, it's too macabre. Haven't you forgotten his fingernails?"

The nurse flushed faintly and slipped the razor back into her pocket. "I'm sorry if you find it amusing," she retorted frostily. "I'm only doing my duty."

"I know, I know," whispered Rachel. "I'm sorry. It's just that it seems so—oh, I don't know."

Slightly mollified the nurse smoothed down the sheet. "You're Doctor Carver's fiancée, aren't you?"

"We've lived together for three years," said Rachel leadenly. "Three years in May. And I'm expecting his child in October. So what does that make me?"

The nurse straightened up and glanced professionally at the slim figure before her. The tight lines around her lips slackened perceptibly. "Oh, he'll come round," she said. "It's just a question of time—of being patient. We're doing all we can, you know."

"Yes, I know," said Rachel. "I really do. It's just

that I haven't slept so well this last few nights. I've been having the most diabolic dreams."

"Haven't you got anything you can take?"

"Nothing that seems to make any difference."

"Come along to the office with me and I'll find you some *Sieston*. It's the best there is. I daresay we could manage a cup of tea too, if you'd fancy it."

It was then that, quite unable to prevent herself, Rachel burst into tears.

Shortly after eight that evening the telephone rang in Dr. Carver's flat. Rachel walked out into the hall and picked up the receiver.

"Is that you, Rachel? George here."

"Oh, hello, George."

"Have you had supper?"

"No. Not yet."

"So if I picked up some exotic concoction from the Chinese take-away and brought it round I might persuade you to share it with me?"

"You might."

"Excellent. Switch on the oven and expect me in about twenty minutes."

The line went dead. Rachel replaced the receiver, wandered through into the kitchen and turned on the cooker almost without realizing she was doing it.

At eight-thirty precisely there was a ring at the front door bell and she opened it to disclose Dr. Richards standing on the threshold with a dripping umbrella in one hand and a paper carrier in the other. From beneath the arm which held the carrier a wrapped bottle protruded. "Chicken and prawn chop-suey and sweet and sour pork with selected trimmings," he announced. "Here, catch hold of the bottle."

Rachel led the way into the kitchen and while she decanted the food into the hot dishes, George found a corkscrew and set to work. "I called in at the hospital on the way," he said, "and had a chat with Phillips. I gather you were up there this afternoon."

"Yes," she said. "I was there."

"They really do seem to have everything under control, don't they?"

Rachel glanced at him but said nothing. The cork emerged with a quiet "plop." George poured a little of the wine into a tumbler, tasted it, swallowed it, and then filled the two glasses. He handed one to Rachel, lifted his own and touched it against hers. "Cheers," he murmured. "To Mike."

Rachel's lips moved but no sound emerged.

"I know," he said. "Come on, let's cart this lot through into the other room."

They sat opposite each other with the tray of food on a low table between them. "I put through a Transatlantic call to Pete Klorner this afternoon," said George, spooning chop-suey on to a plate and handing it to her.

"Who?"

"Pete Klorner. The chap I met when I was over in the States. At Stanford. I told you about him, didn't I?"

"Did you? Oh, yes, I believe you did. Well?"

"He's coming over."

"Oh, is he? Why?"

"He thinks he might be able to help."

Rachel laid down her fork and took a sip at her wine. "Help?" she repeated vaguely. "Help Mike?"

"That's right."

"But how can he?"

"I'm not *sure* he can, Rachel, but I think there's just a chance. So does he."

"And who's paying for this? You?"

"The Department, naturally. I spoke to the Prof about it this morning. He's all in favor."

Rachel nodded. "And what does your Mr. Klorner think he can do?"

"Primarily he believes he can help us establish the nature of Mike's O.O.B. contact."

Rachel stared at him. "You don't mean that."

"Oh, yes, I do," said George. "And so does he."

"And what then?"

"Pete's pretty sure there's a direct causal connection between that contact and Mike's coma. He believes he knows a way of resolving those patterns we taped off the pineal area. I know it sounds incredible, Rachel, but Klorner's not the kind of chap who'd say that if he didn't mean it. All right, so maybe it's a hundred to one shot, but what else is there?"

"I don't know," she said listlessly. "What about that drug you were using?"

"Mike cleared the last trace of Y-dopa from his system more than thirty-six hours ago. I checked with Phillips."

Rachel speared a morsel of chicken and chewed it in silence for a while. "And just supposing, for the sake of argument, that Klorner's right," she said at last. "What happens then?"

"I just don't know, Rachel. We're all groping in the dark. But I suppose it's possible—*just* possible—that if we can manage to track down Mike's contact—track it down in the flesh I mean—then . . ."

"Then what, George?"

Dr. Richards spread his hands helplessly. "At least it'll be *something*," he said.

"Yes, you're right, of course, George," she said. "At least you'll be *doing* something. It's better than sitting around here till it's time to crawl up to the hospital for another session in front of those bloody monitor screens."

"Come on, you're not eating," he said. "Try some of this one. It's really good."

Rachel allowed him to put some more food on her plate. "These O.O.B.'s," she said. "What are they *really*, George?"

"We don't honestly know. Ex-corporeal mind to mind contact seems the best bet. That was Mike's theory anyway."

"So this 'contact' he had—or you think he had—that means what? That he was in someone else's *mind*?"

"We think it's possible."

"Is it, George? *Really?"*

"Well, Mike thought so too, you know."

She nodded. "And if you do succeed in tracking down this—this 'contact'—this other person—what do you expect to find? Mike's *mind* for Christsake?"

Dr. Richards' face was expressive but he only shrugged.

"And what then? Do you say to him or her or God knows what: 'Got you, Mike! I claim my ten thousand pounds in Eurobonds!' or is it: 'Release him! I hereby exorcise ye in the name of Beelzebub!'?"

"You know," said George with a wry grin, "I believe I might even do that if I thought it would get him back to us."

"I'm sorry, George. Honestly I don't mean to be bitchy. It's just that you can't imagine how *useless* I feel—futile. Tell me, when do you expect Klorner?"

"On Friday."

"Will he be staying at the Center?"

"He's booked into the V.I.P. wing."

"Can I get to meet him?"

"Of course. I think you ought to anyway. Why don't we make a date for lunch on Saturday? That'll give him time to get over the worst of his S.S. lag."

Rachel was late for the lunch appointment. Flood water had undermined the foundations of a bridge just outside Petherton and the road was temporarily closed for repairs. Forced to make a wandering detour through a labyrinth of unfamiliar lanes, she arrived at the Center, hot and bothered, twenty minutes adrift, and learned from Reception that Dr. Richards was waiting for her in the lounge.

She found George standing at the bar with his back to her, apparently deep in conversation with a gray-haired, middle-aged man, who was dressed all in black —or at least in a suit of so dark a gray as made no difference. He caught sight of her immediately and murmured something to George who turned round, smiled, and waved her over. "I was just beginning to

THE ROAD TO CORLAY

wonder where you'd got to," he said. "What happened?"

Breathlessly she explained and apologized, while Klorner smiled benignly and told her how he had been surprised by the extent of the flooding around Bristol. "From the air it's beginning to look like the Everglades," he observed. "Your farmers must be getting pretty worried."

Rachel allowed George to supply her with a Campari-soda and set about making herself agreeable. "George told me you'd once been at Hampton, Mr. Klorner," she said. "When was that?"

"The late '60's, Miss Wyld. A long time ago."

"And you haven't been back to England since?"

"Oh, yes. Several times. But only on vacation. I still have family living in Yorkshire."

Rachel was surprised. "Then you aren't a real American?"

"I am now," he said. "But I was born in Sheffield."

George said: "If no one objects I think we might well be advised to take our drinks through into the dining room while there's still some food left."

Over lunch Rachel plucked up the courage to ask Klorner directly how he thought he could help Mike.

"I'm not *sure* that I can, Miss Wyld—I wish I were —but it just so happens that I am the possessor of certain technical data that we researched in Hampton in '68—data which, for a variety of ethical reasons, have never been exploited. My hope is that they may help us to analyze the nature of Doctor Carver's coma."

"And what sort of data are they?"

Klorner laid down his fork, dabbed at his lips with his napkin and took a thoughtful sip at his Reisling. "Basically they are concerned with a technique we discovered for displaying encephalic voltages—'brainwaves,' if you like—in different planes. We called it the 'Encephalo-Visual Converter'—E-V.C. for short. I've got Dr. Richards' team working on it right now."

"And what does it do?"

"Hopefully it will enable us to see what Doctor Carver was thinking."

"*See?*" Rachel was totally astounded. "You don't mean *really* see?"

Klorner smiled and nodded. "It sounds fantastic, doesn't it?" he said. "But that's just what I do mean."

"Not just squiggles and dots and what not?"

"Oh, no," Klorner assured her. "The real thing. If he was thinking of Buckingham Palace then we'll see it—or, more precisely, we'll see his own visual concept of it. Enough, anyway, to give us some indication of what was on his mind."

"A thought-seeing machine," she murmured.

"You could call it that," he admitted.

"Then why hasn't it been developed?" she demanded. "There must be a fortune in it."

"Oh, yes," he said. "I'm quite sure there is."

"Well, then?"

Klorner pursed up his lips and slowly shook his head. "The man I worked on it with at Hampton alerted me to some of its problems—principally, the ethics of the thing. In the wrong hands it could prove far more destructive than any H-bomb. It's only because I sincerely believe that he'd have given me the go-ahead in this particular situation that I'm here today. The Doctor was a truly remarkable man."

"Was?" interjected George "Is Dumpkenhoffer dead?"

"I really don't know," said Klorner. "I completely lost touch with him back in '69 when I went to the States. But if he *is* still around I guess I'd have heard by now. He'd be well on into his seventies."

"How long will it be before you can get this thing working?" asked Rachel.

"Tomorrow or the day after, given we don't run into bad snags. It's mainly a question of wiring up a heap of involved circuits. All the materials we need are here to hand."

"And can I be there when you switch on?"

"I would consider it a privilege," said Klorner graciously. "Indeed, if past experience is anything to go by, I'd say that having somebody on hand who has a close emotional relationship with the subject is pretty well essential when it comes to interpreting the precise nature of the signal displayed."

"That's me," said Rachel. "Floods or no floods I promise I'll be there just as soon as you give me the word."

Chapter Seven

THE LONG ARM of the Sea of Dee which linked the Irish Sea to the Somersea and divided Wales from the Fifth Kingdom, was arguably the most dangerous stretch of water in the Seven Kingdoms. At High Springs the tidal rise in the Midland Gap was close on thirty meters and if a south-westerly gale had piled up the seas in the Severn Reach the consequential clash of raging waters in the narrow defile known as the Jaws of Shrewsbury was utterly awe-inspiring. Not for nothing was the fine white sand which supplied the glass-blowers of Montgomery with the raw material for their crucibles known locally as "Drowned Man's Bone."

Living their lives in such close proximity to death had bred into the Western Borderers a contempt for authority which was almost legendary throughout the Kingdoms. For generations most of the local populace had supplemented their meager livelihood with casual piracy and regular scavenging from wrecks. A line of granite forts which stretched from Stoke in the north

to Cheltenham in the south on one side of the channel, and from Oswestry to Hereford on the other,
testified to the stranglehold which for centuries the
Borderers had exerted on this vital trade route. Indeed, well within living memory, there had been a
period during which no unescorted trading vessel
had been allowed passage through the narrows unless
it had first paid tribute to the self-styled "Lords of the
Isles." It had taken the combined action of King
Dyffed and the Earl of Stafford, a force of a thousand
men and a campaign which had dragged on for the
better part of two years before the area was officially
declared safe in 2997. For two months the headless
body of "King" Morgan fed the crows from an army
gibbet on the walls of Welshpool Castle—a gruesome
tribute to the force of royal arms.

In the twenty odd years which had elapsed since
Morgan's summary execution, the narrows had remained nominally free. Fast Welsh longships now
cruised up and down the channel from their strongly
fortified bases at Wenlock and Oswestry and the passage dues which had previously gone to swell the loot
of the "Lords" on Black Isle now filtered down into
Dyffed's granite vaults at Carmarthen and the tithe
chests of the Church Militant.

Having had ample opportunity to appreciate its
strategic value, Dyffed had allowed Morgan's own
stronghold to remain virtually intact. From the squat
watchtower perched on the shoulder of the granite
outcrop, still known locally as "Morgan's Mount," the
ensign bearing the scarlet gryphon on the Sixth Kingdom now streamed in the wind which blew so steadily
off the scarp of the Long Mynd some thirty-five kilometers to the south-east. Northwards the great Sea of
Dee gleamed in the spring sunshine, dotted with the
sails of fishing smacks and coastal traders and patched
purple with the shadows of scurrying clouds. So clear
was the April air that the watchman's powerful glass
could just distinguish the lower peaks of the far distant

Pennines standing sentinel along the westward flank of the Fifth Kingdom.

One of the boats which the watchman would have observed putting in to Welshpool harbor carried among its passengers that same Advocate Sceptic whom Archbishop Constant had set upon the trail of the Boy Thomas, shortly before issuing his Edict against the Kinsmen. By pure chance, unofficial news of the Edict had percolated through to Brother Francis on the very day that he had first received word that Kinsman Gyre was upon Black Isle.

His immediate reaction on hearing the news of the Edict was to assume that his interim report to the Archbishop had miscarried. A moment's further reflection was sufficient to convince him that his personal situation was now extremely precarious. The prudent course would undoubtedly be to hurry back to York and take steps to safeguard his own reputation. He did not doubt that he could do it. And yet he hesitated. In so doing he provided eloquent testimony to the hold which the heresy of Kinship had established over his imagination. As he cast feverishly about for some course of action which would enable him to fulfill his quest and yet avoid the sin of disobedience, casuistry came to his aid.

The Edict was rumored to have been issued from the Eastern Falconry which would place its execution firmly within the jurisdiction of Simon of Leicester and the Gray Brotherhood. But Archbishop Constant's fiat overrode the authority of the Brotherhood and he, as the Archbishop's personal envoy, was carrying upon his person the sealed letter of authority which Constant had given him to assist him upon his travels. His original term of task still had a little while to run and he had as yet received no overriding summons of recall from the Archbishop. Until he did so, could he really be adjudged to have any significant option other than to remain bound by his original oath to pursue his quest with all the zeal and ingenuity at his command?

That same evening Francis had taken ship at Barrow praying in all humility that he might, by Divine favor, be permitted to reach Gyre before the emissaries of Bishop Simon ran the Kinsman to earth and haled him off to Nottingham for an official inquisition *ad extremis* in the castle dungeons.

Within half an hour of stepping ashore at Welshpool, Francis was once again afloat, this time aboard a local crab boat whose two man crew were more than willing to ferry him across the narrows and round the southern point of Black Isle for a silver quarter. The tide being unfavorable they were obliged to disembark him on the jetty at Stone Cross, a cluster of tumble-down sheds and hovels by the water's edge some two kilometers from the village of Cwymdula which was his destination.

He scrambled up the rusty iron ladder to the top of the sea-wall and found he was the object of curious scrutiny from a group of ragged urchins. He smiled at them, murmured a greeting, and sketched a perfunctory blessing. At this most of them dropped their gaze, but one, the eldest, stared back at him boldly and then, with insolent deliberation, raised his own grubby hand and made the Sign of the Bird, his extended forefinger tracing the outline of a sprawling letter "M".

Francis' heart skipped a beat. "Am I among Kinsfolk?"

Six pairs of eyes regarded him opaquely and then the leader said sullenly: "What's that to en, priest?"

On the point of framing a reply Francis became painfully conscious of the pitfall underlying the deceptively simple question. Out of the mouths of babes. "I come from the far north seeking Kinsman Gyre, my son," he replied gravely. "Will you take me to him?"

There was a moment of hesitation before the child muttered: "Us knows of none such," and the rest of the little group, taking their cue from him, obediently shook their heads.

Casting about for some way to reach them Francis

had an inspiration. Having caught sight of a bedraggled gull feather lying on the jetty he stooped and picked it up. Holding it as high above him as his arm could reach he said: "I am Brother Francis. I come in peace. By the Wings of the White Bird of Kinship I beseech you to conduct me to Kinsman Gyre."

For perhaps the length of a count of ten they stared at him, then at a murmured word from their leader they retreated behind the dismembered skeleton of an abandoned fishing boat and conferred together. Francis was left clutching his frail symbol of Kinship and feeling extraordinarily foolish.

Finally one of the children emerged and approached him. "I's Megan," she piped. "I's to tak en to Dai's place. En's to bide la till us come for en. Dost git?"

Francis nodded whereupon the urchin skipped off ahead of him down the causeway and along the rutted track that climbed toward Cwymdula. Glancing back over his shoulder as he stumbled to keep up with her the Advocate Sceptic was astonished to observe that all the other children appeared to have vanished clean off the face of the earth.

Black Isle, Western Borders
Day of St. Mark. April 3018

"My Lord,

"Your servant's travels in your service have brought him to the Western Borders—a strange, wild land of great tho' savage beauty whose inhabitants seem scarce tame and speak among themselves a tongue as far removed from that of Cumberland as that of Cumberland is foreign to that of York.

"As you will know I came hither in quest of the Kinsman Gyre, believing him to be in possession of the document which the Kinsfolk speak of as 'Morfedd's Testament.' It is my hope that before this night is out I will have had sight of it and will be in a position to communicate to you the gist of its contents if not the actual document itself.

"No word having yet reached me from your hand, my Lord, I have no means of knowing whether my interim report (dispatched to you from the Sanctuary of Kentmere) miscarried. However, the messenger to whom it was entrusted seemed suitably sensible of its importance, and having no reason to doubt his integrity, I must assume that you are now privy to the substance of my inquiries to date."

Having got thus far Brother Francis laid down his pen, read through what he had written, and groaned aloud. The style in which his report was couched with its verbal hummings and hawings, its longwinded circumlocutions and backtrackings, reflected nothing as much as the writhings of his own tormented conscience. It was inconceivable that an eye as cold and as clear as Constant's would not see through it.

He got up from the stool, walked across to the window and stared glumly out over the jumble of roofs to where, across the intervening waters, the distant signal beacon of the North Mynd winked through the gloaming. His oppression of spirit manifested itself in the form of a dull physical ache in the pit of his stomach while the potent question which the child on the jetty had directed at him returned with redoubled force. "Oh God," he whispered. "Sinner that I am, use me for Thy Divine Purpose." And few prayers he had ever uttered had been more heartfelt or more anguished.

Sighing, he turned away from the window to where a cheap tallow candle sputtered on the trestle table and set shadows jigging across the grimy wall above the straw pallet. He picked up the sheet of parchment and read through the final paragraph for the third time. "What is it you're trying to hide, Francis?" he muttered. "In God's name, man, why can't you speak plain?" And almost as though it were a separate voice lisping at his ear he seemed to hear the words: " 'Tis

from fear, Brother. Simple fear." Hearing them he
recognized them. In that instant he learned the bitter
truth that the last enemy to be faced was not Death
itself but the fear of Death. As he raised his head and
gazed into the heart of the candleflame before him
there came a gentle scratching at his door.

Rapidly he rolled the parchment into a scroll, thrust
it under the pallet and opened the door. The boy who
had questioned him on the jetty was standing half-
hidden in the shadows. "Come en wi' me, priest," he
whispered. "An' do en as I say."

Pausing only to snuff the candle, Francis stepped
out on to the boarded landing, closed the door quietly
behind him, and felt his way cautiously down the un-
lit stairs.

Voices were coming from the tap-room but the
door was shut and they slipped past unnoticed to
emerge from a narrow slit of a passage into a small
yard, roofed with stars and piled with dim barrels
and empty crates. There the boy signed to him to halt
and pulling out a dark cloth from inside his leather
jerkin he whispered: "I's to hood en, priest."

"Is that necessary?" Francis protested feebly, then,
sensing that the boy might cheerfully abandon him
there said: "All right. I agree," and bent his head.

There followed a stumbling, bruising journey which
lasted for perhaps twenty minutes until Francis was
warned of steps downwards, felt stone slabs grate un-
derfoot, and heard a door open then close behind
him. Finally, to his profound relief, he felt the hood
being tugged from his head.

He found himself standing in what appeared to be
a sort of crypt—a wide room whose stone ceiling was
supported by stout granite pillars. In a raised recess at
the far end a fire of driftwood was smoldering sulkily.
On the wall which formed the chimney breast someone had sketched in white chalk the image of a bird
hovering with wide wings outstretched.

"Bide en here, priest," muttered his guide and disappeared into a passage which, until that moment,

Francis had not realized existed. He walked slowly forward holding out his chilled hands to the fire and gazing up at the image of the bird. As he did so there came unbidden into his mind a phrase of Katherine Williams': *"for he took my heart from me and breathed his music into it and gave it back to me . . ."* He felt a curious tightening of the skin over his scalp —a sort of electric tingling of apprehension and excitement which was unlike anything he had ever known. Then, hearing the sound of approaching footsteps, he turned, just as a young woman came into the room.

She walked toward him, holding out her hand in greeting. "Well met, Brother Francis," she said, smiling at him. "We were beginning to think you might arrive too late."

In spite of the charcoal brazier glowing in the corner of the room and the thick fleece covers piled on the bed, the man could not stop shivering; it was as though his whole body were a bowstring trapped for ever in the vibrant instant following upon the release of its bolt. Sunk deep in their bony sockets his dark, fever-haunted eyes wandered restlessly from point to point while a faint, chill, dew of sweat pricked out across his deeply lined forehead and glistened waxily in the candlelight. Every now and again he would jerk his head forward from the piled pillows and his face would set itself in an expression of intense concentration as though he were straining to catch some sight or sound detectable only by himself. At such moments one of the other people in the room would approach the bed, bend deferentially over the sick man and ask if there were anything they could do for him. More often than not he would gaze back at them blankly as if unable to comprehend the question, but occasionally he would shake his head and then sink slowly back again. Once he was racked with a fit of coughing which dragged on and on to be ended only when an ominous froth of pink spittle bubbled on his lips and was wiped away solicitously by one of the watchers.

After this the man closed his eyes and appeared to subside into a fitful doze, though ever and again his eyelids would flick open and his eyes, dark and alert, would glance avidly round the room as if searching for someone who was not there.

It was into this room that the boy who had guided Francis slipped noiselessly. He sought out one of the watchers, moved across to her and murmured something into her ear. She nodded, glanced swiftly round at the figure on the bed, then rose and left the room as quietly as the boy had entered it.

No sooner had she gone than a dramatic change came over the sick man. He sighed deeply and those nearest to him noticed that the palsied trembling to which they had grown so accustomed that they scarcely remarked it, had suddenly stopped. His hands rose to his head, thrust back the loose strands of gray hair that had fallen forward, and then with crooked fingers he began combing through his tangled beard. "Would someone open a window?" he said.

An old woman started to protest that the night air would be sure to start him coughing again, but a man silenced her with a glance, rose from the bench on which he was sitting and unfastened the retaining hook on the casement. At once a breath of cool night air surged into the stuffy room bringing with it the soothing murmur of distant surf and the unmistakable iodine tang of rotting seaweed. The sick man smiled and nodded his thanks. "Shall we drink a cup of wine with our guest?" he enquired.

The man said: "Surely, Kinsman," and signed to the old woman who made a gesture which said plainly: "I think you're all crazy," before rising to her feet and shuffling off through a curtained doorway, muttering to herself.

"Gwyn?" said the sick man.

The boy approached the bedside. "Aye, Kinsman Gyre."

"Fetch me my pipes, boy. You know where they are."

The boy nodded and ducked away through the same door that the old woman had taken.

A moment later the young woman re-entered the room, saw at a glance that the sick man was not as he had been when she had left him, and said: "Kinsman Gyre, I bring you Brother Francis."

Francis following a pace or two behind her heard the words but could not as yet see the person to whom they were addressed. He knew Grye by repute to be that ex-Falcon whose sure aim and deadly bolt had ended the life of the Boy Thomas high up on a make-shift scaffolding upon the walls of York citadel all of eighteen years before. Since then the man had become part of a living legend as, in company with Old Peter the Tale Spinner he had roamed the high-ways and byways of The Seven Kingdoms, telling the Tale of the Boy and preaching the gospel of Universal Kinship. Francis' feelings as he stepped over the threshold were a piquant blend of apprehension, curi-osity and awe.

His first thought on seeing Gyre was that he could have spared himself his fears that Simon of Leicester's inquisitors would ever put the Kinsman to the rack. He knew instinctively that this man was living on bor-rowed time and that the debt was likely to be recalled at any moment. He moved forward to the foot of the bed and bowed. "Kinsman Gyre," he murmured, "I am most sorry to find you unwell."

Gyre chuckled sardonically. "A close run thing, eh, Brother? Tell me, how is my Lord the Archbishop these days?"

"He prospers," returned Francis.

"For a little while only, Brother Francis. His race, like mine, is nearly run. But we both have some work to do yet, he and I." He turned his head and beck-oned to the young woman who had brought the priest. As she approached the bed he murmured: "Light an-other candle and place it so that I can see his face more clearly. It is like speaking to a shadow."

While she was carrying out his instructions the boy

Gwyn returned bearing a slender case some half a meter in length made of tooled leather. He handed it to Gyre.

The Kinsman smiled his thanks. Taking up the case he ran his fingers dreamily over the lacings, then said to Francis: "You shall carry these to Thomas of Norwich for me, Brother. They are his by right." He cocked a quick eye at the priest. "Know you what they are?"

"Pipes?" hazarded Francis, wondering at the strange turn the interview was taking.

"Aye, pipes," said Gyre with a sigh. "But not just *any* pipes, Francis. These were fashioned for Tom by Morfedd the Wizard of Bowness. There are none like them in the living world. Would you care to hear them?"

"Very much," said Francis. "I have heard tell of them often on my travels."

" 'Tis not the same as hearing them. These pipes speak a tune like none other." He raised his eyes again and stared hard at the priest. "Is that not why you are come, Francis? To hear what they have to say to you? Speak, man. You are among friends now."

And once again the voice of Katherine Williams was there whispering inside Francis' head: *"He came to show us what we have it in ourselves to be . . ."* For the first time since entering the room he felt the angels' wing caress of real fear; it brushed by him and left behind a chill like melting snowflakes on his skin. The Kinsman's eyes held him fixed and would not let him go. Dark, sardonic and glittering with the knowledge of impending death they seemed almost to be regarding him from across the threshold of another world.

Francis ran the tip of his tongue around his dry lips. "I came hither to ask if I might be allowed to view Morfedd's Testament," he said huskily. "It was for that I have sought you all across the North."

Gyre nodded. "Aye. Think you we know not that? But your quest for the Testament was but to buy you the time you needed from your master. What you are seeking lies in here, Francis," and so saying the Kinsman lifted the case containing the pipes, unfastened the laces that held it closed, and from it removed the curious, twin-stemmed instrument, part whistle, part recorder, that Old Morfedd of Bowness had contrived for the Boy Thomas all those years ago.

Francis leaned forward to see them more clearly and, as he did so, the pipes twisted between the Kinsman's fingers allowing the candlelight to wink from some tiny crystalline facet set deep within the shaft of one of the tubes.

Gyre stroked his fingers slowly all down the length of the gleaming barrels. "You never heard Tom play, did you, Brother?"

Francis shook his head.

"So you will hear only the echo of an echo. And I have not one hundredth part of Tom's skill. But now and again he comes to speak through my fingers as one day he will surely speak through the Child and through Thomas and through you." Raising his head abruptly the dying Kinsman gazed up at the vaulted ceiling and cried with a voice so strong it seemed almost as if it must be coming from some other throat than his: "Boy, show now at the end that I am forgiven! You know that I shot in ignorance of what I did! Speak you now through my darkness that his darkness may become light!"

He drew a deep, panting breath, raised the twin mouthpieces to his lips, and fixing the Advocate Sceptic with an unwavering gaze he began to play.

Beti, the old woman who had been sent to fetch the wine, was on her way back bearing a laden tray when she heard the sound of music coming from the Kinsman's chamber. By her own reckoning she had lived for seventy-seven years and her life's rhythm was far older than the turbulent sea channels among which her days had been passed. Birth, death, hardship and hunger were the fixed stars in her cosmos. Universal

Kinship was a concept beyond her compass. She tolerated it because her son and his wife wished her to. And yet something reached out to her in that dark passage beyond the dying Kinsman's room, reached out and held her heart in thrall. Hearing Gyre play she forgot who she was and why she was there. She stood as if transfixed, listening with ears she had long since forgotten she possessed—the ears of a child who hears for the first time a music which speaks of all the infinite possibilities lying within the grasp of the unshackled human spirit. Time held no meaning for her then. Like a down feather adrift on the dark tides she felt her soul being swept this way and that at the behest of forces immeasurably stronger than herself. In a series of flickering lightning flashes she re-lived moments long since forgotten, when she no longer had an identity to call her own, moments when her girl's heart had seemed to wing out from her body to share another's anguish and she would willingly have given her own life to ease some other creature's pain. She did not even associate her own ecstasy with the sound of the Kinsman's piping. For all she knew a magic key had suddenly unlocked a casket buried so deeply within her that she had long since forgotten its existence, yet from it a fountain of pure joy come welling up to spill over in unregarded tears upon her cheeks.

At last the spell broke. She shuffled on down the passage, elbowed open the door and the curtain beyond it and re-entered the room. She set down the tray she was carrying and peered about her. Dimly she sensed something new and strange rippling among the shadows, as though the room itself were still faintly awash from the departure of an invisible presence. She shivered involuntarily and in a gesture born of a lifetime's superstition, crossed herself.

Gradually, like sleepers coming awake, the other people in the room began to stir. Only the black-robed priest standing at the foot of the bed remained unmoving, his hands hanging limp at his sides, his eyes staring wide open yet unseeing at the figure of the Kinsman before him.

The young woman moved forward and leaned over the bed. "Kinsman?" she whispered. "Kinsman Gyre?"

The Kinsman's dark eyes seemed to swim up toward hers as if from some unconscionable depths. His forked tongue moved slowly along his lower lip. "He came," he whispered. "The Boy came."

She nodded. "Aye, he came," she said, and glanced over her shoulder to where the old woman stood. "The wine, Mother."

Beti filled a cup and brought it to her. The young woman held the earthenware goblet to the Kinsman's lips. He sipped a little, nodded, and then indicated that he wished to be moved higher up on the bed. The woman's husband stepped forward and together the two of them did as he wished.

Gyre drank some more of the wine and a faint touch of color came creeping back into his ashen cheeks. Nursing the goblet in both hands he peered up over the rim of it at the silent priest and nodded his head slowly. "Your soul has been on a long journey, Francis," he said gently. "Welcome back to us."

Nursing the goblet in both hands he peered up over the rim of it at the silent priest and nodded his head slowly. "Your soul has been on a long journey, Francis," he said gently. "Welcome back to us."

Francis opened his mouth as if to reply but no words came.

"Aye," murmured Gyre. "I know how it is with you, Brother. Once long ago on the road to York I heard that self-same song. The door is already open but some of us have grown so to love our iron cage that we must needs be taken out of ourselves before we can bear to leave it."

The young woman coaxed the priest over to a bench and sat him down. Then she fetched another cup of wine and handed it to him. "Come, Francis," she said. "Let us drink wine in Kinship."

Francis took the cup from her and nodded ab-

stractedly. He heard her words as he had heard
Gyre's but it was as if he were overhearing voices in
another room talking of things which did not really
concern him. Like a sleep-walker he wandered, lost
in wonder, through a landscape that was both strange
and yet familiar, conscious only that his life's search
had suddenly ended, that the Grail he sought had
been delivered into his hands, and that this dim, candlelit room contained the Rome to which all the wind-
ing paths of his life had led.

At last he found his voice again. "For how long
have you known that I would come?"

"For many years," said Gyre. "Are you not that
Black Bird for whom we have been waiting? It has all
come to pass as it was written."

"And now that I am here?"

"My own life's work is done, Francis. I can tell
you only that you must seek out Thomas of Norwich
and give these pipes to him."

"And where am I to find him?"

Gyre's voice was growing faint, his breath a rapid
fluttering. "I have sent him to Corlay in the Isle of
Brittany. He was to await the coming of the one
Morfedd speaks of as the Bride of Time. It is all written in the Testament. So go now, Francis. Go to Corlay, and take my blessing with you."

The Kinsman lifted the pipes and made as if to
hand them to the priest, but even as he reached out
they slipped from between his fingers and his head
fell back against the pillows. A second later the wine
cup rolled off the bed and shattered into fragments
upon the stone flagged floor.

Chapter Eight

THE POTTER HAD judged the wind and tide correctly. Shortly before dawn the flood surging up Taunton Race swept Jane's little boat through the channel which separated the westernmost point of Blackdown from the three rocky islets known as the Hag's Teeth and on round into Culmstock Cove. As the cliff of Blackdown Head was drawn like a sable curtain across the sky cutting off her view of the faint mound of Quantock Isle Jane let out her breath in a long sigh of relief and patted the side of the boat in affectionate acknowledgment. "Wake up, Thomas," she called softly. "There is work to do."

Crouched at the foot of the mast with his head sunk upon his bent knees the sleeping Kinsman did not stir. Jane reached out with her foot and prodded him gently. "Wake up, Thomas."

He came to with a gasp, jerking back his cowled head, while his frightened eyes seemed to look all ways at once. "Rachel?" he whispered hoarsely. "In God's name where are we?"

"Culmstock Cove," said Jane. "Were you dreaming?"

The Kinsman peered at her then up at the yardarm swaying above his head. He put out a tentative hand and touched the oaken thwart as though he expected it to dissolve beneath his fingertips. "Jane?" he whispered. "You are Jane?"

"Who else should I be?"

"I am not dreaming?"

"You fell asleep out on the Reach," she said. "I had not the heart to wake you."

Thomas dragged himself to the side of the boat and hung his head over. Then he dipped a hand into the gliding sea and splashed water against his face. The sudden chill made him catch his breath.

Jane watched him, a puzzled frown crinkling her brow. "Who is Rachel?" she asked.

Thomas shook himself like a wet dog and then shivered violently. "Someone in my dream," he said. "I know no one of that name."

Like a wisp of thistledown a recollection ghosted across Jane's memory. She reached out, caught it and drew it in. "Her hair?" she said. "Rachel's hair? Is it dark red, like chestnuts?"

Thomas froze. "How can you know that?"

"She is part of Carver's life," she said. "His wife I think. I saw her when I reached you that first time. Your dream was Carver's dream."

"She is with child by him."

"Is? Or was?"

"I know not what to think, Jane. Who is this man? Some lost soul set wandering for penance who has found lodging in my mind? Am *I* Carver and *he* Thomas?"

"He's lost," said Jane. "That's all I know."

"Did you not say that you had found him?"

"Only in *you*, Thomas. As a part of you." She peered ahead into the darkness of the cove and murmured: "I could try and reach him again if it would help. But only if you will let me."

"What do I have to do?"

"You have only to want my help."

"Nothing is more certain," he said. "Such dreams as that will surely destroy me else."

Jane nodded. "Perhaps Carver dreams of you as you dream of him. He means you no harm, Thomas. That at least I am sure of."

"Nor I him," said Thomas morosely. "But I care not for Kinship with a ghost however friendly."

Jane reached forward and touched his hand. "Be not afraid, Thomas," she said. "Before we part I shall do my best to read you." She sat back and strained to fathom the shadows. "I recall a beach hereabouts where a brook runs in under the trees. We'll lay the boat up there while I set you on the road for Sidbury."

A few minutes later she pointed ahead to where a line of paler shadow glimmered faintly in the wan, pre-drawn light. "That's the place," she said. "We'll drop the sail and row in. There's a sand-bar we have to clear and I can't call to mind how the channel runs. Will you slack off the haul?"

Thomas busied himself about the mast and the wooden yard suddenly descended with an unprofessional rush, smothering him in damp canvas.

Jane laughed and helped him to extricate himself. "I've seen it done worse," she said, "but not often. You're better at the oars."

They cleared the sandspit without trouble and made their landfall under the shelter of a group of waterside oaks just as the first fingerings of dawn touched the sky. Thomas scrambled ashore and between them they dragged the boat up the gently shelving sand and made it fast to an exposed tree root.

Jane stowed the sail and the oars. "I'll have till noon to catch the ebb," she said. "That should give us all the time we need."

"You do not have to come with me, Jane. Just point out the way and leave the rest to me. It would go ill with you should the Falcons find you in my company."

"They'll not find you," she said firmly. "The Magpie will see to that. So let us be on our way, Thomas. We have a climb ahead of us."

Dawn found them well away from their landfall and some three hundred meters up into the Blackdown hills. The breeze which had carried them across

the sea from Quantock had died away without clear-
ing the mist from the valley. It gathered in chill drops
along the twigs of the scarcely budded trees and fell
with a melancholy patter on to the drifts of dead
leaves in the gulleys. Once they heard a dog howling
in some invisible farmstead to the north but they saw
no one and emerged at the top of the combe just as
the first welcome sunbeams came lancing in over the
distant, mist-cloaked wastes of water separating them
from Salisbury and the far-off coast of the Second
Kingdom.

They paused for a moment and looked about them.
Their breath rose in warm, panting plumes in the
clammy air and all away to the north-east the plunging hills thrust their humped backs up through the fog
like a school of whales. "Sidbury's down there," said
Jane, pointing to the south, "but it's best you skirt
round by Yarcombe. That way you'll keep water between you and the Falcon post at Upottery."

Thomas nodded. "And what of this man you call
the Magpie? Does he live at Yarcombe?"

"He lives nowhere special," said Jane. "He has a
house on wheels and travels about all over. But when
he's on Blackdown he lives with his mother."

"A peddler is he?"

"He's a bit of everything," she said. "He mends
things and makes them and he buys and sells. Dad
did him a good turn once and he's never forgotten it.
Some folks say he's touched but he's not really. He's
just different."

"Is he Kin?"

"No," said Jane. "Like I said, he's different. He's
huesh."

Thomas darted her a quick look and nodded his
head slowly. "I shall look forward to meeting him,"
he said with a faint smile.

"Oh, you'll meet him, Thomas. You have to. But
I can't tell you when."

"Where then?" he asked curiously.

"I don't know that either," she said. "It was

strange." She shut her eyes tight, kept them shut for
some seconds and then opened them again, pulling a
face as she did so. "I saw you crouched down beside
him. He was staring into the distance. And I think
there was a pile of old stones or something. It was
just a bright flash. But it's like that sometimes. You
want to see more and you can't. The harder you try
the less you hold. It's no use straining after it."

They set off again making their way over open
moorland with their long dawn shadows trailing after
them through the sparkling dew. An hour later they
topped a rise which gave them a view out over Yarcombe inlet. Jane shielded her eyes and pointed out
the wriggling white line of the high road which followed the spine of the hills, running south-west to
Sidbury. "You can't see Chardport from here," she
said. "It's on the other side of that hill between us
and the Windwhistle Isle. Dad sells pots to a man
there called Sam Moxon who has a shop down by
the quay. Sam's Kin like us so he'd surely help you
on your way."

"Best not to trouble him," said Thomas. "The fewer
the folk who help me the better for their own sakes.
Now let you and I break our fast together, Jane, before we go our separate ways."

He unshouldered the leather knapsack the potter's
wife had given him and led the way to a sheep shelter
of woven bracken. There he spread out his cloak in
the sun and beckoned Jane to join him. "By the Grace
of the White Bird," he said, breaking bread and handing it to her. "Come. Don't look so sad. See, your
mother has given us a veritable feast."

Jane smiled dutifully and helped herself to cheese
and salt. "I wish you had not lost your pipes,
Thomas," she said. "I would dearly love to have
heard you play."

"I promise I shall come back to Tallon and play
for you on your wedding day, Jane. A tune for you
alone. That which I heard last night out there on the
Reach when my heart was full of stars. I have it in

here." He touched his forefinger against his temple. "Safe under lock and key."

"I'll not wed in Tallon," she said.

"No? Then how does the wind blow?"

Jane glanced at him and then away. "Out of Quantock," she said. "I know no more than that."

"You have not met him then?"

She smiled but said nothing.

"Well, what is he like? Is he a fisherman?"

"You could call him that, I suppose. A fisher of sorts."

"A sailor of some kind then?"

Again she smiled. "A very poor one."

Thomas brushed some crumbs from his beard and nosed hungrily back into the satchel. "So how long has he been paying court to you, this sort of fisherman?"

"Who said he had? Not I."

Thomas lifted a smoked mackerel from the bag and sniffed it appreciatively. Holding it by the tail he levered it carefully apart and handed half to Jane.

"You keep it," she said. "You have a hard day's legging ahead of you."

"His brother is in here too," said Thomas, "and you'll not eat again till nightfall. Come. Take it."

Jane took the fish and nibbled at it with her white, even teeth. "What is this place you are traveling to, Thomas?"

"Corlay? A great castle. Lodged high up in the hills. It was given to Old Peter by Queen Elise of Brittany when she became Kin. She wished it to become a second York."

"And will it?"

"Yes. One day. When the Child is born there." He plucked a fish bone from his lips and flipped it into the bracken.

"And when will that be?"

"No one knows. That is why I am carrying the Testament there. The sages will study it and be able to prepare themselves for the coming of the Bride of Time."

"The Bride of Time," whispered Jane and shuddered so violently that she almost dropped her fish.

Thomas blinked at her. "Why, yes," he said. "It's written in the fifteenth verse—

> *Wilderness of woman's woe,*
> *Heart's hurt, grief's groan,*
> *Fashion thy birth bed,*
> *Child chosen, Time's Bride."*

Jane stared down at the ground. When she spoke her voice seemed to come from somewhere far away. "Two nights ago, Thomas, just before you told us about your drowning in the Somersea, you fell into a swoon. Do you know what made you? What it was you saw?"

Thomas frowned. "I know not," he said. " 'Tis often thus. But why do you ask?"

Slowly she lifted her head and turned her eyes to his. "You do not recall asking me about the dark flame and how I came to know of it?"

He nodded. "Yes, that I remember. But no more."

"And if I took you now by the hand and led you back to that moment, would you again take refuge as you did before?"

Thomas felt his heart trip and stumble in its beat. "I know not, Jane," he muttered. "Such things are not mine to command."

"You are afraid?"

"Yes," he said simply. "I am afraid."

"Of me, or of yourself?"

"Of I know not what. Something in you, maybe. Perhaps that strange gift you have. I cannot trust it as I should."

"But I trust you, Thomas. And I trust your gift. Are we not Kin, you and I, both in word and spirit?"

Thomas appeared about to say something and then, seemingly, checked himself. "Aye," he nodded. "In word and spirit both, Jane. What would you have me do?"

"Help me to read you."

"That we agreed upon. So? What must I do?"

Jane flung her half-eaten fish into the open satchel, wiped her fingers on her cloak and said: "Lay your head in my lap."

Thomas pivoted round so that his back was toward her and lowered himself by his elbows. " 'Tis a softer pillow than my last," he said with a grin. "There. Is all well?"

"Most well," she said. "Now close your eyes."

He did so obediently.

She rested her right hand lightly upon his forehead and murmured: "Let your spirit wander to the borders of sleep, Thomas. There is nothing to fear."

Gradually his breathing became deep and regular; the tense lines around his eyes and mouth softened and faded; his heart-beat slowed to a quiet, even pulse.

For a count of a hundred she gazed down upon him and then she too closed her eyes and, like a swimmer lowering herself into the water, slid to join him.

Wandering through the dim and echoing sea caverns of the Kinsman's mind, calling a name. Memories pluck at you like fingerweed as you drift past, sinking down, down, ever deeper into those cold, dark levels beyond conscious recall. Where are you hiding, Carver? Come hither. Come. Sail down like a white sea-bird and settle on my shoulder. Rise up like a silver salmon and leap into my arms. Through tide drift and time drift I have come seeking you . . .

—*Rachel? Oh, thank God . . .*

—*Come to me. Be not afraid.*

—*You're not Rachel! Who are you?*

—*I can be your Rachel if that is what you wish.*

—*Oh my God! What sort of a creature are you?*

—*I am your friend. Did you not dream of me?*

—*The boat! The girl on the boat!*

—*I found you once before but could not hold you.*
—*Am I dead?*
—*I only know you are from the Old Times before the Drowning.*
—*I'm delirious.*
—*How came you to Thomas in the Somersea?*
—*Crazy. Crazy.*
—*Do you not remember?*
—*The contact! You must be the contact!*
—*I know no more than you. I found you within Thomas. Your name is Carver. I heard them calling you that.*
—*Thomas?*
—*The Kinsman. Thomas of Norwich.*
—*The O.O.B.E.! Sweet Jesus Christ!*
—*Is Carver your only name?*
—*This is insane!*
—*Does Rachel call you Carver?*
—*Rachel?*
—*Does she call you Carver?*
—*She calls me Mike . . . Michael.*
—*Michael. Michael Carver. How old are you Michael?*
—*Old? Twenty-eight.*
—*Is Rachel your wife?*
—*What? No. Well, yes. Yes, she is. Why don't you tell me where I am?*
—*You are on Blackdown.*
—*Blackdown? Near Taunton?*
—*Yes.*
—*Sweet God in Heaven! Blackdown!*
—*Where did you think you were?*
—*Holmwood. Near Petherton.*
—*Under the Somersea?*
—*What?*
—*Under the sea.*
—*The sea! . . . The man in the sea! . . . The white bird . . . WHAT YEAR IS THIS!*
—*Three thousand and eighteen.*

So the black wave of his despair lifted you up,

swept you away from him, far beyond his reach and beyond your own, till you rose like a dark bubble through the bright, tumbling cascade of the Kinsman's memories and surfaced at last in the familiar haven of your own self to find that self in tears.

"What is it, Jane? What happened?" Thomas heaved himself on to one elbow and peered up at her.

She shook her head and scuffed the tears from her cheeks with the heel of her hand. "It's all right," she gulped. "It often makes me cry. There's nothing to worry about."

"That's all you can tell me?"

"He's there," she said flatly. "His name's Michael —Michael Carver—and he's twenty-eight years old. Or a thousand and twenty-eight . . . He's from before the Drowning—a place he calls Petherton."

Thomas stared at her in blank astonishment. "You mean you *talked* with him?"

"Dream talk. He thinks he's dead."

"Is he?"

"No. I'm sure he's not. He's still himself, and that must mean his body's alive somewhere. I've never yet read a spirit after the body's died."

"Alive? And from *before* the Drowning?"

"I know," she said. "But I'm sure I'm right." She heaved an enormous, shuddering sigh and shook her head. "Tell me, Thomas. When you dreamed of him last night what was your dream?"

The Kinsman spread his hands. "It's gone," he said. "All I can remember is the girl telling me she was with child."

"And where were you when it happened?"

"Walking with her somewhere. Was it beside a river? A lake perhaps. It was raining. I remember watching the raindrops making rings on the water. She was worried lest I should be displeased."

"And were you?"

"No. I was overjoyed."

"Was it then you woke up?"

"Yes. For a moment I was sure you were her."

"I think Carver may have thought the same. He knows me as the girl on the boat."

Thomas rose to his feet and stood gazing into the distance. "What can you make of it, Jane?" he said. "Is it not most like one of the Old Tale Spinner's yarns? Matter for an ale-house tap room on a winter's evening? Or are we perhaps bewitched?" He tensed, and lifting his hand to shield his eyes from the sun, squinted down at the distant road.

"What is it, Thomas?"

She scrambled to her feet and, standing at his side, saw the sun wink from the polished steel casques of the three horsemen who were cantering, tiny as toy soldiers astride toy horses, over the hill toward Chardport. She reached out for the Kinsman's hand and gripped it tight in hers.

"Time I was on my way, Jane," he said, "or our story may well end before it has even begun."

"Sure they cannot be seeking you," she said. "Who could have alerted them so soon?"

"Perhaps not for me, but the Edict was issued a month ago. None of us is safe now."

He ducked back into the shelter, picked up his cloak, shook the bracken from it and hitched it over his shoulders. Then he stooped for the satchel, caught sight of a half-eaten mackerel and proffered it to Jane with a grin.

She shook her head. "Those black birds have taken my appetite with them," she said, "and left a stone in its place."

Thomas dropped the fish back into the satchel and latched fast the leather toggle. He straightened up and looked at her. But now, when he most wanted fresh, bright words he could find none that were not already tarnished. He stretched out his right hand, and laid it gently upon her shoulder and turned her face toward him. "So," he said. "It is farewell, Jane."

Her lip trembled. She nodded and lowered her eyes.

"You have my blessing. You know that."

She shook her head fiercely and suddenly she had ducked forward and flung her arms around him, hugging him to her so hard that he could feel her quick life trembling all through his own body. He lowered his face and pressed it briefly against the soft, brown helmet of her hair. "Ah, Jane, Jane," he murmured. "What a splendid song there is in you. One day I shall sing it for all the world to hear. So weep no more: go in peace: and let the White Bird wing you safe back home."

He eased her gently from him, touched her downcast cheek with his fingertips, and then turned and strode away down the green hillside toward the Sidbury Road.

She raised her head and, watching him grow smaller in the distance, felt as though all her insides were being drawn out of her. "White Bird, oh, White Bird," she prayed fiercely, "bring him back to me. Let him be the one."

She saw him gain the road then turn and look back up the hillside. His hand rose and waved. She lifted both her arms, spreading them wide as though she could will them into wings and swoop down to him. But nothing happened. With a final salute he turned away, swung off along the white road, and within a minute had vanished behind a distant hedgerow.

Lost to sight in the fathomless April blue, skylarks spilled their silvery songs down upon Jane's head as she made her lonely way back along the moorland path toward the cove. The morning mist had vanished and the sunlight sparkled from the dew-spangled cobwebs. Away to the north Quantock Isle was a heartlifting wonder of emerald green and purple and blue. But Jane had eyes for none of it. She moved like a sleep-walker, conscious chiefly of a numb, leaden weariness of body and spirit, while the sentient part of her trotted in her imagination at the Kinsman's side down the long white road to Sidbury. Hardly aware that she had reached it she found herself at last in Culmstock valley and began the descent to the sea.

Using a fallen tree as a makeshift bridge she crossed the gurgling brook and picked her way down the steep track to the shore. The tide was already ebbing and had left a line of sea-wrack scribbled across the wet sand to mark the limit of its advance into the cove. Where the small waves were creaming across the bar a cluster of sea birds scavenged for shrimps, wheeling and diving, silver-white in the bright, early morning sun. Far to the west the slopes of Dartmoor loomed tawny as lions against the cloudless sky.

She paused for a moment to recover her breath, then following the track of her own footprints along the margin of the brook she rounded a towering bramble clump which had screened her from the boat. It was still lying where she had left it, though the tide had since shifted it slightly to one side. She walked forward and was about to untie the rope which held it fast to its mooring when she noticed hoof marks on the sand.

For an icy moment she stood staring down at them, rigid with shock. Then she raised her head and scanned the beach. The tracks of two horses disappeared round a little promontory no more than fifty paces from where she was standing. The prints were still sharp and clear in the sand, in one place only a matter of meters from the retreating water's edge.

With her heart racing painfully she bent over the rope and struggled to loosen the wet knot. Just as it began to yield, her anxious ears caught the unmistakable crack of a breaking twig. She jerked her head back.

On the bank immediately above her, half hidden in the dappling shadow of a huge oak, a man dressed in a tunic of black leather was staring down at her.

She felt as if a cold net had been cast into her stomach and drawn in tight as a clenched fist, yet somehow she contrived to smile and say: "Oh, you startled me."

The words had scarcely left her lips when she noticed a second man lowering himself down the bank by the promontory. In his left hand he grasped the deadly little crossbow of black metal called the talon which the Falcons favored. It was fully drawn, cocked and ready to fire.

The man above her started to whistle tunelessly between his teeth then he too launched himself down the steep bank. He landed amid a tiny avalanche of dead leaves, twigs and pebbles no more than a dozen paces from where she stood, cutting off her retreat to the brook. Still piping his chill, hissing whistle he beat the soil from his tunic. Then, staring directly at her with a cold and calculated insolence, he unbuttoned his breech flap and began to urinate on the sand before her.

Jane wrenched the rope clear of the root to which it was fastened and flung it aboard. Then she hurried round to the stern and began dragging the boat down to the water. She had moved it less than its own length when the second Falcon shouted: "Hey, hold it there! What's all the tearing rush?"

"The tide's running out fast," she panted. "I don't want to miss it."

"Oh, you'll catch it all right," he called. "We'll see to that. Where are you headed for?"

"Quantock."

"Quantock, eh?" The man laughed. "Hear that, Owen? Our little birdie's a long way from its nest."

The Falcon addressed as Owen sauntered over and leaned his weight against the side of the boat, effectively anchoring it. "Your name, wench?"

"Jane," she said. "Jane Thomson."

"Well met, Jane," said the man with the bow cheerily. "All on our lonesome, are we?"

Jane said nothing.

"I'm Rowley," he said affably, "Sergeant Rowley to you, Jane. And now I'm going to ask what brings you to Blackdown."

"I've been to see my aunt," lied Jane desperately. "She's ill."

"I'm sorry to hear that, Jane. Really sorry." Rowley clicked his tongue solicitously. "Aren't you sorry, Owen?"

Owen bared his teeth in a cold smile.

Sergeant Rowley paced slowly around the boat. He was a head shorter than his companion and had a stubbly bristle of a reddish gold beard which glinted when it caught the sun. His face seemed to be creased into a permanent, fatuous grin. "Quiet place this," he observed. "Very quiet. Just the spot to slip ashore if you didn't want all the world to know what you was about. Like visiting a plaguey aunt, say." He had completed his circuit of the boat and now stood within an arm's length of Jane, his head tilted slightly to one side, eyeing her speculatively. "All right, lass," he said. "Time's up. Where is he?"

Jane gazed at him in feigned incomprehension.

"Where's who?" she said.

"The Kinsman you slipped ashore last night."

"I don't know what you mean."

"No? Then whose are the prints?" He gestured with his bow to the tracks left by Thomas's feet. "Auntie's, maybe?"

Jane shook her head, repeating: "I don't know. I don't know."

Sergeant Rowley stared at her without saying anything, then he glanced back at Owen and gave a little upward jerk of his chin.

The second Falcon rose from the boat, moved round behind Jane's back and seized her by the arms. She started to tremble uncontrollably. "Please," she muttered, "please don't," and winced as she felt a leather thong bite into her snared wrists.

Rowley reached out and tweaked open the toggle of her cloak. She jerked backwards defensively and the garment slipped from her shoulders and slid to the sand. "Come on now, lass," he said. "Be sensible."

Jane shook her head wildly. "There was only my

cousin," she gasped. "He came down to meet me. There wasn't anyone else."

"You're lying, Jane," said the Sergeant. "And that's very silly of you. We don't take kindly to liars. We don't like them one little bit."

He took half a pace forward and with his right hand smacked her hard and very deliberately across the face, first one side and then the other. Her head rung like a smithy and her eyes filled with tears.

"So where is he?"

She shook her head helplessly and whispered through swelling lips: "There was no one. No one. Let me go. Please let me go."

"Come on, girlie," said the Sergeant. "You'll tell us in the end and we're bound to pick him up anyway. So let's just be sensible, hey?"

He reached out, pulled undone the bow which held the lacing of her bodice and twitched the panels aside to expose her breasts. Then he caught hold of her chin in his hand and tilted her face upwards. "You know what you've got coming to you if you don't," he murmured.

Jane's eyes were wide with terror; her bruised lips trembled; but no words emerged from them. Suddenly she felt Owen's arms grip her round the waist. She was swung off her feet and flung down backwards on to the hard sand beside the boat so that all the breath was knocked out of her. Dark against the bright sky the Sergeant stooped and ripped her dress apart all the way down to her ankles.

A sound most like the harsh scream of a gull rose from somewhere deep within her and curdled the air. Blind with terror she kicked out wildly only to have her ankle gripped and then ground down into the sand beneath the Sergeant's spurred boot. Owen reared up over her, one hand fumbling at his breeches flap, the other grasping her free leg. Then he was down upon her, crushing her into the sand. She felt his yard jab brutally against her cringing belly and a pain like a hot iron drove burning into her left breast. Dimly she heard the Sergeant shout and then the crushing agony of his boot on her ankle was suddenly gone.

Owen lay sprawled full length upon her, his hungry stubbled face pressed flat against hers, his eyes, grotesquely enormous, staring wide open as though in supreme astonishment. She felt one tremendous spasmodic shudder ripple through him and she shrieked aloud from the fire in her breast.

There was a heavy thud against the boat; a scrabbling scratching of nails against wood; and a long, low spluttering, bubbling sound. Then, mercifully, she lost her hold upon her swimming senses and drifted off into dark oblivion.

She came to just as the dead Falcon was being dragged from on top of her. The steel tipped bolt which had pierced his back protruded half a finger's length beyond his chest. It was, his own dead weight which had driven it down into her breast. With the point withdrawn the wound began to ooze blood.

She felt rough but kindly hands drawing her ravaged dress together over her bruised nakedness and then she was being rolled over on to her side and the thongs were being slashed from her wrists.

Three paces away the Sergeant was lying sprawled with his back to the boat. His booted legs were spread wide, his startled eyes gazing blindly up at the sun. Dark blood dribbled from his mouth in a thickening stream and a feathered bolt jutted out of his neck just where it joined his shoulders. Seeing him thus Jane felt her stomach suddenly contract and before she could prevent herself she had vomited violently on to the trampled sand.

The ragged, gray-haired man who had released her unhooked a leather flask from his belt, unstoppered it with a deft finger twist and, having coaxed her up into a sitting position, held it to her lips.

She swallowed, choked, and then at his urgent bidding, swallowed again. "Bravely, lass," he murmured. "And now let's see what those black devils have done to you." He drew the torn and bloodstained dress aside and made a little, worried, clicking sound with his tongue. Unwinding a cloth from around his neck he splashed brandy on to it from the flask and gently sponged the bright blood from the wound. "Ah, you'll live, Janie. 'Tis but a nasty scratch. 'Twas well I *hueshed* this when I did though, hey?"

Jane leaned against him shuddering while the tears coursed down her pale cheeks and dripped unheeded from her chin. He waited until her trembling had abated a little then patted her shoulder, rose to his feet and fetched her cloak. "We must away from here, lass," he said, draping the garment over her shoulders and fastening the toggle. "There's no way we can stay and face this charnel out. Our best hope is to sink the carrion in the channel. That way we'll maybe buy ourselves a day or two's grace. Come, help me get this cockleshell afloat."

He pulled her to her feet and together they dragged the boat to the water's edge. Then he ran back and lugged the corpse of the Sergeant down to her. "Run and fetch me a big flat stone, Janie," he panted, wrestling the barbed bolt free from the Falcon's neck. "Hurry now, lass."

Jane seemed to come awake at last. She ran back to the bank, prised loosed a slab of sandstone and carried it down the beach to him.

"A right Christian tombstone that," he grunted. "Now help me get the bastard aboard."

Jane lifted the corpse by its booted feet and between them they contrived to tumble it over the gunwale. "Shall I come too, Magpie?" she asked.

"No. I'll manage. Go you and find another pebble like that last." He thrust the boat out, scrambled aboard and seized the oars.

Janie hurried back up the beach and began hunting for a second stone.

In half an hour the job was done. The Falcons' tethered horses had been turned loose and their erst-while masters, lungs and bellies thoughtfully paunched by the Magpie's knife were lying five fathoms deep feeding the crabs in Culmstock Cove.

The Magpie laid his crossbow in the boat, helped Jane aboard and then hoisted the sail. "If our luck holds the next tide'll wipe all clean and none the wiser," he said. "How fares the bosom?"

"It aches."

"Aye. 'Tis only to be expected. But we'll soon have that put right." He shook out the sail and settled back at the tiller. "So tell me. What brought you hither, lass?"

Jane told him. By the time she had concluded they were clear of the cove and the boat was heeling to the mid-day breeze which blew down off the distant Dartmoor slopes. "He'll be lucky to get away to sea from Sidbury," said the Magpie. "They're combing every ship in the port."

"You'll find him," said Jane. "Like you found me."

He cocked a quizzical blue eye at her. "Oh, so that's the way it is," he said thoughtfully. "I had wondered."

"You haven't *hueshed* him, then?"

"No, but there's still time. I only picked you up yesterday. It had to be Culmstock."

"You were waiting there?"

"Aye," he said. "For an hour or more. You passed within an arm's length of me down by the brook."

"Then why didn't you . . . ?"

"I durst not break the spell, lass. I'd *hueshed* the carrion upon you. It began and ended there. Had they but known it they were dead before they ever rode out this morning."

"Does it always come true for you?"

"Always. Sure you must know that."

Jane drew her cloak tight about her and shook her head. "I *hueshed* Thomas drowned, Magpie. He was to be washed up in The Jaws. That didn't happen."

"It will," he said. "If you saw it truly it will. There's no power on earth can alter it."

"I thought that too," she said, "until I found

Carver. Now I'm not sure about anything any more. Not death, or life, or *huesh,* or anything. It's all fallen apart."

"And him? The Kinsman? How does he fit in?"

"I *hueshed* him with you, Magpie. Before we left Quantock."

"Where's it to be?"

"I don't know. On the moors somewhere, I think. Nowhere I knew."

"That's all you saw?"

She nodded. "There was a pile of stones. Gray stones. It was just a flash."

The Magpie chewed his lower lip. "Little enough," he said, "but I've known less. And it seems we'll get to him before they do." He stretched out his hand, laid it across Jane's shoulder and gripped her comfortingly. "Don't fret over it, lass. We'll find him. Sooner or later, we'll find him."

"Let it be sooner," she said.

Chapter Nine

THE BLINDS IN No. 5 lab at the Post-Graduate Research Center had been drawn down shutting out the dismal noontide prospect of lowering clouds and incessant drifting rain. Internal illumination was provided by one bluish neon strip and the amber cones of three strategically placed bench lights. Rachel closed the door quietly behind her, blinked to accustom her eyes to the gloom, and then made her way carefully toward the group of men who were gathered around one of the lights at the far end of the room. Almost at once she snagged her heel on one of the heavy-duty electric cables that snaked across the floor, and her muttered, "Damn" drew their attention upon her.

"Ah, there you are, Rachel," said George affably. "Glad you could make it."

She greeted them collectively, picking her way gingerly up the littered aisle between the ranked benches. "I'm not too late then?" she inquired.

"No, no," Peter Klorner assured her. "We've had a dry run over the first phase just to check things out and now we're all ready to go. So far everything looks good."

"You haven't discovered anything?"

"We've discovered that the E-V.C's feasible," said George. "You're looking at three converted skeptics."

"What did you do?"

"We guineapigged Ian and were treated to a very interesting tour of the night life of Amsterdam. It really does *work*, Rachel. You'll be astonished."

"But how can it work for Mike if he isn't here?"

"We got all his last session down on tape. Pete's linking it in now. Sit yourself down here. If anything does show up it'll be on the big center screen."

George pushed another chair into the semi-circle. Aware of a tightening sensation in the pit of her stomach, Rachel sat down obediently. "Does anyone mind if I smoke?"

"Go ahead," said George.

Rachel unzipped her shoulder bag and went through the familiar calming ritual of extracting a cigarette from the pack and lighting it. As she clicked the lighter shut Ian said: "All clear here, Mr. Klorner."

"O.K.," said Peter. "Well, I guess this is it then. Let's have the other lights off."

Ken, the second technician, flicked off the switches leaving Peter Klorner pooled in the amber glow from one bench light. "Here goes," he said, and pressed a button on the console before him.

With a faint, dry whisper the tape began to unreel from its spool. As it did so the cathode ray tube came to life, glowing with a cold, bluish light. Rachel stared at the screen and felt the skin all down her back and shoulders crawling into goose flesh.

"We picked up our first clear trace just after twelve," said George. "That would be about forty seconds in from here. We were recording only from our four P. points and it's possible the impulse may not register at all."

"I suspect it will," said Klorner.

The screen flickered and dimmed precipitately, then just as their eyes were adjusting to the new gloom, it blossomed into a myriad twinkling points of light which danced and quivered and rocked up and down in an incomprehensible swirl of chiaroscuro. The coruscation lasted for precisely thirty-two seconds and then faded away.

"Could anyone make anything of that?" inquired Klorner.

No one could.

"The second trace showed up about an hour after the first," said George. "There wasn't anything in between."

Klorner nodded and slipped the recorder into rapid forward. It hummed on smoothly until the screen once again jerked into brightness. Then he stopped it and back-tracked a little, allowing himself a ten second overlap. "Well, here's number two," he said. "Let's hope it's more comprehensible than number one."

A shape, vague and yet curiously familiar, filled the upper right quarter of the screen. It seemed to advance and recede and then suddenly it lurched into sharp focus. As it did so the hooked beak opened in a silent squawk of alarm, the powerful wings lifted and spread and the gull swept away to vanish against the blinding white glare of the sun.

Like a camera panning slowly round, the screen next became a quiver of jostling images of waves, then a dim line of coast, and finally, just before the picture lapsed into darkness once again, there came a vivid close-up of a man's forearm, a section of a spar, and far away beyond it something that could just possibly have been a sailing ship.

Klorner stopped the tape. "We'll take another look at that," he said. "Does it mean anything to anyone?"

Ken said: "That first trace we saw could have been the sun reflected off water, couldn't it?"

"I don't understand any of it," said Rachel. "Is that supposed to be what Mike *saw?*"

"What else could it be?" said George.

"Well, a dream or something. For Christ's sake, George, Mike was *here*—lying on that trolley over there. He wasn't floating in the sea, was he?"

"I don't know, Rachel. Let's have another look at it. Maybe we'll spot something we've missed."

The pictures reformed upon the screen. The gull's cold eye peered into theirs; the waves glinted and sparkled in the April sunshine; and flickering far away on the northern horizon the coaster "Kingdom Come" dipped and rose as it came beating up into Taunton Reach.

As the images faded and died for the second time Ian said: "If I didn't know it was impossible I'd swear that those were the Blackdown Hills. I've stared at them from my bedroom window for the past fifteen years."

"He's right, you know," said Ken. "That could well have been Staple Hill."

"Oh, come off it!" said George. "It could have been *anywhere!* And since when has Blackdown been a seaside resort?"

"Do you want another look at it?" said Klorner. "Or shall we press on to the next?"

"Let's go on," said George. "We can always come back to it again."

The third and final vision was, if anything, even more incomprehensible: a brief but extraordinarily vivid close-up of an old man with white whiskers and

wind-blown hair leaning down toward them and
reaching out to trace some mysterious mark upon
them with the extended index finger of a right hand
that loomed so huge as to completely block out the
sky.

Over lunch in the canteen the four men tried to make
sense of what they had seen. Rachel listened to their
talk of psycho-kinetic fields, pineal points and O.O.
B.E.'s while she pecked dispiritedly at her plate of
egg mayonnaise. Finally, when there was a lull in the
conversation, she said: "I don't know whether there's
any point in my mentioning this but I'm sure I've
dreamed of that weird old man."

The others eyed her speculatively. "Well, who is
he?" asked George.

"I don't know," she confessed. "All I know is that
for the first two nights after Mike went into his coma
I had the same extraordinarily vivid dream. I was sitting with a lot of other people on a hillside somewhere
and we were listening to that old man. He was telling
us a story about a mysterious white bird that would
somehow change us all into something else—something marvelous. I know it sounds crazy but it wasn't.
It was—I don't really know how to describe it—as
though everything suddenly made sense for the first
time in my life. I knew what I was *for*—who I *was*."
She flushed, shook her head in confusion and muttered: "Sorry. God knows what made me tell you
about it."

Peter Klorner frowned. "You're quite sure it *was*
the same man?"

"Oh, yes," she said. "Quite sure. I couldn't be mistaken about that."

"And you've never seen him apart from those
dreams?"

"Never. Until just now, that is."

Klorner plucked his lower lip thoughtfully. "Well,
there must be a connection somewhere. The question
is where?"

"Inside Mike, presumably," said George.

Klorner nodded. "Have you checked to see if he's still registering in the pineal area?"

"No," said George. "Do you think we should?"

"Yes, I do. Presumably the hospital will co-operate?"

"I'm sure they will. After all, Jim Phillips is at least as concerned about Mike as we are."

"Then I suggest we make arrangements to take a specimen recording for an E-V.C. processing. If he's still registering we could see about transferring our set-up to the hospital. It shouldn't be too difficult."

"O.K.," said George. "I'll go and phone Jim right away."

When Dr. Richards had left the canteen Ian said: "You know, the more I think about it the more convinced I become that those *were* the Blackdown Hills."

"And how do you explain the sea, Ian?" demanded Rachel.

"Yes, I know," he said. "But did you by chance see that 'Forecast' program on the telly last week?"

"No," she said. "What about it?"

"Calder and Winkley and some others were doing an extrapolation of climatic changes. They had this big relief model of the British Isles in a huge tank. They turned on the tap to show what would happen if the ice-caps melted. One of the first places to go under was Somerset."

"So."

"So we'd be under the sea, wouldn't we? And Blackdown would be the new coastline."

Rachel smiled. "It's an ingenious idea," she said. "But you're forgetting one thing. It hasn't happened."

"Not yet," he agreed. "But it might. The point they were making was that it's beginning to look as if we're on the brink of some pretty dramatic weather change."

"Are you trying to suggest that Mike's O.O.B. experience—if that's what it was—is some sort of *future* contact?"

"I don't know *what* it was," he retorted. "Do you?"

She stared at him, and for a moment her eyes were wide with speculation. Finally she turned to Peter Klorner who was listening to their conversation and was not smiling at all. "Does it make sense to you, Peter?" she asked.

"The climatic change certainly does," he admitted. "There's been a lot of speculation along those lines in the States recently. As for the rest, let's just say I prefer to keep my options open till we've got more data to work on."

Rachel was astonished. "You mean you can conceive it as a *possibility?* I don't believe it!"

Klorner regarded her somberly. "From my experience I'd say that what takes place in the pineal zone of the human cortex is beyond the present scope of our natural philosophies. It's a land with laws of its own. I must confess that I *can* conceive of our tidy linear time scale being of little or no consequence there." He permitted himself a quiet smile. "Has it ever occurred to you that we are the virtual prisoners of our acquired perceptions? Anything that doesn't fit we prefer to discount or ignore. It's very easy to say it *can't* happen, therefore it doesn't."

"But time . . ." protested Rachel and then faltered to a stop.

"Yes?" he prompted gently. "What about it?"

Rachel swallowed. "Yesterday: today: tomorrow. For me that's time."

"And how about 'Now'?"

"What do you mean?"

"I suggest that Now is no more than our projected awareness of the immediate future, extrapolated from our memory of the past. In fact Now does not exist. It is an abstraction. A philosophical concept. We live in a perpetual state of becoming and having been. It is perfectly conceivable that all forms of time are but one and the same time observed from differing viewpoints."

"Not to me it isn't," Rachel averred stoutly.

"And how if that old man of your dream should

prove to exist only in the future or the remote past?"

"Oh, that's impossible."

"But not inconceivable?"

"All right. Hypothetically he might. But not *really*. And the same goes for Ian's sea."

Ken laughed. "Be sure to have a good look at Sedge Moor when you're driving back to Bristol. It might make you change your mind."

"Whose side are you on?" she retorted. "I'm beginning to think I'm the only sane person here."

Ian grinned. "You're forgetting that we outnumber you three to one, Rachel. In questions of sanity the majority view constitutes the norm. If you can't beat 'em, join 'em.".

Twenty-four hours later they ran the second tape through the E-V.C. It yielded two indisputable contacts spaced approximately three hours apart. The first was a glimpse of a star-embroidered tapestry of a night sky against which the dimly shadowed figure of a girl could be perceived sitting at the helm of a sailing boat which rose and dipped over a plum-dark sea: the second was a curious amalgam of two intertwined visions; one of Mike himself walking with Rachel in the rain beside the river Avon; the other of the girl in the boat leaning over him with anxious eyes. Neither contact lasted for much more than a minute, nevertheless, in Klorner's opinion, they constituted sufficient evidence to justify transferring the E-V.C. equipment to the hospital and maintaining a constant monitor program.

Chapter Ten

AT NOON THREE days after taking ship from Welshpool, Brother Francis stepped on to the quay at Chardport having successfully completed the first stage of his journey to Corlay. Obeying the instructions he had been given by Kin at New Bristol he inquired the whereabouts of Moxon's shop and was directed down a cobbled alley beside the fishmarket.

He found the Harbor Stores easily enough and guessed, rightly, that the gaunt, leather-aproned man who was stooping knee-deep amid a litter of straw unpacking pottery from a wooden crate was Sam Moxon in person. As Francis approached, the shopkeeper straightened up and eyed him curiously.

"Mr. Moxon?"

"Aye, sir. The same. What can I do for ye?"

"A word in private with you, sir, if it is not inconvenient."

Moxon hesitated for a second and then nodded. "If ye'll just step inside the shop I'll be with ye directly." He took a charcoal stick from behind his ear, made a check mark against a list, then picked up four earthenware mugs in either hand and followed the priest into the shop. He kicked the door to behind him, set the mugs down on the counter, glanced round to make sure they were not overheard and said: "Your servant, sir."

"I come in Kinship to ask your help, Mr. Moxon. Your name was given to me by Mistress Peel in New

Bristol. I was directed to her by Sarah and David Lloyd of Black Isle on the Western Borders."

Sam Moxon's eyes flickered over the priest's black habit. His doubt was plain to see. "The Western Borders," he murmured. "And what was a gentleman of your calling doing in those parts, if ye don't mind me asking?"

"I went there in search of Kinsman Gyre."

Alarm scrawled anguished lines across the shop-keeper's face. "Wisht, man!" he hissed. "Speak lower if ye must. Know ye not that the whole of Blackdown is under Falcon curfew?"

Francis shook his head. "I stepped ashore but ten minutes ago," he said. "Apart from my inquiry to seek you out I have spoken to no man."

"The Bird be praised for that," muttered Moxon. "The Gray Falcons are stooping everywhere and their beaks are red. You see those pots before you? The man who made them was hanged by the neck on Quantock just two days back and his house fired for the crime of harboring a Kinsman. Speak of Gyre and, priest or no priest, ye're like to find your tripes dangling from a drawing knife."

It was Francis' turn to stare. "Gyre is dead, Mr. Moxon," he murmured. "It is for that I am come here."

"God rest his sad soul," sighed Moxon. "Old Peter gone, and now Gyre. Where will it all end?"

"The Falcons did not find him," said Francis. "He died of a fever on Black Isle. His last act was to lay upon me the task of seeking out Kinsman Thomas of Norwich and delivering into his hands the Boy's own pipes. I have them here with me in my satchel."

"Then you are indeed true Kin?"

Francis nodded and with one accord the two men embraced. As they did so Sam Moxon gave vent to a deep, pent up sigh of relief. "Faith, Brother, but ye had me sorely perplexed," he confessed. "How comes it that ye still wear the blackbird's plumage?"

"I have served the Church all my life," said Francis,

"and would be serving her still had she not been struck blind. Now I must use what time I have left to undo the wrongs which are being done in her name. I must to Corlay in Brittany and you must speed me on my way."

"Corlay?" echoed Moxon. "Why Corlay?"

"Gyre dispatched Thomas of Norwich there a month ago."

Moxon frowned. "So? Then something has surely gone amiss. It was for sheltering the same Thomas that the good potter was hanged on Tallon last Tuesday. Rumor has it that the Kinsman ye seek is now in hiding here on Blackdown. It is for that the birds of prey have been flocking in this past two days."

"You are sure of this?"

"Aye. The whisper which reached me was that the potter's daughter ferried Thomas of Norwich across from Quantock two nights back. Since then a couple of Falcons have seemingly vanished clean off the face of the earth. Their horses were found wandering up on the hills above Clayhidon, but of the riders not a trace."

"But surely they cannot be laying that at the Kinsman's door?"

"Any stick will do to beat a dog, Brother, and sorcery has served the Church well enough in the past."

Francis nodded. "You have no idea where he might be?"

"Well clear of Blackdown, I trust. I'd not give him much longer for this world else. 'Tis said there's close on a hundred Falcons out scouring the hillsides 'twixt here and Sidbury. They've nailed a price of thirty royal crowns on his live head."

"Thirty crowns!"

"Aye. I heard them crying it in the market yesterday. They must want him badly, poor fellow. Dos't know why?"

"The Lloyds told me he carries a precious relic to Corlay."

"No doubt that would explain it," said Moxon. "But thirty royal is a lot of gold in our part of the world."

"In any part, Mr. Moxon."

"It won't tempt the Kinsfolk," said Moxon, "but they're scattered thin hereabouts. Mind ye, there's little enough love felt for the Falcons either, so I'd lay he still has a chance."

"And you've heard no whisper of his whereabouts?"

Moxon shook his head. "Only what I've told ye, and that came to me direct from Tallon on Quantock."

"What about the girl—the potter's daughter?"

"Vanished likewise it seems."

Francis picked up one of the mugs from the counter and turned it over abstractedly in his hand. "So what can you advise, Mr. Moxon? Where should I go to seek him?"

The shopkeeper plucked a straw from his apron and set it between his lips. Then he took the charcoal stick from behind his ear, cleared a space on the counter and drew a rough outline of the Blackdown coast. "My guess is that he'd try to slip across to Dartmoor hoping to ship out to Brittany from Tavistock or Buckfast. He'd surely have guessed that Sidbury would be sealed off. So he might well be making for one of the coast villages over here to the west—Broadbury, say, or Orway. There's Kinsfolk in both. Most likely Broadbury because the coasters call there regularly."

"And how would I get there from here?"

"Ye might find a boat to take you, but I doubt ye'd get passage till tomorrow. Your quickest way would be along the high road to Yarcombe, then on to Upottery and from there due west to Dunkeswell. From Dunkeswell it's even-stevens to Broadbury or Orway."

"How far is it?"

"Ye'll not have much change out of thirty kilometers. But the *Brass Bells,* hard by the West Gate, will hire ye a nag to Upottery and like as not ye'll get another from there on to Dunkeswell. With luck that'll see ye in Broadbury afore curfew."

"Ah, the curfew," said Francis. "I had forgotten that."

"Your garb will surely shield ye from any trouble of that sort," said Moxon. "Now when you come to Broadbury seek out Saul Jenkins the shipwright. He's Kin like I said and maybe he'll have heard something."

"Saul Jenkins," Francis repeated. "Very well. You place me in your debt, Mr. Moxon. I am truly grateful for your help."

As he turned to the door the shopkeeper laid a restraining hand on his arm. "Before ye go, Brother," he murmured, "would ye allow me just a glance at the true pipes?"

Francis unshouldered his satchel and laid it on the counter. From it he withdrew the leather case that Gyre had given him. He untied the laces and folded back the tooled flap to expose the gleaming instrument lying within.

Moxon wiped his hand on his sleeve and laid his forefinger reverently on one of the stops. He held it there for a few seconds then removed it. Gazing upon his fingertip with a look of wonder he raised it slowly to his lips. "Thank ye, Brother," he murmured. "I am deeply beholden to ye."

Francis smiled, retied the laces and restored the case to his pack. "Is it far to the West Gate?" he asked.

" 'Tis scarce a hundred paces past the church," said Moxon. "Come with me. I'll set ye on your road."

A kilometer beyond Yarcombe Francis encountered an improvised barrier of hurdles drawn up across the road. He reined in his horse and awaited the approach of the helmeted soldier who glanced from the priest's cowl to the post horse and back again. "Good afternoon, sir," he said civilly. "May I ask whither ye're bound?"

"For Upottery," said Francis.

"And your business?"

Francis stared at him coldly. "By whose right do you ask?"

"Lord Simon of Leicester's," returned the soldier.

"Know then that I travel on the personal service of Archbishop Constant. His business is no concern of Lord Simon's."

"Your clapper, priest."

"What?"

The soldier opened his mouth, stuck out his tongue and pointed to it as though he were making signs to an idiot. "Show us yours," he said, "or your journey ends right here."

Francis gazed across at the grinning Falcons who manned the barrier, then protruded the tip of his tongue between his lips.

"Further, man! Are ye shy or something?"

"Your name and rank, soldier?"

Their eyes met and the soldier was the first to look away. "Open up for his reverence!" he yelled and sauntered back to his post while the hurdles were dragged apart and the priest rode through.

The experience was repeated once more with minor variations before Francis eventually topped a rise and looked down upon the narrow creek which separated him from Upottery. His sole consolation lay in the reflection that Thomas of Norwich must still be at large. Gazing across at the hills he would have to cross before he reached Broadbury he saw sunlight winking from polished steel as a mounted patrol combed through the wilderness of gorse. The far off yelping of dogs was carried to him on the back of the breeze. He shivered involuntarily and breathed a prayer for the Kinsman's safety.

As his horse clip-clopped over the wooden bridge at the foot of the hill Francis saw a posse of mounted troopers, uniformed in gray leather, cantering toward him. In their midst rode a red-bearded monk clad in a gray habit. He drew in to the side of the road and waited for the troop to pass, but as they came abreast the monk reined up his horse and raised his right hand in greeting. "Whither away, Brother?" he called, then, screwing up his eyes cried: "Francis! By the holy powers!"

Francis raised a hand to shadow his brow. "Andrew?"

"Who else? And what brings you to Blackdown of all places?"

"Do you need to ask?"

"What? Has his Lordship sent you scampering all the way from York?"

"Is Leicester so much nearer?"

Brother Andrew grinned and shrugged. "And how was it up in Cumberland?"

"Wet," said Francis concealing his astonishment as best he might.

"You stay in Upottery?"

"Passing through only. And you?"

"I have some Edict business to conclude here. It won't detain me long. Which way are you headed?"

"Dunkeswell, if I can get horsed."

"We'll meet again for sure then, Francis. I ride that way tomorrow. A safe journey to you."

"And to you," responded Francis, lifting his hand in farewell.

Brother Andrew laughed, slapped his horse's hindquarters with his looped reins and clattered off in pursuit of the soldiers.

Francis stared after him conscious of a coldness lingering like an invisible eddy on the sunny air. For a moment he was moved to wonder at the notion of a man being condemned to dwell for ever in a strange, silent world of his own where he read men's speech from their lips. Did that perhaps help to explain Brother Andrew's passionate persecution of the Kinsfolk to whom music and song were the very key to life itself. And how, in Heaven's name, had the monk known of his mission to Cumberland? Could it mean that Constant himself was under secret surveillance? Or had his interim report from Kentmere been intercepted on its way to York? If that were so then he himself must surely have been picked out as suspect by the Secular Arm.

The tomb-like chill left by Andrew's presence found a lodging in Francis's bones and made him shiver. For the first time since leaving Black Isle he saw the path he had been chosen to follow stretching out before him in an unwavering line direct to the inquisitorial rack and the martyr's pyre. But even as he contemplated it stonily he was suddenly overwhelmed by a flood of wholly irrational happiness whose lifegiving springs welled up from a candlelit death chamber far away on a rocky islet on the Western Borders. He laughed aloud, shook up his horse into a lumbering canter and headed for the town gate.

Chapter Eleven

JANE NEVER *hueshed* her father's murder. The news of it was gleaned by the Magpie. After lying low in Dunkeswell for forty-eight hours he had gone down to Broadbury in the afternoon to seek out a fisherman who could be trusted to carry a confidential message to Tallon telling the potter that Jane was safe and would be returning in a day or two. It so happened that the first likely man he set his eyes upon in the waterfront tavern was "One-Eye" Jonsey, skipper of the "Kingdom Come."

The Magpie paid for two mugs of ale and carried them over to the high-backed settle where Jonsey was sitting gazing despondently out across the harbor. He set a mug down in front of the coaster. "What's up, old friend?" he asked. "You look as if you've bought yourself a bellyful of vinegar."

Jonsey's one eye swiveled round and focused on the Magpie. "Oh, it's you, Patch," he grunted.

The Magpie eased himself down into the settle at Jonsey's side. He touched his own tankard against the one he had set before the coaster and raised it to his lips. "Well met, One-Eye," he murmured. "Fortune's kind to me."

"Then you're the only one," responded Jonsey morosely.

"I'm sharing it with you. Drink up, man. Your health."

Listlessly Jonsey lifted the mug and swallowed a token mouthful.

The Magpie glanced around then put his lips close to the coaster's ear. "Dos't make for Tallon, friend?"

Jonsey shook his head. "We were there yesterday. Haven't you heard?"

"Heard what?"

"The Grays hanged Pots Thomson on Tallon quayside."

The Magpie's hand descended on the coaster's wrist and gripped it like a steel vice. *"What?"*

"It's true, Patch. They swung him for harboring a heretic—a poor, drowned bugger of a Kinsman Napper and me fished out of the Reach last week."

The Magpie felt as if his skin was shrinking all about him. "Are you sure of this?" he hissed.

"Sure?" echoed One-Eye. "Man, we found the poor sod dangling there when we docked. I've not slept a wink since. It's like I noosed his neck myself."

"And Susan? What of her?"

"They fired the cottage with her in it. It was still smoking when we tied up."

The Magpie groaned aloud in an agony of impotent rage. "Who blabbed?"

"They screwed it out of some youngster who'd gone down to tip Pots off that the birds were on the way."

"They didn't find their Kinsman then?"

Jonsey shook his head. "The whisper is he's here on Blackdown. And the wench too."

"What wench?"

"Pots' lass."

"Pots told them that?"

"He told them nothing," said Jonsey. "He kept them stalled for six hours till they gave it up as a bad job and strung him up. They've bought themselves a load of hate on Quantock by that day's business. He was a real good man was Pots, as brave as they come."

The Magpie nodded while his thoughts darted off in all directions. Only the knowledge that Jane had *hueshed* him with the Kinsman had kept him chained to Blackdown. Now that her own life unquestionably depended upon his getting her away, Thomas would have to take his own chance. "Where's your next port of call, One-Eye?" he asked.

"Buckfast. But we've missed our tide. There should have been a cargo of cider waiting for us in Todd's warehouse but it isn't there. Napper's away now trying to find out what's become of it."

"Have you steerage room for a passenger?"

"Aye. Of a sort. What of it?"

"Hold it for me, old friend. And set a steel lock on your tongue."

Jonsey turned his head and scrutinized the Magpie's face with his single, shrewd eye. Whatever he read there he kept to himself.

The Magpie raised his tankard, touched it once more against Jonsey's and murmured: "To Pots Thomson and his lass."

Jonsey stared at him hard and long. "Aye, Patch," he responded, "I'll drink deep to that. I'll hold passage till flood tide tomorrow eve. Will that do you?"

"It'll have to," said the Magpie. He swigged off his ale, gripped One-Eye by the shoulder and slipped out of the tavern by a back entrance.

On his way back to Dunkeswell the Magpie glimpsed a Falcon patrol riding down to the port he had just left and he made a wide, looping detour which took him up through the hanging woods and out over the brow of Windhover Hill. It was an area of scrub land, of gorse, brambles and bracken, with a scattering of wind-twisted thorn trees which somehow contrived to cling to the thin soil despite the ceaseless efforts of the prevailing westerly gales to uproot them. Hundreds of years ago a priory had stood there but it had vanished long since and most of the stones had been pillaged for sheep shelters. A few obstinate scraps of ruin still remained providing nesting sites for the buzzards which circled high in the turbulent air currents above the hill crest.

The Magpie was about to stride on past when something made him pause. He stood still for a moment, peering uneasily about him and then, without quite knowing why, began moving toward the most substantial fragment of the ruins. As he did so he suddenly knew what it was that had reached out and drawn him to this desolate spot. "A pile of stones," he murmured. "Gray stones."

No sooner had he recalled Jane's *huesh* than he was gripped by it. At that moment he could no more have turned and gone back than he could have willed his own heart to stop beating. He ghosted forward to where a patch of brambles all but concealed an opening in the crumbling masonry and called out softly: "Are you there, Kinsman?"

A jackdaw squawked from a cranny high up in the ruin; the wind droned fitfully round a broken corbel; but that was all. He tried again. "It's the Magpie, Kinsman. The potter's daughter *hueshed* you with me."

A dislodged pebble rattled faintly in some invisible cavern and a voice whispered hoarsely: "Are you alone?"

"Aye, man, there's no one but me."

A hand appeared at the opening, gripped the lichened stone, and then the Kinsman's apprehensive face was peering out at him.

"Come on out, songster. I'll not harm you."

Thomas dragged himself up and crawled out from under the brambles. "The dogs," he muttered. "Where are the dogs?"

"Drawing the woods away below Cotleigh," said the Magpie, reaching down and pulling the Kinsman to his feet. "How came you to hole up here?"

"I doubled back and swam the creek below Upottery last night. I hoped to throw them off my scent. I've been here since before dawn."

"Did you not make Sidbury, then?"

"No," said Thomas and shuddered.

"They'd have nailed you for sure if you had," said the Magpie cheerfully. "Your only chance now lies to the west. God man, you stink like a rutting polecat!"

"So would you if you'd bedded where I have," retorted Thomas with a flicker of spirit. "I'm sorry if it offends you."

The Magpie laughed. "We'll find you a change of garb presently. Till then I'd hold it a kindness if you'd keep downwind a pace or two."

As they emerged from the shelter of the ruins the Magpie called out softly: "Hey up! Hold still, man!"

Thomas dropped to all fours. "What is it?" he whispered.

The Magpie edged past him and stared down the eastward slope of the hill to where a solitary, black-robed figure was riding up the dusty road from Upottery. "A lone blackbird," he said. "He'll not harm us, but we'd best keep our heads down till he's past."

He made his way back to Thomas and, squatting down beside him, plucked a long grass stem and chewed at the stalk. "My lighting upon you will maybe help to ease the burden I'm bearing back to Jane," he murmured. "That lass thinks the world of you."

"Jane?" echoed Thomas. "Is she not on Quantock?"

The Magpie shook his head. "The crows were lying

in wait for her at the cove. Had I not *hueshed* it she'd like as not be as dead as they are by now."

Thomas made a low moaning sound deep in his throat. "What happened?"

The Magpie recounted it without embellishment and then added: "But there's worse to follow," and told him what he had learned from Jonsey.

The Kinsman sat completely stunned with horror. "I am to blame," he groaned. "It was I who killed them. I carried their deaths within me."

"Nay, Thomas," said the Magpie. "Take it not upon yourself, man. What will be, will be. The pattern is drawn and none of us has the power to alter it. 'Tis Jane we must be thinking on now."

Thomas raised his bowed head and stared bleakly up at the buzzards wheeling below the high, thin tissue of cloud. "The pattern *was* altered," he said dully, "and now the innocent are being called upon to account for it. Had I been left to drown none of this would have happened."

The Magpie glanced at him out of the corner of his eye. "She told me she'd *hueshed* you washed up in the Jaws," he said curiously. "I thought she must have dreamed it. It does sometimes happen that way."

Thomas made no response. With a shake of his head the Magpie rose to his feet and ascertained that the coast was clear. "Come, Thomas," he said. "Bestir yourself. We've half an hour's brisk legging ahead of us."

Jane was helping the Magpie's ancient mother to prepare a meal against her son's return when she heard the sound of voices coming down the track toward the cottage. The old woman cocked her head on one side and grinned. "'Tis my boy," she said. "Don't fesh yourself, pet!"

"There's someone with him."

"What of it? But ye'd best set out another bowl and scrape a few more tatties."

Jane nodded, picked up a basket and turned toward

the door. As she opened it she saw the Magpie and Thomas walking toward her down the garden path. The basket dropped from her hand and she flew into the Kinsman's arms like a bird to its nest. "I knew he'd find you!" she cried. "Didn't I say so? Didn't I?"

"You did, Jane. It all came true just as you said it would."

"I prayed to the White Bird to bring you safe back," she said.

"And here I am."

"But what happened, Thomas? Where have you been?"

"Oh, scampering about like a fox. Up hill and down dale."

"Was there no boat from Sidbury?"

"I never got to Sidbury. There were Falcons everywhere. I all but ran head first into a patrol an hour after we parted."

He felt her shiver against him. "We're both safe now," she said. "That's all that matters."

Unseen by Jane, Thomas caught the Magpie's eye and shook his head to signify that he could not tell her now. "Is there a pump handy?" he asked. "I am sorely in need of a wash."

"There's a pool yonder," said the Magpie. "Jane will show you. I'll see if I can't scratch you up some clean traps."

He vanished inside the cottage to re-emerge a moment later with a lump of soap which he shied toward them.

Jane retrieved it and led the Kinsman by the hand down the flagstone path to where the brook had been dammed up to form a washing place. "Did Magpie tell you what happened?" she asked.

"Yes," he said, unfastening his cloak and dropping it to the ground. "Do you want to tell me about it?"

"No, not really. It was like a nightmare and I couldn't wake myself up. Everything seemed to happen so slowly."

"And the wound?"

"It doesn't hurt any more. Mother Patch sewed it up for me. Look." She dropped the soap on to the stones at her feet and untied the bow on her bodice. Drawing aside her dress she exposed the outward slope of her left breast. In the center of a livid purple and yellow bruise the lips of the wound made by the blade of the Magpie's bolt had been drawn together by three neat little knots of black horse hair.

Jane contemplated it wistfully for a few seconds then pulled her dress together and retied the laces. "There'll hardly be a mark when I get back to Tallon," she said.

The name jerked Thomas back to the horror of what he knew. It was as though a hand gripped him by the throat and was squeezing the breath out of him.

Her alarmed eyes scanned his face. "What is it, Thomas? Are you ill?"

He shook his head dumbly. "Sick at heart, Jane," he whispered. "I don't know how to tell you. I have no words."

"Something's happened." Her eyes were huge with apprehension. "What is it, Thomas?"

He reached out and took her trembling hands in his. "They came for your father the morning after we fled," he said. "There's nothing left for you at Tallon any more, Jane. Nothing at all."

Her lips parted and a little faltering sigh crept out between them. "Oh no," she whispered. "Oh no, oh no."

If Thomas could have died at that moment and spared her such pain he would have done it a hundred times over. His aching heart reached out to her and he drew her to him and held her close and cherished her, murmuring he knew not what to comfort her. But it was as if the finger of the Ice Spirit had touched her on the breast and she could feel nothing. Her eyes were dry, wide with the shock of irreparable loss, and she lay as stiff as a wooden doll in his arms. "Fly with me to Corlay, little bird," he murmured.

"There will be no more pain there; no more fear. There everyone will love you and I will sing my songs to you all the day long."

She spoke then, quite calmly, but in a strange, dead little voice. "Were they both killed?"

"Yes," he said. "And your house is burnt to the ground. There is nothing there for you now."

"Then I must go back and bury them."

"You cannot, Jane. You are a fugitive like me. They would only kill you too."

"They've done that," she said. "What more could they do?"

The Magpie emerged from the cottage with a bundle of clothes under his arm. As he came down the path toward them, Jane loosed herself from Thomas's arms and turned to him. "Is it true?"

Magpie's eyes flickered to the Kinsman's strained face and then back to the girl. "Aye, lass," he said. "It's all true. I had it from the lips of 'One-Eye' Jonsey this afternoon."

"You did not *huesh* it?"

He shook his head.

"Nor I," she whispered. "Oh, Magpie, why not . . . *why not that?*" Her face crumpled and she sank to the ground and smothered her pain in the Kinsman's discarded cloak, shuddering and whimpering like a wounded animal with the anguish of it.

Thomas crouched down beside her and laid his hand upon her quivering shoulder, praying as he had never prayed before in his life. As he did so he discovered words upon his lips that no conscious thought of his had placed there: *Wilderness of woman's woe: Heart's hurt, grief's groan . . ."* The world rocked all around him and in one single, pulsing, inrush of awareness he remembered what it was he had glimpsed in the lamplight of the potter's kitchen an eternity ago. All became fused, inchoate, glowing as though the evening light in the little valley were rushing downwards, draining into them both, leaving behind a wrack of insubstantial shadow. The burden of the mystery was lifted and the still air all about his head became awash with the tumultuous sighing downrush of huge invisible wings. For a timeless moment they hovered all about him and then slowly, slowly faded away, to vanish far off among the imperceptible reaches beyond the stars.

Beneath his hand he felt Jane stir. Opening eyes he scarcely realized he had closed he saw her lift her head and turn it slightly to one side as if she too were listening.

"Jane?"

Her tear-streaked face turned slowly and her wondering eyes met his. "It came," she whispered. "The White Bird came."

Thomas nodded. "Yes," he said. "It came for you."

After supper that evening the Magpie told Jane all he had learned from Jonsey. She listened to him in silence then rose from the table and walked out into the cottage garden. Thomas half made as if to follow her but the old woman waved him back. "Let her weep her fill, Kinsman," she said. "She'll ha' need o' thee presently."

The Magpie fetched a jar of strong spirit and poured it out for them. "Jonsey's holding the 'Kingdom Come' till night tide tomorrow," he said. "I'll lift you both down to Broadbury in the van and slip you aboard at dusk. He's bound out for Buckfast. You'll surely find a Frenchie there who'll ship you both to Brittany. Jonsey might do it himself if he can find a cargo to carry."

"You think she'll come with me?"

"What other choice has she, poor lass? They'd burn her to ashes the moment she set foot on Quantock."

"It's not Jane they want," said Thomas. "It's me."

"So?"

"So if I gave myself up to them . . ."

The Magpie's mouth dropped. "Are you crazy, man? Dos't think to strike a bargain with the devil? And even if you did, what's to become of her after?

What sort of life could she lead in Tallon? She saved your skin, Thomas, but not to buy back her own. She needs you alive, man—alive and warm in her bed."

"He's right, Kinsman," chirped the old woman. "Ye owes her all o' that."

Thomas flushed. "But she already has a sweetheart. She told me so herself."

"So now she has another," said the Magpie, jerking back his head and swallowing off his liquor at a gulp. "Better a bird in the hand any day. Sure you must know that it's you she's sweet on, man! Go, seek her out. Heal her hurt and let her know it hasn't all been in vain."

Thomas looked from the son to the mother then picked up his own cup and drained it off. The harsh bite of the raw spirit made his eyes water. He thrust back his stool and stood up.

The old woman grinned and lifted her claw-like hand in an archaic love-sign. "There's all the sweet hay ye'll need in the barn, Kinsman. An' us'll not be botherin' ye."

Thomas stepped out into the fast-gathering dusk and closed the cottage door behind him. To the west, behind the distant moors, the sky still glimmered with a few, faint, coppery-green streaks of dying day. Among the dark trees higher up the valley an owl hooted derisively and bats flickered to and fro like falling leaves in the still air. He walked slowly down the path toward the stream, peering about him into the shadows, until finally he caught sight of Jane sitting crouched beside the edge of the pool. Her head was resting upon her bent knees, her fingers laced behind her neck so that she appeared as if folded in upon herself like a sleeping flower. So poignant was her attitude of grief that for some minutes he stood still, not daring to intrude upon it, until above the faint bubble of the water he heard her muffled sobbing. As though released from a spell he ran forward, knelt down beside her and took her into his arms.

For a moment or two she remained, passively

weeping, then he felt her face turning toward his. The taste of salt came sharp upon his tongue as her warm, wet mouth sought and found his own.

Hours later Jane opened her eyes, saw the crescent moon shining in through the slit window of the barn and felt a sigh like some enormous, left-over wave of her storm of grief, rise shuddering through her to ebb away upon the quiet air. Thomas's right arm lay diagonally across her pale nakedness. Gently she touched his shoulder with the fingers of her left hand, dreamily tracing the line of slack muscle down to the elbow and then on along the scarred forearm and wrist to where his fingers lay cozily bedded down between her thighs. She spread her own hand to cover his and stroked it softly, whereupon he stirred, mumbled something in his sleep, and opened his eyes.

They lay and looked at one another by the dim moon-glow then she leaned over him and pulled his cloak across to cover them both. "I did not mean to wake you, love," she murmured. "Go back to sleep."

His answer was to seek her mouth with his own. Nor was she averse to his finding it.

Chapter Twelve

CONSIDERING THE COMPLEXITY of the operation the transfer of the Encephalo-Visual Converter from the laboratory in Holmwood House to the Intensive Care Unit of the General Hospital was effected remarkably smoothly. The equipment was housed in a small ward which adjoined the one in which Michael Carver was lying. Peter Klorner supervised the installation which was completed almost exactly forty-eight hours after the initial monitoring of the second tape. The first unmistakable "contact" was obtained and video-recorded at 16.52 hours, a bare fifteen minutes after the circuit went live.

It soon became apparent to the rapt observers that an alteration had taken place in the nature of the signal. The new "direct" image had a quality of depth that was wholly remarkable. None of the watchers doubted that the girl, whom they all recognized as the one they had seen on the boat, was in some manner contributing to the change. They first saw her emerge from a cottage doorway carrying a basket. As she turned to face them the basket dropped from her hand and she scampered toward them. At the instant her laughing face filled the screen, two curious aspects of the vision struck all the watchers: the first was her remarkable facial resemblance to Rachel Wyld: the second a faint but unmistakable attenuation of the atmosphere immediately surrounding her. This latter feature almost made it appear as if she were sheathed in some strange, refractive aura whose effect was slightly to distort the immediate background against which she was being seen.

No sooner had Peter Klorner observed this than he announced: "I think we'd better watch out for p.k. backlash."

"You've met this before, have you, Peter?" asked Dr. Richards.

"Something rather similar," said Klorner. "Be ready to throw the main switch the moment I give the word. How's Doctor Carver, Ian?"

"Just the same," called Ian from the next ward.

"No sign of R.E.M.?"

"None that I can see."

"Why aren't I a lip reader?" said Kenneth. "What do you suppose she's saying?"

"God, he's right!" exclaimed George. "Why the hell

didn't I think of that? It might give us just the lead we need. Where can we get hold of one?"

"Social Services maybe?" suggested Kenneth.

"By the way, where's Miss Wyld?" asked Klorner. "I think she should be here."

George glanced at his watch. "She said she had an appointment at the ante-natal clinic for 3:30," he said. "She ought to be along at any minute. Do any of us recognize this place?"

"I suppose that *could* be Dartmoor in the distance," said Kenneth.

"What intrigues me is their clothes," said Ian. "Who wears that sort of gear nowadays? Hey! What's the kid up to?"

Standing beside the pool Jane was fumbling with the laces at her throat, tugging open her dress to expose the wound in her breast.

"How about that?" murmured Ian, sipping in his breath with a painful hiss. "Has she been *stabbed* or something?"

"It looks like it," said George. "And not so long ago either, I'd say."

"What do you suppose happened, Doc?"

"God knows," said Dr. Richards. "All I can assume is that we're seeing this through the eyes of Mike's O.O.B. contact. But who is he? And *where* is he?"

"And *when* is he?" supplemented Ian. "If this is supposed to be happening *now,* I just refuse to believe it."

"Then what's your alternative? Some sort of archetypal memory of Mike's?"

"I hadn't thought of that," Ian admitted. "I suppose it could be."

"I've been thinking along those lines," said George. "I was reading up one of Walker and Sutherland's papers last night. They're working with deep hypnosis up in Newcastle. They've come up with some pretty impressive evidence of historical imprinting."

"She looks pretty upset about something, doesn't

she?" said Kenneth. "Hello. Here comes that other bloke again."

At that moment there was a tap at the door of Michael's ward and Rachel came in. "I see you've got it working," she said. "Has anything happened?"

"It certainly has," said George. "We're in continuous contact. Come and tell us what you make of this."

Rachel made her way past the foot of Michael's bed and entered the room where the four men were gathered around the E-V.C. screen. She stared at the picture in astonishment. "Who is she?"

"You don't know?"

"No," she said. "She does look a bit like me though."

"Except for the hair I'd say she could be your twin," said George.

"Was she the one who was in the boat?"

"We think so."

"And where is she? Where's it happening?"

"We've no idea. We thought maybe you'd know."

"I haven't a clue," said Rachel, shaking her head. "What's going on there?"

"We've no more idea than you have, but he's obviously said something to her which has upset her. Good Lord! Look at . . . What on earth—?"

"Cut it!" cried Klorner. "Quick!"

As George snatched at the main switch there was a dull report from one of the metal servo-cabinets and the screen died. At the same instant they all heard Michael Carver cry out in sudden pain.

In the two hours it took them to replace the blown inductor and to make the necessary repairs and modifications to the circuit, Dr. Richards succeeded in locating a teacher at a school for handicapped children who was an expert lip-reader. She was perfectly willing to co-operate and, shortly after six, he fetched her to the hospital, sat her down in front of the video-recording and switched it on. "It's a long shot, Mrs.

Huddlestone," he said. "For all we know they may be talking Anglo-Saxon."

She nodded, adjusted her spectacles, and gazed at the screen before her. As they watched Jane running yet again into the Kinsman's arms, Mrs. Huddlestone said clearly: "I knew he'd find you. Didn't I say so? Didn't I?"

"Marvelous!" cried Dr. Richards. "That's just what we've been hoping for! Do, please, carry on."

The interpreter nodded. When she reached the words: "Was there no boat from Sidbury?" George stopped the film and said: "Sidbury? Are you sure of that?"

"Not absolutely," said Mrs. Huddlestone. "But I don't think I was mistaken."

"Would you mind taking another look at it?" he said. "It's just the kind of clue we're after."

She scrutinized the re-run and said firmly: "Yes, Sidbury. No doubt about it."

She took them right through the whole sequence, faltering only occasionally when Jane spoke with half-averted head. By the end Dr. Richards had gleaned the two names "Sidbury" and "Tallon" and a word which Mrs. Huddlestone thought might be "hesh."

"Hesh?" he repeated. "Does it mean anything to anyone?"

The others looked blank, and Ian said: "If that's Sidbury near Sidmouth in Devon, I don't really see how he could have caught a boat from it. It's about three miles in from the coast."

"And what about Tallon?"

"Never heard of it."

"Still we do seem to be getting somewhere at last," George insisted. "Mrs. Huddlestone, could we possibly prevail upon you to sit in for a little bit longer?"

"Why, of course, Dr. Richards," she said. "I confess I'm finding the whole thing absolutely fascinating."

"Splendid. How much longer will it take you to fix things, Ken?"

"Any moment now."

Ian said: "You know, Doc, I have a feeling we've just seen your archetypal memory hypothesis shot down in flames."

"I don't see why," said George.

"Well, I could be wrong, of course, but I suspect the catching a boat from Sidbury ties in with Blackdown being on the edge of the sea. Somerset wasn't the only place they sank in that 'Forecast' program. The whole of the Exe valley was under water. Devon and Cornwall were an island."

"What I don't understand," said Rachel, "is what happened when everything blew up. What *is* p.k. backlash, Peter?"

"Psychokinesis invariably manifests itself through the pineal area," said Klörner. "With a direct link from the contact to Dr. Carver's mind there was nothing to prevent it breaking out."

"Is that why the picture went out of focus just before it happened?"

"It seems likely."

"And she was responsible?"

"There's no way of telling," said George. "But Peter recognized the aberration phenomena as soon as the girl appeared."

"That sort of glow, you mean?"

He nodded.

"Do you think she's somehow connected with it?" asked Rachel. "Responsible for Mike's coma?"

"I wish I knew, Rachel. The fact that Mike responded physically to the p.k. discharge would certainly seem to indicate something of the kind. A psychological affinity maybe. The truth is we're all still groping around in the dark."

"You can say that again," grunted Ian.

Rachel walked through into the adjoining ward and looked down at the man whose unconscious head was now encapsulated within its studded plexiglass helmet. That there could be any direct connection between him and the scenes she had just witnessed demanded an act of pure faith. And yet in some odd way she sensed that it *was* true, that the cry she had heard had been wrung from him by the intensity of his involvement in the anguish of that unknown girl. *"It was like a nightmare and I couldn't wake myself up,"* she murmured, quoting Jane's words down at him. "Is that how it is, Mike? Or is it that you don't *want* to wake up?"

Contact was reestablished at 1903 hours. The picture was less sharp but still perfectly adequate for Mrs. Huddlestone's purposes. Soon she was retailing details of the conversation which had taken place in the cottage just after Jane had walked out. The names "Broadbury," "Brittany" and "Quantock" made the men look at each other with a wild surmise. What followed shortly after made them not look at each other at all; their attention was wholly absorbed by what was taking place on the screen. There was little for Mrs. Huddlestone to interpret but a great deal for her to observe. "Well I never!" was the only comment she permitted herself. Perhaps fortunately, once Jane and Thomas had transferred to the barn the picture became too dim for lip-reading. Klorner switched over to record and they all trooped down to the hospital canteen.

On the way they passed through the Outpatients' waiting room. One wall was decorated with a large scale relief map of the whole area surrounding Taunton. Ian walked over to it and contemplated it thoughtfully. "Look here," he said. "Just supposing this area was all flooded, the Quantocks would be an island and so would the Blackdown Hills."

"He's right, you know," said Kenneth. "And damn it, Broadbury *would* be on the coast! And so would Sidbury!"

"What about Buckfast?" asked George.

"Assuming it's Buckfastleigh it's too far over to the west," said Ian. "Out here somewhere. But I don't see why it shouldn't fit. It's on the edge of Dartmoor, isn't it?"

Rachel stared at them incredulously. "What are

you trying to say?" she demanded. "That all this is supposed to be happening somewhere out there in the future?"

"That's right," said Ian. "What's more I'm almost prepared to take a bet on it."

"You're crazy, Ian!"

" 'Time present and time past,' " said George,
" 'Are both perhaps present in time future
And time future contained in time past.' "
T.S. Eliot. Unquote."

"Don't say you've joined them, George."

"No," he said. "It's just another hypothesis so far as I'm concerned. I don't think it's possible."

"Thank God for that," she said. "It's bad enough having to think that Mike might be making love to someone else, let alone someone who hasn't even been *born* yet! Has it occurred to you that he might not *want* to come back?"

"No," said George with a smile, "I confess that hadn't occurred to me."

"Well, this evening it occurred to me," she said. "And frankly, George, it's scaring me to hell."

Chapter Thirteen

A BELT OF rain drifting eastward from the Irish Sea crossed over Dartmoor and reached Blackdown by the middle of the afternoon. Standing just inside the barn doorway the Magpie surveyed the sagging

clouds and grunted with satisfaction. "This will keep
the crows caged," he said. "We'll take the coast road
round. It's an hour longer but there's less chance of
fouling a patrol. Janie, you shall ride up front alongside me. Thomas must keep his nose down within.
When we get to Broadbury I'll run the van straight
down to the quay and into Jenkins' yard. We'll lie up
there till dusk and I'll slip you aboard when Jonsey
gives me word. Are you with me?"

Jane and Thomas glanced at one another and
nodded, whereupon the Magpie spat for luck, hefted
the leather scuttle of his cape over his head and
squelched off through the rain to harness up the horse.

Jane wandered over to the nest of hay and gazed
down at it wistfully. "Do you remember how you
promised to play for me on my wedding day,
Thomas?"

He turned to her and smiled. "Aye, love," he said.
"When you were spliced to that certain poor sailor
you would not name. Well, so I shall. I have tunes
singing within me which will set the very stones skipping. Corlay will have a wedding to remember all its
days."

"Corlay," she murmured. "Corlay can never be so
sweet to me as this has been."

"Far, far sweeter," he insisted. "We have but fingered a prelude to our joy. The best is yet to come."

He moved across to her, put his arms around her
and kissed her softly on the back of the neck. "My
love," he whispered. "My own true love. Sweet bride
of time."

She shivered and clasped her arms tight across his
own, imprisoning them. "Why do you call me that?"

"Because that is what you are. My pride for eternity. I shall immortalize us both! You have unlocked
my soul, Jane, and set it winging free! Even the Boy
himself could not have sung the song that I shall sing
for you! You have given me the power to set the whole
world free!"

"Do you truly mean that?"

Thomas laughed. "Mean it? I shall *prove* it to you! Ah, Jane, do you not feel it trembling in the very air about us? Was it not for this that the Bird brought us to one another? Why, even the very ship which carried me to you is waiting now to waft us both in triumph to Corlay! The 'Kingdom Come'! Ours is the kingdom, Jane, and we are come to claim it!"

He lifted her off her feet and whirled her round in the air like a child on a May swing until she surrendered to his infectious happiness and the barn rang with their laughter.

Twenty minutes later the Magpie had shackled the last trace to the shafts of the covered van and Jane and Thomas had said farewell to Mother Patch. Just before she clambered up to take her seat beside the Magpie, Jane saw the old woman beckoning to her from the cottage doorway and ran back to her.

The crone nodded her close and whispered: "Last night I *hueshed* ye a bonny boy, my pet, wi' all the stars a'crowdin' round his cradle. Sure he shall be a mighty wonder to the world."

Jane kissed her impetuously on the wrinkled cheek and skipped back through the puddles to the van with her heart singing. The Magpie reached down, pulled her up beside him, and a moment later they were away, bumping and lurching down the rutted track to the coast road.

He glanced at her bright eyes and grinned. "Mam told you, did she?"

Jane nodded and flushed to the tips of her ears.

"And what shall you call him?"

She laughed. "Do you need to ask?"

"Lord save us! Not *another* Thomas?"

"There's no better name in all the Kingdoms," she averred stoutly. "And I could not call him 'Magpie' could I?"

"I have another name," he said. "For what it's worth it's Jack."

Jane put her head on one side. "I never knew that," she said. "Why don't you use it then?"

" 'Twas my pig of a dad's," he said, "and I want no more part of him than he did of me." He turned his head and spat as though the mere thought of his father had left a bitter taste upon his tongue. "Shall you wed at Corlay?"

"Yes," she said. "And you, dear Magpie, shall be Guest of Honor at our wedding feast. You shall sit at my left hand and drink from my own cup. And Thomas shall compose a special song in praise of you and everyone will sing it."

"That sounds too good to miss," he said with a grin. "When is it to be?"

"Soon," she said. "The sooner the better. Oh, Magpie, it *will* happen, won't it?"

He flicked a quick glance at her. "Aye, Janie," he said. "Of course it will. Just like Mam *hueshed* it."

"Did she *huesh* that too, then?"

"Why, yes," he said. "You mean she didn't tell you?"

"No. Not a word. Only about the child—our boy."

"It must have slipped through her old sieve. Why, all last night she was brimming over with it."

Jane sighed a deep sigh of happiness. Closing her eyes she tilted back her head and murmured: "Oh, blessed White Bird, I thank you with all my heart."

As he heard her quiet prayer the Magpie silently absolved himself from the sin of his kindly little fiction.

They reached the outskirts of Broadbury without having had sight or sound of a Falcon. The only indication of the official presence lay in the black flag flapping wetly from its pine standard above the stone fort which overlooked the little harbor. But as the van turned down toward the quay, Jane plucked at the Magpie's sleeve and pointed to the road which led over the hill to Dunkeswell. A band of five, gray-clad troopers was jogging down toward the harbor. The off-sea wind came curling across the waterfront houses and carried the cold jingle of metal with it.

"Fear not, lass," muttered the Magpie. "Mark my words, they'll be bound for the shelter of the keep."

And so it proved. The troop reached the point where the road forked and trotted briskly over the cobbles toward the gates of the fort.

Jane let out her breath in a long gasp of relief. "The black ones are bad enough," she muttered, "but those gray ones . . ." She shuddered and left the sentence unfinished.

"They're but mortal men," said the Magpie, grimly. "And if needs be they can die to prove it."

"I don't want them to die," she whispered. "Just to leave us alone. We've never hurt them."

"There's hurt and hurt," said the Magpie. "In their world it's eat or be eaten. These days the crows are flying in fear of their black souls. They know their time to quit the roost is nearly up."

The leather curtains behind them parted a fraction and Thomas peeped out. "What is it?" he whispered. "Have you seen something?"

"Keep your head down, man," growled the Magpie. "Do'st seek to spill the cup before you've even tasted it? I'd not put it past those vermin to have a glass trained on us this minute."

Thomas vanished precipitately and the iron shod wheels of the van squealed and rattled on the wet stones. Jane huddled down inside her damp cloak and clutched at a rope stay to steady herself. As she did so she was granted a sudden brilliant vision of a golden castle set high among brown and purple crags. She knew at once that it must be Corlay even though it was trembling as though she were viewing it through a shifting lens.

Wholly captivated by her *huesh* she was blind to the two Falcons who broke away from the group approaching the fort and came galloping back along the road on the far side of the harbor. Unfortunately the Magpie was concentrated upon his driving and did not notice them either.

"One-Eye" Jonsey and his brother were swinging

barrels of cider aboard the "Kingdom Come" using a primitive windlass they had set upon the edge of the quay. They looked round as the Magpie's leather-covered wagon came bouncing over the cobbles toward them but neither brother did more than give the newcomers a covert nod as they rattled past and on down the quay to the yard owned by Saul Jenkins the shipwright. There the Magpie reined up his steaming horse, jumped down from the driver's seat and set to work dragging open one of the huge timber gates.

He had just walked back to the horse's head and was about to lead the animal into the yard when he heard the staccato clatter of steel-shod hooves on the distant cobblestones and a bawled command: "Stand, carter, on your life!"

The Magpie was caught in two minds. His cocked cross-bow was lying bolted up and ready to hand behind the leather curtain in the van. To attempt to retrieve it now could only mean disaster for them all. As though ignorant that the command had been meant for him he lugged at the horse's bridle and was rewarded with a bolt which hummed past his ear and buried itself in the timbers of the gate. "Are ye mad?" he yelled. "What need ha' ye to shoot at an honest, God-fearing tradesman?"

"So do as ye're bid!" cried the trooper who had loosed the bolt. "Stand means stand still, ye fool!"

He reined up his snorting horse and swung himself to the ground. Then he slid a fresh bolt into his bow and cranked the lever back to cock it. "Who's the wench?"

"My niece, Patty. My sister Betsy's lass."

The soldier grunted. "What are ye carrying?"

"A load of chairs, master. All of a long winter's honest toil."

"Show me."

The Magpie touched his temple with an obsequious finger and clambered up on to the wagon. "Come,

Patty," he said. "Look sharp! Let the gentleman see what fine goods we carry to Master Jenkins."

Jane nodded and began to fumble with the toggles on the curtain. The Magpie twitched aside the lower portion of the flap, groped inside, and dragged out a bentwood chair which he thrust toward the soldier. "I have a round dozen of 'em here, Master," he whined. "All alike as podded peas. Do'st wish to see the lot?"

The Falcon glanced round doubtfully at his companion, seemed about to climb back on to his horse, then changed his mind. "Aye, man," he growled. "Open up."

The Magpie handed Jane the chair he was holding, unfastened the rest of the toggles and pulled back one of the flaps. The soldier placed a booted foot on the step, pulled himself up with one hand and peered in. "Aye, well," he muttered, " 'tis as ye say." On the point of clambering down he took a cursory prod at the second flap with his cradle bow and knocked it just far enough aside to disclose the Magpie's own weapon. He frowned, dragged the bow out and called to his companion: "Keep an eye on these two, Brad. I'm going to take a poke around inside."

The second trooper ordered Jane and Magpie down on to the quay. As they stood staring up at him they heard a yell from within the wagon followed by the triumphant cry: "We've struck gold, boy! I've got me a live snake!"

Brother Francis was returning from a fruitless expedition to a family of Kinsfolk who lived in an outlying farm high in the hills behind Broadbury when he saw two armed and mounted Falcons riding slowly along the harborside road toward the fort. Stumbling between them, their wrists bound behind them and their necks shackled by a length of stout cord, were two men and a girl. A few curious bystanders had braved the steadily falling rain to watch the melancholy little procession wend past, and Francis hastened to join them. Selecting a woman who appeared sympathetic he murmured: "Who are they?"

"They do say as it's the Kinsman they've been hunting for all over, sir. The other man's the Magpie."

"And the girl?"

"Reckon she'll be the potter's lass from Tallon. They hanged her dad, poor wench."

"A sorry sight," muttered Francis. "But no doubt 'tis God's will."

The woman stared at him, noted his priest's habit and murmured a grudging: "Aye, no doubt," before moving away down the street.

Francis waited until the prisoners and their escort had left the waterfront and were ascending the distant incline toward the fort, then he hitched his knapsack up on his shoulder and set off after them. He had no particular plan of action other than somehow to keep himself on hand and, hopefully, attempt to intercede on their behalf should an opportunity present itself. He thought he might just possibly contrive to buy them a little time by the judicious use of Archbishop Constant's seal reinforced by threats of his Lordship's grave displeasure. But he did not delude himself that these would prove more than a token shield to set against Brother Andrew's implacable fixation and the Gray Brotherhood's pragmatic license, backed up, as they were, by the whole grim machinery of the Secular Arm.

The iron studded doors of the stronghold had been shut and bolted by the time he reached them. He hammered at the wicket gate until the shutter behind the metal grille was drawn aside and a pair of suspicious eyes stared into his.

"Your business?"

"I travel in the service of my Lord, Archbishop Constant. I seek immediate audience with your commander."

"Your name—sir?"

"Brother Francis of York."

"Let's see your authority."

Francis delved into his satchel and produced the *laisser-passer* to which was affixed the primatial seal. He unfolded it and held it up, guessing that the doorkeeper could not read. There was a pause, then the shutter was clapped to and he heard the sound of a bar being withdrawn from its brackets. The wicket opened and Francis stepped through into the arched gatehouse. As he did so there was a shout of "Open up there, man!" from the inner courtyard and a helmeted Falcon came running toward them leading his horse by its bridle.

The doorkeeper hurried to drag back one of the doors. With a curt nod of acknowledgment the trooper vaulted up into his saddle and galloped away down the road.

Francis stood to one side as the keeper shoved the door back into place, thumping at the huge bolts and cursing monotonously under his breath about the sodding Gray who seemed to think they owned the whole sodding world and every sodding creature in it. When the last bolt had been rammed home Francis asked the man where he could find the officer in charge.

"Across the yard yonder and through t'other arch. Cap'n Arnold's the second door."

Picking his way among the pungent litter of horse droppings, Francis crossed the cobbled courtyard. Four steaming horses were standing tethered to iron rings along one wall. An ostler emerged from a stable doorway bearing an armful of hay which he began thrusting into a bracket manger. He was followed by a trooper carrying two wooden buckets. Of the three prisoners or their escort there was no sign.

As Francis gained the arched entrance to which he had been directed he heard raised voices coming from behind the first of the two doors on his right. A moment later the door swung open and a stocky, gray-haired man wearing boots and breeches but no jacket stormed out, bawling back over his shoulder: "Those are my orders, dammit, and don't you forget it!"

"Captain Arnold?"

The man's head jerked round. "Yes? I'm Captain Arnold."

Francis bowed from the neck. "Permit me to introduce myself, Captain. Brother Francis, envoy *privatus* to my Lord Archbishop Constant of York."

"*Cardinal* Constant?"

Francis' eye flickered in momentary astonishment. Then he nodded.

"I'm delighted to make your acquaintance, sir. Will you step into my office? Forgive this undress. Everything's got a bit out of step today."

Francis made a little, open-handed gesture indicative of sympathy and understanding, and followed the Captain into a surprisingly comfortable room. A wide mullioned window looked out across the harbor and a log fire was burning brightly in the grate. Hanging on the back of an inner door was something which looked remarkably like a woman's petticoat.

"A glass of wine, sir?"

"Thank you," said Francis. "That is very kind of you."

The Captain produced two glass goblets and a green bottle. "Bojerlay," he said with a smirk of pride. "I trust it's to your liking?"

Francis nodded and smiled. "You have an excellent cellar, Captain. Your health."

"And yours, sir. Now, how can I be of service to you?"

Francis sipped his wine and prayed desperately for inspiration. "I am here on a matter of some considerable delicacy, Captain Arnold. However" (here he glanced about him), "I am convinced that I can count upon your absolute discretion. My Lord the Archbishop—that is to say *Cardinal* Constant . . ."

Captain Arnold nodded and tapped his forefinger against the side of his nose.

"*Cardinal* Constant has entrusted me with a confidential mission concerning a man who passes under the alias of 'Thomas of Norwich,' a member of—"

The Captain's glass had paused on its way to his lips. His mouth had opened. He was staring. "*Who* did you say?"

"Thomas of Norwich. Needless to say that it is not his real name. He is, in fact, a member of my Lord's private intelligence service who was infiltrated privily into the Kinsman's sect several years ago. For reasons which, unfortunately, I am not at liberty to divulge— much as I would like to—it is imperative that this man should not be allowed to fall into the hands of the Gray Brotherhood."

"Go on, sir."

Francis hesitated just long enough to recall the mut- tered imprecations of the gatekeeper. He took a wild chance. "My Lord the Cardinal considers that the Brotherhood has exceeded both its terms of license and its secular authority. These wanton excesses are bringing the whole of our Secular Arm into disrepute, throughout the Kingdoms. We are soldiers of Christ, Captain Arnold, not butchers!"

The Captain nodded. "Ah, true, sir, true," he mur- mured. "The Grays do indeed exceed all license."

"So, Captain, if you should by any chance happen to learn the whereabouts of this man, my Lord Cardinal would certainly consider it an act worthy of the high- est esteem—of secular promotion, indeed—if you could do your utmost to see that no harm befalls him. The man is to be transferred direct to York under my personal supervision."

Captain Arnold moistened his lips with the tip of his tongue. "And what would you say, sir, if I were to tell you that a man answering to the description of this very Kinsman had been brought in here as a prisoner not above a quarter of an hour ago?"

Francis acted out a delicate little pantomime of utter astonishment, concluding with: "Alas, you see fit to jest with me, Captain."

"Not I, sir, upon my faith! Two of the Grays

winkled him out down by the harbor yonder along with a couple of his companions—a Quantock wench and a local peddler. We have all three locked up in a cell against the arrival of Bishop Simon's chief inquisitor."

"Brother Andrew?"

"Aye, that's the chap. Do you know him?"

"We have met," said Francis. "And you say he's coming here?"

The Captain nodded. "One of his own men has just ridden off to Dunkeswell to fetch him. I gave orders that none of the prisoners was to be interfered with in any way until he arrived."

"You have acted both wisely and humanely, Captain. My Lord Cardinal shall certainly hear of it from my own lips. Now perhaps the best and simplest course would be for me to sit down and write you out the official *receptum* which will relieve you of all further responsibility. But first my credentials." He produced his letter of authority and held it out.

The Captain gave it a perfunctory glance and nodded. "It all seems perfectly in order," he said. "But hadn't you better make sure he's the right fellow first?"

"Yes, of course. A word with him in private will suffice. It should not take me more than a moment."

The Captain drained off his glass, banged it down and strutted briskly to the door. "If you'll be good enough to follow me, sir," he said, "I shall be glad to conduct you to him personally."

Chapter Fourteen

FOUR GRAY FALCONS were sprawled around an oak table throwing dice from a leather cup. A stone flagon of ale was warming in the embers on a raised hearth and bread and cheese were scattered on a bench beside it. As the door opened and Captain Arnold strode in followed by Brother Francis the troopers glanced up then continued with their game.

The Captain's face turned puce with rage. "On your feet, you insubordinate dogs!" he roared.

Slowly, with calculated indifference, the lounging soldiers heaved themselves up and stood eyeing the two men insolently.

"The key."

The Falcons glanced at one another and the man who had been responsible for capturing Thomas said: "They're our prisoners, Captain. Not yours."

Captain Arnold did not argue. He was a full head shorter than the trooper but he skipped two rapid paces toward him and smashed the man stunningly across the mouth with his fist. "The key, you dog!" he snarled.

The Falcon licked his split lip then slowly reached inside his tunic and produced an iron key. He held it out to the Captain.

"Open it!"

The man walked over to the inner door, thrust the key into the lock and twisted it. Then he raised a booted foot and kicked the door open with such violence that it crashed thunderously against the stone wall of the cell.

Captain Arnold chose to ignore this. He gestured to Francis. "They are down below, sir," he said. "Have a care for the steps."

Francis nodded, squeezed his way past the trooper and stepped down into the dimly lit cell. He peered about him. "Which of you is Thomas of Norwich?" he whispered. Then, as his eyes grew more accustomed to the gloom he saw that they all had strips of rag bound across their mouths.

"They are gagged and bound, Captain," he called. "I cannot question them like this."

"I gave no such order," said the Captain. "You have my permission to release them."

Francis unknotted the cloth from the girl's mouth and then moved to the first of the two men. "I am Kin," he whispered urgently. "I am come to save you. Which of you is Thomas of Norwich?"

The Kinsman opened his freed mouth and flicked apart the two halves of his strange tongue. He did not say anything.

Francis bent over him. "My name is Francis," he murmured. "I come from Gyre. I have persuaded the Captain that you are a secret agent of Cardinal Constant's. Once I have positively identified you he is prepared to release you all into my custody."

"From Gyre, you say?"

"Aye, Thomas. I watched him die on Black Isle four days ago."

"What proof have you?"

"The pipes. The Boy's own pipes. Gyre gave them to me in trust for you. I have them here with me."

"Can'st free my hands, Francis?"

"I have no knife."

The Magpie shuffled close and as Francis tugged off his gag he whispered: "In my left boot. Quick man!"

"Well?" called the Captain. "Are you satisfied, sir?"

"One moment, Captain." Francis seized the knife,

sawed desperately at the Kinsman's bonds and felt the ropes begin to part.

Thomas jerked his wrists free. "The pipes, man!" he hissed. "Give me those pipes! And if you hear me play stop up your ears."

Francis thrust the knife into Thomas's hand and wrestled with the latch of his satchel. "I have to go and sign an official *receptum* for you," he whispered. "I shall be back anon."

"The pipes!"

"Aye, they're here." He dragged free the tooled leather case, dropped it into the Kinsman's shadowed lap and scrambled to his feet. "This is certainly the man, Captain," he called. "We can proceed."

"Very well, sir. Will you come with me?"

Francis climbed the steps to the cell door and pulled it shut behind him.

The Captain turned the key in the lock then removed it and placed it in his own breeches pocket. As the two men left the guardroom they heard the Falcons muttering among themselves. "Mutinous dogs," growled the Captain. "If I had them in my own troop they'd soon be yelping to a different tune."

While Captain Arnold poured them each another glass of wine Francis dipped a quill and scrawled: *"I, Brother Francis, envoy* PRIVATUS *to his Lordship Cardinal Constant of York, do hereby undertake full charge and responsibility for*—he paused and recharged his quill—*Brother Roger known as 'Kinsman Thomas of Norwich' and the two prisoners taken into custody with him."* He dated it, signed it with a flourish, sprinkled sand over it and shook it dry. Then he lifted his glass to the Captain and tossed it off in a single gulp. "I shall make it my business to see that you receive due recognition for your service, Captain Arnold. Remember, I have the Cardinal's ear."

The Captain started to grin then changed it into a sober frown. "I try to do my loyal duty, sir. But I confess that I have always striven to temper justice with mercy."

"I can well believe it, Captain." Francis briskly rolled up the receipt and handed it over with a smile. *"Consummatum est,"* he said. "Now shall we conclude the formalities? I am certain you must have far more pressing duties to attend to."

He picked up his satchel, slung it over his shoulder and followed the Captain back into the guardroom.

The first thing Francis noticed on entering was that the troopers were no longer at their dice. Two were stationed beside the outer door, while the man with the bruised and swollen lip was standing alongside a companion and had his back to the hearth. Both men were nursing crossbows.

If Captain Arnold was aware of the change he gave no sign. He marched up to the cell door and thrust the key into the lock. As he was about to turn it the ringleader said: "What are ye up to, man?"

The Captain pivoted slowly on his booted heel. "Man?" he whispered. "Did you call me 'man'?"

"Aye," replied the Falcon sullenly. "And ye'll not filch my prisoners though I hang for it."

"Oh, you'll hang all right," the Captain assured him. "Though I have to rope your neck myself, you'll hang." So saying he wrenched the key round in the lock, thrust open the cell door and cried: "Come out here, you three!"

"The first one who sets foot in the doorway dies!" shouted the trooper. "I know my orders."

"This is mutiny." Captain Arnold spoke the words very slowly and deliberately but with an undertone of quiet savagery which was truly impressive. "You realize that all four of you can swing for it. This holy priest is Cardinal Constant's personal envoy. Take good note of that, you treacherous dogs!"

"Let it be, Jan," muttered one of the Falcons. "Us'll all be crucified, man."

"We'll not be crucified, boy, nor hanged neither. Old Stone Lugs'll see to that. He'll be here directly. Shut that door, lads. We'll all stand fast and sweat it out till he comes."

As the outer door banged shut there came drifting up from within the shadowy throat of the cell a sound so ineffably sweet and pure that at first Francis could only suppose that he must be imagining it: a single, sustained, trilling note of an insufferably exquisite, crystalline clarity. Another followed, and another, each as pellucid as a diamond drop, till his whole head seemed to vibrate in maddening, trembling sympathy. At the same moment he became aware that something extraordinary was happening to the light in the room. Each tiny pinpoint of fireglow or reflection had begun to branch and sparkle like a filigree of rainbow frost on a winter windowpane; leaping outwards in slim, twinkling spearshafts of subtle scintillation till every person and every object in the room was clothed in a shimmering web of bejewelled brilliance. As the intensity of the illumination increased, so the agony in his head multiplied until it had crossed the threshold of measurable pain and become transmuted into an ecstatic anguish, a sensation so purely elemental that he knew he was about to disintegrate and become one with the air and the fragile tissue of the light and the very stones of the walls. No longer consciously hearing or seeing anything he yet heard and saw everything. Untethered his entranced soul soared up like a hawk, swinging outwards in wider and ever widening circles, ranging further and further abroad until, incredibly, he found himself back once again upon Black Isle watching the flickering fingers of the dying Gyre beckoning him forward along the path of the Song of Songs toward the paradise of Eternal Kinship where there was no more fear.

Francis recovered consciousness to find the girl bending over him and shaking him. He seemed to float up toward her as though from some unimaginable depth and then, unable to prevent it, continued insanely on until he had drifted right into the calm gray ocean of her own eyes. There she held him for a moment, quietly suspended, before she gently released him. " 'Tis all as he said, Thomas," she called. "Will he be able to walk?"

Hands grasped Francis by the upper arms and he became aware that he was being dragged up into a sitting position. Though he was barely conscious of any physical sensation he knew that his back must be resting against the rough stone wall of the guard-room.

"Can you stand, man?" inquired a brusque male voice.

By an immense effort of will, Francis succeeded in lifting himself an inch or two off the stone flagged floor and then sank back.

"Again, man," urged the Magpie. "Try again. Up! Up!"

The grip on his arms tightened, his feet scrabbled vaguely at the floor and somehow he was standing, rocking drunkenly and gaping about him in dazed astonishment. The two Falcons who had been stationed before the hearth were still standing there, but gazing upwards with vacant, idiot eyes at the raftered ceiling. Captain Arnold was stretched out, apparently asleep, upon the floor beside the cell.

"Try to walk, Francis," urged the girl. "We'll help you. Come."

Francis willed his wooden legs to move him forward, managed a single, lurching step and would certainly have pitched on to his face had not Jane and the Magpie steadied him.

"Again."

He essayed a second step, and then a third.

"Good. Good," she encouraged him. "It's coming back to you."

With a tongue that felt like a swollen bladder he contrived to ask what had happened.

"Why did you not stop up your ears like Thomas told you?" she said. "Had you not heard Gyre play you would surely be as they are now."

Their shuffling progress brought them up to the two

Falcons by the door. Francis peered at them and saw that their eyes were focused on some distant point that only they could see. "Will . . . they? . . . Are . . . they?" he forced out.

"We do not know," she said. "Thomas has only done this to animals before. He thinks they will recover by and by."

In the distance a door banged, followed by the harsh clatter of steel-shod boots on stone. The girl jerked round and all but lost her grip on Francis' arm. "Thomas!" she called. "They're coming!"

"Fear not, love," replied the Kinsman. "Look you to him."

Chapter Fifteen

DR. RICHARDS ARRIVED at the I.C. Unit with Rachel and Mrs. Huddlestone to discover that news of what was happening had leaked out and that at least half a dozen unfamiliar, young, white-jacketed figures had crowded into the side ward and were clustered around the E-V Converter. "What *is* this?" he protested. "Who gave you people permission to come in here?"

Sheepishly they shuffled back, still with their eyes fixed on the screen, and one said: "Is it a fact that this is a genuine O.O.B.E., sir?"

"We don't know *what* it is," said George, "and unless you ladies and gentlemen clear out and let us get on with our work we're not likely to find out, are we? So, with your kind permission . . ."

"Couldn't we just stand in at the back, sir?" pleaded one. "I promise no one will know we're here. After all it isn't every day we get a chance to see medical history in the making."

"Out!" growled George, and held the door open until they had all trooped through it. Then he called the spokesman back. "Go and find me a 'Strictly No Admittance' notice for this door," he said. "If you're back with it inside two minutes I'll allow you inside. But only *if* and *only* you. Understand?"

As the young intern scuttled off down the corridor, George said: "Have there been any new developments, Peter?"

"The three of them were picked up by some soldiers down on the quay," said Klorner. "They've been brought in to a sort of fort and locked up in a cell. The light's very dim."

"Mrs. Huddlestone won't be able to help us much either," said Ian. "They've all been gagged."

"Good Lord! Really?" George peered into the screen. "Still no sign of any R.E.M. from Mike, I suppose?"

"Not a thing."

"How about aberration?"

"Just that same trace on the girl."

Dr. Richards nodded. "I'm going to try out something which occurred to me last night," he said. "Rachel, I want you to go through and touch Mike—take hold of his hand or something. Careful you don't dislodge the drip."

Rachel entered the second ward and walked across to the bed. "Now?" she asked.

"Now," said George.

She lifted Michael's wrist and held it lightly in her hand.

"Right," called George. "Now let go."

"I've done that."

"Again."

She picked up the inert hand for the second time

and heard George say: "Am I imagining it, or is that trace aberration fluctuating?"

"Yes, I think you could well be right," said Ian. "Can you try it once more, Rachel?"

The action was repeated and this time everybody who was watching the screen agreed that the faint, hazy aura around the image of the girl's head dimmed perceptibly for as long as Rachel was in direct physical contact with the unconscious man. Before they had a chance to discuss the significance of the effect the ward door opened and the young intern reappeared. Simultaneously Klorner said: "Hello. It looks as if something's happening at last. Who's this?"

Mrs. Huddlestone did her best to enlighten them, but with Francis talking to the prisoners in a whisper and the light so dim in the cell, she was unable to do more · than offer a few speculative words and phrases. However, it soon became clear that at least one of her guesses was correct, for no sooner had Francis left the cell than they all saw the instrument in Thomas's hands.

"Yes, those are pipes right enough," said George. "But what on earth are they all so excited about?"

They watched fascinated as Thomas freed first the girl and then the other man and then sat down crosslegged on the floor directly facing the cell door and set the pipes to his lips. Fascination turned to utter incomprehension as the picture suddenly flicked to one side to show them Jane and the Magpie squatting down with their fingers apparently jammed into their ears.

For a minute or two nothing happened then they saw the cell door swing open to reveal Captain Arnold standing at the top of the cell steps. His lips moved.

"Come out here, you three," relayed Mrs. Huddlestone distinctly.

They saw the Captain turn to one side, apparently addressing someone who was invisible to them. Mrs. Huddlestone was beginning to apologize for being unable to read what he was saying when the whole surface of the screen began to tremble as though they were viewing it through a heat haze. At the same instant the figure of the Captain seemed to flick from positive to negative as if all the shadows and the highlights had suddenly transposed themselves. The screen itself brightened precipitately and then blacked out almost completely, though they were still able to make out the dim figure of the Captain in the doorway. As they stared at him the man appeared to buckle slowly at the knees and slide to the floor.

"What's happening, Peter?"

"I'm absolutely baffled," said Klorner. "But we're picking up strong traces of p.k. Nothing the torus can't handle though."

"I don't like it," said Rachel. "Are you sure Mike's all right?"

"Nothing unusual registering anywhere," Kenneth assured her.

"Then why's the screen gone so dark?"

"It must be something to do with the contact's own physical perception," said George. "Yes. Look. It's changing back again."

As he spoke the picture brightened, reverted to normal and swung around. They saw the two crouching figures rise to their feet and make for the steps. As the scene transposed into Thomas's vision of the guardroom Ian said: "I'm pretty sure those two by the fireplace are the ones who brought them in, Doc."

"What's the matter with them?" asked George. "Are they drunk?"

No one was in a position to enlighten him. They watched Jane and the Magpie reviving Francis, but whatever words passed between them were too far away for Mrs. Huddlestone to interpret. Suddenly the door flew open and another soldier strode into the room. Immediately the same extraordinary transposition effect took place on the screen. This time it lasted less than a minute. As the picture cleared they observed that a second figure had emerged from the shadows. Dressed in a gray monk's habit he was standing just inside the doorway and in his hands he was holding what appeared to be a cross-bow. It was pointed directly at them.

Thomas heard the cold command to cease piping and glanced up to find himself looking directly along the shaft of the talon which Brother Andrew held trained upon him. The fifth Falcon was already standing as still as if he had become one stone with the flags beneath his boots.

"Release them from this spell, mage."

"They are your birds, priest, not mine. 'Tis for you to whistle them home."

The monk took a pace further into the room and caught sight of Francis. "Well, well," he said. "I might have guessed what brought you scampering to Blackdown. Your master never did choose his epithets lightly."

Francis stared at him blankly. "Epithets?" he echoed. "I do not follow."

"No? Then let me enlighten you. Constant penned one word across that report you sent him from Cumberland. *Apostata!*" The word dripped like venom from the monk's lips and hissed among the shadowy corners of the room. "Indeed you have much to answer for, Francis."

"That may be," returned Francis calmly. "But not to you or Lord Simon."

"We shall see. We shall see," said the monk. "These are friends of yours, I take it?"

"They are."

"Devil's spawn!"

"Nay, Andrew, as Christ is our judge you wrong them utterly."

"I do? Then how, pray, do you explain this?" The monk gestured round with his bow at the mesmerized Falcons. "Is that not the devil's own handiwork, Francis? Or has he offered you some other plausible explanation?"

"The only devil here is within you, Andrew. This sacred mission of yours is but a compensation for your own infirmity."

The monk's lips tightened into a thin, pale line. "Ah, but you shall pay dearly for that, Francis," he whispered.

"Do you fear the truth so much, Brother? Look into your own heart, man. What nourishes it if not the morbid pleasure you derive from inflicting pain upon the innocent?"

The monk had begun to tremble as though he were afflicted with a sudden palsy. "Have a care," he chattered. "Have a care."

But Francis was relentless. "You are sick, Andrew. Sick unto death. The plague rages in you not in the Kinsfolk. Can you not see that it is yourself you are striving to destroy?"

The monk's face had contorted itself into a truly horrifying grimace of pure hatred. He leveled his bow at Francis then, even as his knuckles were whitening on the trigger, he half turned. There was a sharp, metallic twang; a flicker like a trace of black thread on the air; and a cry of anguish from Jane. Before anyone else could move a muscle the Magpie had launched himself full length across the room. He struck the monk just above the knees and brought him crashing to the ground. A knife blade glinted briefly in the shadows; there was a choking cough, and then nothing more.

Francis struggled to his feet, found himself once again in effective command of his own body, and turned to the Kinsman. He saw that he was leaning back against the wall with Jane beside him. His eyes were closed and his right hand was clasped across the left side of his chest.

"Are you hurt, Thomas?"

"Aye. Sorely. I fear he's just writ amen to a prayer he penned in Newbury."

"His black soul smokes in hell for it," said the Magpie. "We'll get you aboard ship, Thomas, and doctor you there."

· "I'm past all doctoring, friend. I durst not draw the bolt." Thomas groaned in sudden, wrenching agony and gasped: "Ah, Jane, love. Has it come to this after all?"

"No, no," she whispered passionately. "Carver will save you, Thomas. Only let me reach him."

Thomas let go of the feathered shaft, gazed down ruefully at his blood bright fingers and muttered: "Your knife, Magpie."

"Nay, man!" The Magpie was aghast. "I cannot do it. Do not ask me."

"In this shoulder," panted Thomas. "The Testament is sewn here. Quick, man! Cut!"

The Magpie stepped close and pricked the knife point along the seam of wax-toughened threads till the stitching on the shoulder of the leather jerkin gaped apart. Thomas fumbled inside the rent and with scarlet fingers drew out a slim packet sealed in oilskin. His eyes sought for Francis. "Speed you to Corlay with Jane," he panted, thrusting the packet into the priest's hand. "Take Tom's pipes and the Testament and guard all three with your life. Away now, all of you."

"I'll not go!" cried Jane. "You cannot make me!"

The Kinsman's life tide was ebbing fast, the color draining visibly from his face as he turned his pain-darkened eyes to hers. "Did you not *huesh* it, little witch?" he whispered with a ghost of a smile. "What will be, will be."

She took his face between her hands. "All I beg is that you let me try to reach him," she pleaded. "Oh, my love, my own love, let me try."

Thomas looked down upon the face that was so dear to him, saw through the fast-gathering shadows that her eyes were aswim with tears and could not find it in his heart to deny her anything. He nodded. "Help me, friends," he muttered. "Lay my head in her lap."

Francis and the Magpie managed it between them,

wincing inwardly as they saw the Kinsman's face go ashen gray with pain.

Jane stroked the lank hair back from a forehead already chill with the cold dew of hurrying death and, leaning over him, cried soundlessly into the shadow-filled depths with all the force of her terrified spirit: *Help us, Michael! Help us! Do not let him die!*

The ward was so silent that the faint hum of the video-recorder sounded almost intolerably intrusive as the E-V.C. screen became filled with the brilliant image of Jane's face and the wonderstruck watchers found themselves seemingly drifting upwards imperceptibly into her eyes. As the pupils grew ever more huge and lustrous Rachel suddenly cried out: "Stop her! Stop her!" and wrenching herself away stumbled through into the ward where Michael lay and flung herself across his unconscious body moaning: "Don't, Mike! Don't! Don't!"

In a second the surface of the screen had dissolved into a slowly swirling vortex which deepened and darkened until it was reaching upwards and outwards —a weird, interminable tunnel of shifting shadows among which faint points of light could be perceived twinkling like far-off stars in some remote and unfamiliar heaven. Around these points drifting wraiths of cloudy shade seemed to coagulate, forming and dissolving like figures in a fevered dream: faces became animals became mountains became castles became ships became birds, but none held their shape for more than a moment. They formed and reformed with no apparent purpose, no real substance, and drifted past and away like ragged tatters of dark mist.

At last all sense of movement ceased; the light dimmed to an almost total blackness apart from one minute needlepoint of brightness far off in the upper right hand corner of the screen. The stillness became a pregnant moment of trembling, rocking indecision, and then, quick as a fish darting, they were flickering off toward the solitary light point. An instant later there was a concerted gasp of astonishment as he observers perceived in the depths of the screen before them a nebulous shape distilling itself into the spectral outlines of the face of the man who was at that very moment lying unconscious on a bed ten feet away in the adjoining ward.

—*Michael? Michael?*
—*Rachel?*
—*Help us, Michael! Help us!*
—*You're not Rachel.*
—*I am! I am!*
—*You are The Bride of Time.*
—*Save him, Michael. Don't let him die.*
—*I cannot save him.*
—*You can. You did before.*
—*I had no choice then. The Bird . . .*
—*Oh, Michael, you must help. I need him so.*
—*You already have him.*
—*I need him alive, Michael.*
—*He is alive within you.*
—*No, no. Not like that.*
—*He's in the child. I have done what I had to do.*
—*I love him, Michael.*
—*I know.*
—*Must he die?*
—*We must all die. Even you.*
—*And you?*
Silence. Darkness. Her heart bled like a wound.

The Kinsman's eyelids fluttered like weary wings. Overcome with despair Jane let her forehead sink until it was resting upon his. Through her sobs she heard him whisper faintly: "Nay, love, it's right we let him be. We owe him a death. I'll not cheat him now."

He shivered violently in her cradling arms, opened his eyes for the last time and murmured: "Sweet bride . . . Our song is sung," and lay still.

Chapter Sixteen

AT TEN MINUTES past seven in the evening, Michael Carver opened his eyes to find Rachel bending over him. As he did so the E-V.C. screen next door became filled with the image of her own face.

"Mike?"

The screen flickered and for a bewildering moment Rachel's face seemed to merge into Jane's and then slowly resolved into her own again.

"Mike?"

"Hi, there," he whispered. "It really *is* you, isn't it? We finally made it."

She bent down and kissed him on the mouth. At the same moment she felt the child in her womb kick lustily and she cried out in sudden ecstatic delight: "Oh God, God, I thought I'd never see you look at me again!"

The others came crowding in and clustered round the bed. Dr. Carver blinked up at their smiling faces until gradually it dawned upon him that he was not lying on the trolley in the lab. He dragged himself up on to his elbows and gave a yelp as the taped drip needle pulled itself free from his arm. "What the hell's going on?" he demanded hoarsely. "Where am I?"

"In the General Hospital," said George. "You've been out a long time."

"How long?"

"The best part of a fortnight."

"A fortnight!"

"Just about."

"*Jesus!*"

"Some O.O.B.E., eh?"

"*You know that?*"

George turned to Peter. "Mike," he said. "Let me be the first to introduce you to a genius—Peter Klorner."

"Klorner? Klorner from Stanford?"

"How do you do, Doctor?" said Peter, reaching out and shaking the bewildered man by the hand. "May I say that it's a unique experience to meet a bona fide time traveller in the flesh."

Michael gaped at him. "Then you *do* know?"

"Let's just say we know enough to have guessed some of the rest," said Klorner. "But there's still a whole lot more for you to tell us."

"But *how . . . ?*"

"We picked up your O.O.B. contact, Mike," said George. "We've got the whole thing on video."

"On *video?* I don't get it."

"Nor will you till you see the E-V.C."

"E-V. C.?"

"Encephalo-Visual Converter," said Ian. "It's out of this world, Doctor! Fantastic!"

Mike flopped back on to the pillow and closed his eyes. "Are you telling me it really *did* happen? That it wasn't just an incredible Y-d. trip?"

"All we've got is what we took off your P. points," said George. "But just wait till you see it, Mike. If that's a Y-d. hallucination, what's reality?"

"You mean you know about Jane? And the Kinsmen? And the Drowning?"

"We've pieced some of it together. But not much."

The young intern who had been hovering on the fringes of the crowd said: "I think we ought to let him get some rest. He looks just about all in to me."

There were immediate murmurs of contrition and they all backed away from the bed leaving Rachel isolated.

Michael opened his haunted eyes and looked up at

her. "So who the hell *am* I?" he whispered. "Do *you* know?"

"You're Mike Carver," she said. "And I love you."

As the rain clouds drew away eastwards from the high moors they left behind them a swathe of sky as clear as golden wine. Standing at the helm of the "Kingdom Come" young Napper glanced back over his shoulder at the purpling hills of Blackdown and raised his right fist in a timeless gesture of silent defiance. The waves slapped against the heeling hull and fell back in a hush of spray. The wake became a long glimmering line drawn further and further backwards till it melted and was lost in the shifting currents of the channel. The boy drew a deep breath and began to sing one of the songs which it was no longer prudent to sing when ashore:

> *"Oh, white wings, strong white wings,*
> *Ye'll bear my heart across the sea . . ."*

The sound of his cheerful voice carried down into the hold where his brother Jonsey sat with Francis and Jane. "He can sing all he likes out here," said Jonsey. "We're well clear of Blackdown now." And he called out: "How's that sky, boy?"

"Sweet and coming up clear from the west!" cried Napper.

"Seems like luck is starting to favor us all again," observed Jonsey. "We'll have a star to steer by, and if this wind holds up we might even count on a sight of the French coast by dawn."

"You hear that, Jane?"

Jane nodded.

"From St. Brieuc it is but a day's ride up to Corlay," said Francis.

"Is it safe to go up on deck now?" she asked.

"Aye," said Jonsey. "There's naught to fear now, lass."

She pulled her cloak about her and climbed up the

companionway steps. As she emerged on deck Napper grinned at her. "You're wiser than they are, Jane. It's fresh up here."

"That song," she said. "Will you sing it again?"

"Which one?"

"White Wings."

"Ah, you know it, do you?"

She nodded.

"Then do you sing it along wi' me, lass. Two's better than one. Come, sit you here beside me."

She shook her head. "I can't, Napper," she whispered. "My heart is too full of hurt. You sing it and I'll listen."

She made her way forward past the creaking mast and sat down on the very net where, though she did not know it, her dead lover had once lain. Resting her aching head upon the gunwale she murmured: "Why did you not take me with you? Why? Why?" and the tears she had not thought she had left in her to shed, rose scalding in her eyes while the boy's clear voice sang—

> *"Oh, white wings, strong white wings,*
> *Ye'll bear my heart across the sea,*
> *Ye'll bear my heart across the mountains,*
> *To where my true love waits for me."*

In the second week of May a gale began to blow from the north. For three days and two nights it howled down the Sea of Dee through the Midland Gap to burst out screaming across the wide wastes of the Somersea. Low over the cowering Mendips the flayed clouds streamed unbroken while below them the rain squalls lashed like black whips and clawed handfuls of spume from the backs of the waves in Taunton Reach. They flew like tufts of fleece to lodge among the thorns and scrub oaks of Blackdown and skein the seaward forests on the North Dorset shore.

By the evening of the third day the clouds began to break and, as night fell, stars could be seen pricking through the flying rents and tatters. Later the moon arose and the wind dropped abruptly. But the seas still ran high, raging blackly under the fitful moonshine and roaring among the groined caverns of Quantock Isle.

At dawn, as the tide withdrew, the combers crept out from Tallon to scratch for gleanings among the high-piled wrack and sea-drift which littered the coves. In a rock-fanged gulley known as "the Jaws" they stumbled upon the naked, weed-shrouded corpse of a Kinsman. He had been dead for weeks and the splintered stump of a cross-bow bolt protruding from between his ribs testified as to how he had met his end.

As was their custom they dragged him down to the water's edge and cast him back into the wayward currents. For what use is a drowned body to any man?